"WHAT SIZE WAR SHOT DID HE AUTHORIZE?"

"A one point five kiloton," Brognola replied.

"That's a baby nuke," Katz commented, "but it should do the job. I'll talk to Striker about how they're going to designate the target. That might be a little tricky this time."

"Why?" Brognola looked surprised. "They have a laser designator, don't they?"

"No. There was no need for it on this mission, and they used the weight allocation for extra medical supplies and ammunition. They're going to have to use the lock-on function on the GPS to mark the spot."

"That means somebody has to be there with it, doesn't it, up to and including detonation?"

Katz simply nodded.

"Goddamn."

DON PENDLETON'S

MACK BOLAN.

STONY MAN™

Hostile
INSTINCT

A GOLD EAGLE BOOK FROM

WORLDWIDE.

TORONTO • NEW YORK • LONDON
AMSTERDAM • PARIS • SYDNEY • HAMBURG
STOCKHOLM • ATHENS • TOKYO • MILAN
MADRID • WARSAW • BUDAPEST • AUCKLAND

First edition April 2000

ISBN 0-373-61930-8

Special thanks and acknowledgment to
Michael Kasner for his contribution to this work.

HOSTILE INSTINCT

Printed in U.S.A.

Hostile
INSTINCT

CHAPTER ONE

Congo

Screams of anguish rose above the pounding of drums and the chanting of the near naked men dancing around the late-night fires at the edge of the jungle clearing. Inside the wood line, a cluster of ragged men and women huddled on the ground, guarded by more seminaked men armed with AK-47s. Most of the prisoners were black, but there were also a few whites from what had been a nearby missionary medical station. Most of the prisoners were beyond fear by now, made nearly catatonic by what they knew lay in store for them.

One at a time, a man or a woman was dragged into the clearing to stand in the light of the fires. At a shouted command, the chanting warriors hacked at them with machetes and beat them with the butts of their rifles. Then, while the unfortunate victim was still alive, chunks of his or her flesh were eaten either seared in the fires or raw. As the warriors ate, they roared into the night like lions.

The warriors roared like lions because they were Simbas, followers of the savage, mystical cult that had once driven the white colonials out of much of Africa. Most people thought that the days of the Simba were long past, but the cult had been revived and a new Simba army was on the rampage in the Congo.

A STENCH OF FRESH BLOOD mixed with voided bowels and roasting meat wafted up to the small hill on the other side of the clearing where a small detachment of UN peacekeepers had taken refuge from the slaughter. In all the years of his long career as a UN peacekeeper, French Commandant Yves Larmont had never seen anything as unremittingly savage and barbaric as the scene that was taking place below.

It was ironic, he thought, that Africa was considered to be the location of the legendary Garden of Eden, the original peaceful home of humankind. Right now, most of sub-Saharan Africa could more properly be likened to the deepest pits of hell with this particular clearing as its epicenter. But not even in the worst hell he could imagine did men eat other men with such pleasure.

The former foreign legion officer was fully aware, though, that there was absolutely nothing that he and his fifteen-man peacekeeper detachment could do to stop the Simba ceremony that was taking place in front of them. To order his men down the hill would be to sentence them to a death that few in modern times had ever suffered. Cannibalism was rare nowadays, and being eaten alive was almost unrecorded in all of history. No one had told the Simbas that, though, and their ceremonies had always involved eating their kill like the lions they had named themselves after.

Larmont's two lieutenants, Georg Pernovski and Ian Benchley, both had tears of frustration and horror in their eyes. Nonetheless, neither one had any desire to try to rescue the few remaining hostages, either. A deep primal fear had frozen them in place. Benchley lost his battle with his fear, turned away and vomited the contents of his stomach onto the red earth.

"Don't let them see your fear, man!" Larmont snapped at Benchley, the young British officer.

"I'm sorry, sir," Benchley said as he wiped the sour slime from his mouth.

Larmont was sorry that anyone, even novice peacekeeper officers, had to witness this. But this was Africa, and the Simbas were very much a part of the African tradition. If you were going to work in Africa, you had to take what came with the job. If he and Benchley survived this, he would strongly suggest that the young British officer find another way to serve the international organization.

But first they had to survive until morning.

THE TALL BLACK MAN at the center of the Simba ceremony wore a khaki uniform with a black Sam

Browne belt and red epaulets bearing the gold crown and crossed swords of a colonel in the old Zairean army. On his head, he wore a lion-skin headband with white feathers. In one hand, he held a bloody machete and in the other an elephant-hair fly whisk, the traditional mark of African royalty.

Colonel Charles Taibu was aware of the effect his Simba ceremony was having on the panicked United Nations troops on the hill, particularly on their white officers. He could almost smell the acrid reek of their fear over the stench of the carnage. He had only to raise his hand and his Simbas would overwhelm them in an instant. But he wasn't going to do that; he was going to let them live. Not from any sense of humanitarianism or respect for the UN, but rather so they could spread the word of what they had seen here. Since there was no TV crew on hand to record what was taking place, Taibu needed witnesses.

By the same token, there would also be black survivors of this Simba ceremony. Taibu was half-white, but he was all African and he knew his mother's people. The black survivors would do more to spread the word of him than all the Western TV broadcasts in the world. The Simba cult had once driven the whites from Africa in droves, but it had been dormant for several decades. Now, under his control, it was making a comeback with a vengeance.

Africa of the Millennium was a continent almost devoid of older people. The average age of the black population of sub-Saharan Africa was under twenty. The typically high African birthrate, combined with years of Western medicine, meant that the normal population demographics had been destroyed. To the average young African, the Simbas weren't a living memory; they were a legend they had heard about from their fathers and grandfathers. The young of the Congo Basin would soon learn, though, that the Sons of the Lion were more than a legend and they would join them or they would die.

The smell of rotting blood hung heavy in the thick night air. The remnants of the bodies hadn't started to smell yet, but the night had been hot and blood decomposed quickly. Taibu did not mind the smell, though; in fact, he rather liked it. To him it was the smell of victory, the smell of his greatness yet to come. As the old man had predicted, he would be the best-known African since Chaka the legendary Zulu king. Since the prediction had come with the man's dying breath, it would come to pass.

It wasn't just the dying words of an old juju man that gave Taibu his sense of purpose. For years, he had felt that he was destined for greatness. His earliest memories were of his mother telling him that he had a destiny that only the sun itself could stop. She had been a priestess, and had the Belgians not held the Congo in their grasp, she would have been a queen among her tribe. Instead, she had been a whore for the white men. Even so, she had instructed her only child in the ways of her people and never let him forget that he was from a royal background.

His father had been Belgian, an officer of the Tribal Affairs Office of the colonial government who paid well to keep his mother as his exclusive mistress. Of his father, he remembered little except that he was a fat, balding white man who had ordered him out of their spacious Elizabethville apartment every time he came to visit his mother. The young Taibu discovered that he had a knack for languages and learned French so he could talk to his father, but he had exchanged few words with him.

He was in the lower grades of the colonial school when Belgium relinquished control of the Congo, but his mother insisted that he continue his education. In his teenage years, he joined the local Communist party and became a runner for them. His facility with languages came to the attention of the Russian advisers in his country when he quickly picked up Russian, and he was chosen to attend the Patrice Lamumba University of International Communism in Moscow. It was there that he really learned to loathe whites.

The Russians made a great show of treating the non-Caucasian Communists as their brothers in Marxism, but it was only a show. In reality, the

Russian and European Communists openly called the African students inferior and made sure that they knew their place in the Marxist scheme of things. Even the Asian, Arab and Latin American students went out of their way to segregate themselves from the blacks, particularly the women.

Communist doctrine stated that all goods and services were to be equally available. What wasn't stated openly was that the doctrine of sharing the wealth included the services of the women, too. It was considered to be dangerously reactionary behavior for a female student to refuse a sexual request from one of her fellow Marxists or for a male to refuse a female's request. Since Taibu was a fine figure of a man by any standards, a few of the white women had sampled him. But these had been empty encounters for Taibu, as the women had used him as a sex toy rather than submitting to him as a woman should.

When Taibu left Moscow after five years, he was a changed man. He had learned a great deal during his stay at the university, but mostly he had learned to despise whites regardless of their nationality or politics. He had also learned to equally hate Latin Americans, Arabs and Asians.

He had also absorbed the tenets and tactics of Marxism and was burning to put them to practice when he returned to his native land. But as he soon learned, African politics weren't the orderly process he had learned in Moscow. Marxist dialectic didn't count for much when tribalism dominated what so often passed for government in Africa. Being a half white from a minority tribe, he quickly found himself in trouble with the rulers of his country.

When he fought to institute a worker's socialism, he threatened the tribal rulers and was forced to flee for his life to the jungle. There, he met others who had been exiled for various reasons or who had fled to escape persecution for their crimes. Gathering these outlaws to him, he abandoned Marxism for something purely African and, remembering the stories his mother had told him of the old days, resurrected the ancient Simba cult.

It had taken him years to make his comeback, but he now had an army loyal only to him and the Way of the Lion. He played the Marxist to bring the people to his cause and to gain sympathy in the Western liberal media. He was a Communist, all right, like Pol Pot, Fidel Castro, Daniel Ortega and the other nationalist leaders who had used Marxist terms to explain their dictatorial rule. Like them, he would claim that he had to eradicate the remnants of colonial bondage before he could institute a Marxist worker's paradise where all would share the wealth. He didn't bother to mention that this process would take his entire lifetime.

So far, his Simba army had been cutting a zigzag path through nations weakened by decades of intertribal fighting, civil wars and corrupt governments. Most of them were still at war with someone, but he took no sides in these conflicts and welcomed all who wanted to join him regardless of their tribe or nationality. In the end, he expected to become the sole leader of half a dozen nations in the Congo Basin. From there, his Simbas would strike south and bring even more nations under his control.

Seeing that his men had finished killing the latest victim, he pointed the machete at the wood line, and another unfortunate was dragged out into the light of the fires. This one was a white man, one of the Christians who had run the missionary hospital. Taibu loathed Christians and stepped forward to take the first cut himself, smiling as he swung his blade.

COMMANDANT YVES LARMONT waited until the Simbas' fires had burned down before evacuating his men from the hilltop. Earlier that evening, three of his Ethiopian contingent had deserted, but that was to be expected. He had operated in Africa long enough to know that most of the show the Simbas put on was for the edification of the blacks in his unit, not himself and his officers. They would tell everyone who would listen of what they had seen and further undermine the morale of the UN peace-keeping troops in the region.

Not that there was that much morale left in the UN troops to destroy. The role of the once effective UN forces had deteriorated to the point that there was nothing left for them to do. Even the term *peacekeeping* was little more than a grim joke. Before this latest incarnation of the Simba cult, there had been precious little peace to be kept in any of Africa. Tribal wars, insurrections and wars of aggression had turned Central Africa into one vast killing field. The people had died by the tens of thousands, and now that the Simbas were back, there would be no end to the slaughter.

As Larmont led his men off the hill and into the jungle, he spared a thought for his house back in Provence. He spent a month and a half each year there, and until now, that had been enough for him. What he had seen over the past two years, though, capped by this run-in with the Simbas, had changed his mind for him. He was too old to fight another war in Africa, particularly against Simbas. He would submit his immediate resignation as soon as he got back to the UN compound.

As far as Larmont was concerned, the whole damned continent could go to hell, taking every white and black with it, and he wouldn't shed a tear. He'd had enough of trying to keep Africans from killing one another.

COLONEL CHARLES TAIBU woke with the dawn and smiled when he saw that the UN peacekeepers had fled their hilltop. By the time they got back to their base camps, his army would have grown in their minds to thousands and the panic would spread.

Like lions attacking a herd of antelope on the plain, panic aided the Simbas. The first thing he did was to send his scouts along the path he wanted to take next. His revolutionary-activities classes in Moscow had taught him the value of reconnaissance and up-to-date field intelligence in guerrilla operations.

When his scouts reported back at midday, Taibu gathered his Simba officers and went over the reports. Of all the targets in his path, only one of them really stood out—a UN-sponsored World Health Organization medical research compound at a place called Donner's Station. So far, his targets had mostly been native settlements and small towns. The Western facilities he had hit had all been sponsored by religious or charity organizations. He hadn't yet brought his version of the new African order to any of the United Nations facilities. But for his dreams to be realized, they, too, would have to feel the strength of the lion and learn to fear the name of Simba.

Reading the map, he saw that there were enough small villages along the route to support his lion warriors until they reached the UN research station. A thousand-man army needed to eat and drink and find amusement. At his command, the Simba army disappeared into the dense jungle like a snake with two thousand legs.

When his army emerged again, blood would flow.

CHAPTER TWO

Stony Man Farm, Virginia

Hal Brognola was glad that the threat board was clear for a change. As the leader of America's premier clandestine strike force, the Sensitive Operations Group, his days and nights were spent keeping track of the world's hot spots and dealing with threats to America's security both at home and abroad. It was a grueling task that he shared with the men and women of Stony Man Farm. But right now he had something closer to home he needed to focus on. And in his mind, it was just as important as dealing with any international crisis.

The time had finally arrived for the Stony Man Farm facilities to be expanded beyond their original boundaries and capabilities. This undertaking was going to be a major clandestine mission in itself, involving grand deception, heightened security and a cast of hundreds, all of whom had to be prevented from knowing what they were doing even while they were doing it. It was going to be nerve-racking enough to pull this off without having to worry about an ongoing overseas operation at the same time.

If the gods of war were good to him and Stony Man Farm, it would stay quiet for the next few weeks.

The Annex, as the expansion was being called, had been in the planning stages for years. Stony Man had long since outgrown its humble beginnings and even more humble physical layout. The farmhouse that housed the SOG operatives had been adequate in the beginning, but the march of technology had added equipment not even dreamed of when Stony Man first went active. Now that the twenty-first century was upon them, the technology necessary to stay abreast with ever more sophisticated enemies required even more space that they didn't have.

The original farmhouse would remain as the primary offices and living quarters for the Stony Man crew. But, Aaron Kurtzman's computer facilities, the blacksuits' communications center and the War Room would all be moved to the new underground Annex. In addition, a new security center would be built to monitor the entire complex and serve as a tactical operations center in case of attack.

The Annex itself was a forty-eight-acre parcel of land adjoining the northern boundary of the Farm. Currently, the land was planted with an orchard of apple trees that were well past their prime. The cover story that Stony Man's Barbara Price was putting out to the locals in the nearby town was that the orchard would be cut down and the land replanted in a pulpwood plantation. Growing poplar trees for wood pulp was a booming industry in the South, and the story was believed.

A second advantage of growing poplar trees rather than putting in a new apple orchard was their phenomenal growth rate. Within two years, the trees would be tall enough to completely shield anything that went on behind them from casual view. They would also provide a perfect place to hide a new network of sensors, video cameras and warning devices to protect both the new perimeter and the old. The openness of the Farm had always presented a serious security challenge for the blacksuit security force, and that would be considerably lessened now.

A primary feature of the new tree farm was going to be the wood-chipping facility situated in the center of the grove of trees. This was to be a one-stop wood-processing operation—the trees would be grown, cut down and processed into wood chips all on-site. The chip mill and wood-chip storage bins would also provide the best concealment in the world for the Farm's new underground facilities. The new operations center would, in effect, be built in the basements of the aboveground wood-processing buildings.

Considering the level of security that always surrounded any Stony Man Farm activity, the job wouldn't be easy. The plans had been well thought out, but it would be difficult to conceal the purpose and extent of the construction from the men who would be doing the work. That was where the Stony Man crew had their work cut out for them, particularly the blacksuit security force.

STONY MAN'S SECURITY CHIEF, Buck Greene, wasn't having a good day. Keeping the Farm secure was his top priority, and having so many uncleared people inside his perimeter was making him edgy. To keep to the construction schedule Brognola had laid out, Barbara Price had given permission for the logging crew to breach the perimeter fence where it adjoined the Annex so they could take the cut trees out by the main road. It made practical sense to do it that way, but it went against the grain with him.

In keeping with the Farm's long-standing rule of going the extra mile to keep good relations with the locals, Price had contracted that part of the job to a local company. She knew that exposed them to an additional risk, but for this phase of the project, it was a slight risk and she felt it could be taken. Greene, however, wasn't so sure and he had his blacksuit security force keeping tabs on them.

The Farm's security force got their nickname from the night combat suits they wore when they patrolled the Farm's perimeter after dark. A team from the daylight shift, the boots-and-jeans detail, named from their farm-clothes uniform, were swinging chain saws right alongside the local loggers. To keep the other workmen from asking awkward questions, they had their weapons stashed in the lockboxes of their pickup trucks. They had their com links hot, as well, and were keeping an eye out. One of the first requirements for being a blacksuit was to be professionally paranoid, and nothing would escape their attention.

CARL LYONS AND HIS Able Team had been called to the Farm to help Buck Greene oversee the construction phase of the Annex project. The work would be done by contractors who were already cleared to work for the Defense Department, the FBI and the CIA. But that didn't mean that their workmen wouldn't need to be watched over. This job had to be done in such a way that when it was over, no one would be able to publish a diagram of the Annex on the Internet as had been done with the CIA headquarters at Langley. And accomplishing that wasn't going to be easy.

Aaron Kurtzman and his Computer Room staff had drawn up the blueprints for the entire job, but none of the three construction crews would ever be allowed to see a complete set. The work had been parceled out into subjobs that would be handled by different crews who had no knowledge of what the others were doing. And on each subjob, a part of the construction would purposefully be left undone or done wrong, and would have to be corrected later by a blacksuit crew when the outsiders were gone.

"This is like having them do a damned puzzle with a blindfold on," Lyons muttered as he read the complicated schedule. This wasn't within the former LAPD cop's usual field of expertise, and he was having to take Kurtzman's word that it was all going to somehow work out at the end.

"We could always kill them after they complete their part of the job so they can't talk," Hermann "Gadgets" Schwarz suggested. As Able Team's technician, he specialized in electronics and gadgets, not construction. "That's what the pharaohs did with the guys who built their tombs, wasn't it?"

"I really don't think Hal will let us do that," Rosario "the Politician" Blancanales said dryly. He was Able Team's front man and would be the main point of contact with the work crews and their supervisors. "I think the construction unions have a clause in their contracts about that."

"It would make our jobs a hell of a lot easier, though," Schwarz insisted.

"If you two are done jacking your jaws," Lyons snapped, "we need to get back to work. This shit isn't going to get done by itself."

"You got it, Ironman." Schwarz grinned.

If there was anything Lyons hated, it was the kind of paranoid hand-holding necessary to keep the separate construction crews from learning about what the others were doing. And that was only after they had completed doing new background checks on all of the workers themselves.

CARL LYONS STOOD with Buck Greene, watching a truckload of retired apple trees drive past the equipment shed on its way out down the main road through the Farm. This was the second load of the morning, and the day was still young. At that rate, the work was progressing a little ahead of schedule, but Lyons knew that wouldn't last long. Somewhere along the line, something would get screwed up and they'd fall behind. When was the last time anyone heard of a construction job coming in on time?

"Goddammit, Ironman," Greene said, shaking his head. "All it's going to take is for one asshole to get in there and we'll be compromised."

"I know, Buck," Lyons said wearily, "I know. But it's what we have to work with."

The two men had had that conversation at least once a day since the project had been given the go-ahead. Each time it came down to the fact that they were exposed in a way they never had been before. But they were taking extra precautions. To Lyons, it was an acceptable risk. To Greene, no risk was acceptable and nothing would change his mind until he had the Farm completely under his control again.

"Look at it this way, Buck," Lyons said. "We have another day, two at the most, on the damned trees, and then the locals will be out of here. After that, we'll be working only with cleared personnel. Gadgets and Pol are running double checks on their backgrounds, and we'll pick up on any problems with them.''

For years, background checks had been the basis for all levels of government security clearances, and Greene had sworn by them. Then he'd had the first serious breach of security at the Farm when a deep-cover KGB agent had been hired on as a probationary blacksuit. The man had passed all of his federal background checks, even those that were Stony Man specific, with flying colors. After all, he'd spent the previous ten years as a federal marshal, and Greene personally chose him and brought him into the Farm for his first tour of duty.

Fortunately, the man had been unmasked before he had been able to inflict any serious damage on Stony Man. He had, however, been able to make good his escape. Even though no damage had been done, Greene had taken the incident personally and had tendered his resignation. Both Brognola and Price had turned him down flat, but he took a vow never to get sucked in again. He had also launched a massive manhunt to find this man, but failed to get even a glimmer of where he had gone.

The failure ate at him, and he was determined not to screw up this time.

THE INTERMITTENT WHINE of the industrial laser cutters in the Computer Room was driving Aaron

Kurtzman out of his mind. The constant hum of the ventilation fans was no better, but at least the fans didn't cut off and on. Worse even than the laser whine was the acrid stench of the vaporizing concrete. The vent fans were doing their best to keep the gases sucked out of the Computer Room, but it wasn't working.

The only thing he could say about this high-tech solution to cutting concrete was that it didn't raise much dust. Jackhammers could have easily done the work in a more traditional manner, but it wouldn't take much concrete dust to destroy the cyber center that made Stony Man what it was.

The core of SOG was the vast electronic network Kurtzman and his staff used to keep watch on the world. There was hardly anything that existed in a cybernetic or electronic form that they couldn't eavesdrop on or break into. Anything from secret bank accounts in the Grand Caymans to a terrorist's cellular phone calls and coded transmissions from deep-space spy satellites could be accessed and decoded at Stony Man Farm.

Even with everything that was going on around him, Kurtzman wasn't letting his end of the stick swing in the wind. Keeping track of the world's current and potential trouble spots required a round-the-clock attention from both his staff and the banks of computers that crowded the Computer Room. The only good thing he could say about this Annex mess was that when it was finished, he and his people were finally going to have a decent place to work. He was also going to have the room to install some additional equipment he had wanted. One of the most difficult parts of his job was keeping abreast of technology, and maybe now, he would actually be able to get ahead for a change.

The old Computer Room would become the terminal for the underground electric rail cars that would connect the farmhouse and the new Annex. That was what the concrete cutting was all about. As soon as the opening in that wall was completed, a blacksuit crew would start doing the underground excavation out of sight of the crews working above them. It would be more irritation, but hopefully a little less annoying than that damned laser.

KURTZMAN WASN'T the only one who had already had more than enough of the construction work both at the farmhouse and at the Annex. Barbara Price was finding it difficult to stay focused on her job, and she was almost ready to get physical with Hal Brognola for allowing this to happen. She knew that the Farm desperately needed to be expanded, and the project had been in the planning stages for years. But she had always hoped they could just keep limping along as they were until after she retired.

Being the Stony Man mission controller wasn't the extent of Barbara Price's job. She was also the de facto head honcho of the Farm operation. Hal Brognola's name was at the top of the organizational chart, but he did most of his Stony Man work from the Justice Department building in Washington. His cover job as a special liaison to the White House meant that he had to maintain an office close to Capitol Hill like the rest of the inside-the-Beltway Feds. That put the burden of the everyday managing of the Farm on Price's shoulders.

Having Able Team working with Buck Greene was a help, but the security concerns weren't the only things that were out of whack. All of the Farm's routines had been disrupted, and she was having to really struggle to focus.

As THE LAST of the old orchard was being taken out, Schwarz and Blancanales were working with a surveying crew that was mapping out the excavation site in the center of the Annex.

Unlike the logging, this job had been given to an outside firm on government contract that was used to keeping closemouthed about its work. Even so, the company was going to do only half of that phase. Once the excavation was completed, they would build the forms, lay the conduits for the electrical power and plumbing, pour the concrete and depart. A second firm, also cleared for sensitive government employment, would excavate a second site, do the same work and also leave.

Later, a blacksuit crew would cut through the

walls and join the two separate underground chambers.

A third firm would come in and build the wood-processing facility that would be erected on what was actually the roof of the underground chambers.

It was a complicated and time-consuming way to build the new facility, but there was a very good reason for doing it that way. With three crews doing the work, none of them would know what the structure they had built was going to be used for.

CHAPTER THREE

*WHO Medical Research Facility 64,
Donner's Station, Congo*

Dr. Frank Bullis looked around his primitive but homey office. There was little in it that the average American doctor would recognize as belonging in a medical facility. But the average American doctor wasn't working at a remote medical-research facility in Africa. Bullis almost hated to admit it, but he was really going to miss the place. It had been the center of his existence for almost two years now.

There was much of the realities of working in the Congo Basin, though, that he wouldn't miss—the almost unbearable daily discomfort of heat and insects, the Stone Age sanitation, the never-do-today-what-you-can-put-off-indefinitely mentality of both the locals and the local governments. Nonetheless, he had learned to operate within the realities of Africa and was actually making progress, more progress than he would have been able to make if he had stayed back in his comfortable Atlanta office.

Bullis was a medical-research superstar. Any medical institution in the world would have been proud to have had him on its staff. He could have easily obtained the funding to open his own facility had he wanted. But he was a virologist with the Centers for Disease Control in Atlanta, Georgia, and he had requested to come to this remote UN research station to conduct his research on the Ebola virus. The fact that he was an African American might have had something to do with his choice, but mostly he had come because this was where the bugs were.

Africa was the breeding ground of the most dangerous viruses in medical history, and there was no shortage of them in the Congo Basin, the darkest heart of Africa. This was the birthplace of AIDS, Ebola, hemorrhagic fever and a dozen other deadly diseases that had made their appearance in the past few decades. And these were just the ones that had been identified.

The World Health Organization sponsored Bullis's research, and his staff had come from a dozen nations, most of them in the West. There were Africans on his staff, as well, but most were in support and nursing positions rather than involved in primary research. The African medical community had been forced to come up to speed very quickly as far as dealing with Ebola patients was concerned, and they were doing the best they could with an impossible situation. But they didn't have the education necessary to do the research to try to find a way to stop the virus.

Once Western medicine could find a way to combat these killers, the African doctors could then take over and try to protect the population. But a cure for Ebola wasn't yet in sight. And if the political situation in the area didn't stabilize, it might never be found. The reports of a Simba uprising were particularly troubling, since none of the regional governments could take the time from their never-ending internal conflicts to unite to battle the Simba cult.

It was the Simba threat that had Bullis evacuating his station. He had no idea how long he would be gone, but the reports clearly indicated that it was no longer safe for Bullis and his staff to stay. There were some things in Africa that were even more dangerous than Ebola, and the Simbas fell into that category.

Captain Ian Connelley, head of Bullis's UN security force detachment, put his head around the corner of the door. "Doctor," he said firmly, "we have to leave now. The Simbas are on the way and I can't wait any longer."

Bullis reluctantly picked up his briefcase, bulging with papers and computer disks, and left the office. Outside, the UN troops were putting the finishing touches on the defenses around the compound. To Bullis's mind, there were far too few men, only twenty-eight, to adequately defend the facility. He had requested more forces from the regional UN commissioner, but had been told that his wasn't the only facility that was being threatened by this most recent crisis and that no more troops were available.

That might have been true, but there were few sites that presented the danger that his operation did. There was no way that he could break down the containment room and take the samples of live Ebola with him. Hopefully, the facility would be bypassed and he could return. If it was attacked by Simbas, the security detachment would defend it and, again hopefully, the soldiers would be able to keep it from being destroyed.

He couldn't allow himself to even consider any other outcome.

BULLIS WAS STEPPING into the jeep when he heard an inhuman scream of agony from the woods in the direction of their escape route.

"Bloody hell!" the Irish captain muttered. "The bastards got around us."

"What do you mean?" Bullis asked

"We're surrounded, Doctor. Get the rest of your people back inside and pray that we can hold them."

Clutching the briefcase to his chest, Bullis ran back into the facility. The dozen or so remaining support personnel had taken shelter in the laboratory, the largest of the camp's structures. It was no more defensible than the other buildings, but it did have the viral containment facility, the one thing that had to be defended.

The next half hour was right out of the pages of a horror-movie script. The bloodcurdling scream Bullis had heard was only the first of many such screams that echoed from the jungle around the compound. The screams would suddenly stop, and a few moments later, a bloody body barely recognizable as being human would be thrown into the open.

Captain Connelley calmly went from one defensive position to the next, reminding his troops to save their ammunition for the assault. As with most peacekeeping companies, his command was made up of troops from two different nations, New Guinea and the Ukraine. While he would have rather have had a company of the lads of the Irish Rangers, his old regiment, he knew he was luckier than many UN commanders. At least he didn't have Pakistanis and Indians to try to keep separated or Arabs and damned near anyone else.

Both of his contingents were from warrior cultures and not only did they get along smashingly, but they were also ready to fight. In particular, his New Guineans were descended from head-hunting cannibals, and they weren't intimidated in the least by the Simbas' bloody antics. In fact, they saw them as laughably overdone. On the other hand, his Ukrainians weren't accustomed to seeing men being skinned alive, but their Cossack ancestors hadn't been cupcakes, either. Both groups would fight to the death so as not to disgrace the people back home, and it looked as if they were going to get that chance today.

Connelley didn't have to be a psychic to see that there would be no way out of this for any of them. From just what he was able to see in the jungle, he estimated that they were outnumbered four to one, and he knew there were more Simbas he couldn't see. This wasn't the battle he would have chosen, but his ancestors had been fighting lost causes for hundreds of years.

Suddenly, the jungle around the research station erupted with screaming, chanting Simbas racing for his position.

"Steady, lads," Connelley called out. "Wait for them."

When the first of the Simbas were in range, he pulled his pistol and shouted, "Fire!"

The shock of the opening volley staggered the Simbas, but it didn't stop them. Leaping over the bodies of the fallen, they charged the perimeter. The detachment had only two light machine guns covering their perimeter, and their sandbagged positions were overrun first by a solid mass of Simbas. Once the defensive ring was broken, even the faintest chance of the situation having a good outcome vanished.

The New Guineans had taken to wearing African machetes with their battle kits. When the Simbas got in too close for them to use their FN assault rifles, the big knives went into action. Men who had grown up slicing coconuts with a single blow now used their blades to sever Simba heads. The heads toppled as fast as the knives could flash, but again the sheer numbers told the story.

Standing back-to-back, the Ukrainians fought like tigers, their bayoneted rifles stabbing like spears. The Simbas again ignored their losses and clambered over the wall of bodies to get at their enemies. Their old Cossack ancestors would have been proud of them as they died in place, their faces to the enemy.

Like the Irishman he was, Connelley also went down fighting, but taking as many of the invaders with him as he could. When he had exhausted the ammunition for his Beretta pistol, he picked up an FN assault rifle from one of his fallen Ukrainians and continued to fire. When he was rushed, he ran out of ammunition and, not having time to change the magazine, he died swinging the rifle like a club.

There was a pause after the last of the UN troops went down, but it was brief. Setting up a victorious howl, the surviving Simbas turned and raced for the buildings of the research station. Bullis watched in horror as they forced the door and stormed into the lab, their rifle butts and machetes swinging.

Though the medical staff offered no resistance, two of them were hacked to death. Shards of glass-ware flew through the air and crunched underfoot as the workbenches were swept clear of the equipment.

When one of the Simbas slammed a rifle butt into the glass of the door to the containment room, red warning lights flashed and sirens wailed, announcing that the seal had been breached. The crazed troops rushed in, their rifle butts and knives swinging in an orgy of destruction.

When Bullis rushed to stop them, a rifle butt to the chest knocked him to his knees.

IN THE CONFUSION, one of Bullis's African male nurses, Joseph Bodo, stripped off his lab coat, shirt and shoes. His cotton pants were a little cleaner than those of the average Simba, but that was all. Slipping out the back of the lab into the kitchen, he stopped by the gas grill the cooking staff used and ran his hand over it to collect as much grease and soot as he could. Spreading it on his face and hands, he looked a lot more like a Simba when he was done. He didn't have a weapon, but some of the men he had seen didn't either, so he hoped that he wouldn't be questioned.

Outside, he headed away from the buildings trying to look as if he knew where he was going. Now that the fighting had ended, the Simbas were busy looting and stripping the bodies of the UN troops. Two of the female nurses had been taken from the lab and were being used by the Simbas. Bodo knew that they would be killed afterward and, as a Christian, he offered a silent prayer for them.

"I see you, brother," one of the Simbas called out to him in greeting.

"I see you, too," Bodo replied.

"A good kill today. We will eat well tonight."

The nurse kept from gagging and forced a smile on his face. "I hope so. The march was long."

The Simba laughed and continued on his way.

Bodo faded into the jungle and headed in the direction of the setting sun. If he could avoid the Simbas, he should reach the next UN outpost in less than two days. They had to be told what had happened at Donner's Station so the WHO and the CDC could be warned of the danger.

WHEN TAIBU WALKED into the lab, the red lights were still flashing and the siren howling. At his shouted command, they were shot out. At the far side of the room, he saw the white doctor on his knees as one of Taibu's Simbas hefted a machete over his neck. The colonel raised his hand, and the Simba stepped back. Another lion warrior hauled the doctor onto his feet and held on to his arm.

The Simba leader studied this American black for a long moment. It was easy to see that the man was African in name only. There was more white blood in him than black. Being half-white himself, Taibu had no idea why this Yankee had left the comfort of America to work in Africa. He had to be mentally defective, like so many of the other Americans he had met. For being the richest and most powerful people in the world, they could do the most stupid things, like come to Africa to try to change things. Taibu's explanation for this strange behavior was that these Americans had to be mentally ill. It was the only answer he could come up with.

"Please tell them to stop," Bullis gasped as he tried to explain in French. His chest ached from the rifle-butt blow he had taken, but he couldn't tell if he had a cracked rib. "Everyone who goes in there will get Ebola and die. Please stop them."

"We can speak English if you would like," Taibu said. "I am Colonel Charles Taibu."

"Frank Bullis," the doctor said as he sucked in another deep breath.

"You are the doctor who is experimenting with the bleeding disease?"

"Yes, I am," Bullis replied. "The men who went in there—" he pointed to the breached containment area "—they might be contaminated with the Ebola virus that causes that disease. They must be kept apart from the other troops, or they will infect them and everyone will be at risk of dying."

"How long does it take for them to get sick after they have been infected?"

"They will start feeling feverish in a day or two, and that is when they will be the most dangerous to the other soldiers. Anyone who is in contact with them then will become infected, too."

When Taibu didn't immediately reply, Bullis continued. "Then they will start bleeding and die in another two or three days."

When the Simba leader still didn't reply, Bullis got frustrated. "Dammit man! You have to isolate those people before they kill you all."

Taibu turned to one of his subordinates and spoke in French rather than one of the many dialects spoken by his ragtag army. "Take the men who went in there and have them dig their own graves. And make sure they dig them deep."

"As you command," the Simba said.

"But you can't just kill them," Bullis pleaded. One of the reasons he had been selected to run this station was his ability to speak French. In much of Africa, it was still the lingua franca of the educated classes, and he had understood the exchange.

"Why not?" Taibu shrugged. "If what you say is true, they are dead men already, are they not?"

"Good God, man." Bullis recoiled. "Let me check the containment seals on the samples first. They might not have broken them. If they didn't break, they might not be infected yet."

"You have until the graves are dug."

Bullis glanced at the grinning Simba guards watching his every move. "I have to get into a biohazard suit before I can go in there."

"You have my permission."

Watching the doctor get into the white biohazard suit amused the Simbas, who had never seen anything like it. They laughed and clapped their hands as if he were putting on a show for them.

Holding the portable air supply, Bullis picked his way through the debris and entered the area. When the warning had reached the station, he had shut down the experiments, returned the virus samples to the biohazard container and sterilized the work areas. If the Simbas hadn't cracked the container, they should be okay.

To his relief, the thick metal box with the red warning labels appeared to be undamaged. The lock was still intact, and through the thick glass window, he could see that the twelve Ebola vials were intact, as well. Taking the box with him, he backed out of the wrecked room. Even though the glass was broken, he closed the door after him.

Taking off his helmet, he turned to Taibu. "The vials are safe." The relief was plain in his voice. "You can let those men live now."

"You say that these vials contain the live Ebola virus?" the Simba leader asked.

"Yes," Bullis said, nodding emphatically. "I can't even begin to tell you how dangerous they are. They're the most deadly thing on Earth, and there is no cure for the disease they cause. If this virus gets loose, tens of thousands of people might be killed."

"Good." Taibu smiled. "And now they are mine."

In a flash, Bullis realized what he had done. He

had just given this power-crazed madman access to the most dangerous biological weapon in the world.

"Oh, dear God!"

Taibu leaned closer to Bullis. "Yes, Doctor." He laughed. "I am God now. I have the Ebola virus."

Bullis fell to his knees and covered his face with his hands.

CHAPTER FOUR

Stony Man Farm, Virginia

Joseph Bodo, Frank Bullis's African nurse, made good his escape from the slaughter at Donner's Station and ran into a roving UN peacekeeper patrol the next morning. His report came one day before Taibu's Simbas overran two more remote medical-care facilities, taking a large number of Western hospital and charity workers captive. With that move, the new Simba threat moved to the top of the list of UN African crises. Charles Taibu finally had the attention he had wanted.

For the past several years, the United States hadn't paid much attention to the perpetual chaos in Africa. The Middle East, the Balkans and Asia had taken precedence as American's chief concerns. There had always been trouble in Africa, and the official view was that it wasn't in America's interest to get too involved. Since nothing was ever solved there, the risks simply weren't worth taking. Now that Frank Bullis and several other prominent

American medical and relief-agency personnel were being held captive, however, the White House was forced to take notice.

Aaron Kurtzman had picked up on the first of the Simba reports through his UN contacts. He had opened a working file on the topic and had kept up with the latest developments as they came in. When the names of prominent Americans started showing up on the lists of the dead and missing, he briefed Hal Brognola on what he had.

After checking in with the White House, Brognola got back to Kurtzman. "So far," he said, "we're not being tasked on this one. The Man has given it to the Joint Chiefs, and they're sending in the Special Operations Command. A joint Air Force and Delta Force operation is being put together to do a snatch."

"Better them than us," Yakov Katzenelenbogen, Stony Man's tactical adviser, said.

"When are they launching?" Kurtzman asked.

Brognola glanced up at the bank of digital clocks on the wall. "The troops are in the air now to Morocco, and they'll launch from there after refueling."

HOSTAGE RESCUE WAS the type of mission the Special Operations Command did well, and the mission profile was right out of their playbook. An AC-130 Spectre gunship would pave the way with its stunning flying arsenal. Computer-aimed 20 mm Vulcan cannons, 40 mm Bofors automatic guns and a self-loading 105 mm howitzer would clear the landing zone at the local airstrip for the two C-130 Hercules troop transports carrying the Delta Force assault team.

Once a perimeter had been established at the airfield, a third cargo aircraft would deliver three Bradley armored personnel carriers for the run into town. Once the hostages were recovered, they would be rushed back to the airstrip, loaded into the C-130s and flown out. It was a routine mission the SOC units had done several times before. But working in Africa had a way of turning even the best planned operation into a dud.

This time, the awesome sight of a charcoal-gray AC-130 Spectre spitting high-explosive fire like an aerial dragon didn't panic the locals. Taibu's Simbas were more afraid of him than they were of any aircraft. Among the weapons he had managed to secure for his ragtag army were several Russian Strella shoulder-fired antiaircraft missiles. While not as sophisticated as the U.S. equivalent Stinger missiles, they were more than adequate to take out a large, low-flying, turboprop aircraft in broad daylight.

Three Strella missiles arched into the sky almost at the same time. One of them missed the Spectre completely, one slammed into the aft fuselage and failed to detonate, but the third homed in on the port-side inboard engine. The resulting explosion tore through a fuel tank, and the blast destroyed the gunship's controls on that wing.

The low-flying Spectre did a slow wing-over and slammed into the ground.

Firing flares to confuse any more Strellas that might be heading their way, the two orbiting C-130s carrying the Delta Force troops did a speedy one-eighty and fled back to the safety of the southern Atlantic. It wasn't the Special Operation Command's finest hour. The African factor had struck again to foil a good plan.

IT WAS A CRUEL happenstance that a CNN news team was on hand doing a story on the Simbas when the AC-130 was shot down. The cameraman got a fleeting shot of the aircraft as it plummeted to the ground. The 20 mm Vulcans and 40 mm Bofors were still firing as it came down, but the rounds were going wild.

When the news crew reached the crash site, they were able to tape the aftermath, and it was a scene only too familiar to their American TV audience. With the aircraft wreckage forming a backdrop, jeering crowds dragged the corpses of the U.S. flight crew from the twisted metal, stripped and mutilated them.

This time, though, the audience got the added benefit of seeing the result of putting servicewomen in combat positions. One of the naked corpses that was seen being hacked to small pieces with machetes was that of a young blond woman, Air Force First Lieutenant Tracy Wells, the AC-130's flight engineer.

The one-time high-school class president and Air Force Academy honor graduate had been badly burned in the crash and was barely recognizable even before the jeering Simbas started hacking at her face.

That part of the footage didn't go over the air on the regular CNN *Headline News* programs. But Stony Man Farm intercepted CNN's raw feed from the satellite and got it all in bleeding color.

The Stony Man crew were no strangers to the brutal realities of the world. Their job required that they deal with it on almost a daily basis. They also dispensed brutality themselves, but never in this particularly barbaric fashion. When the Stony Man warriors went into action, they brought death swift and certain, but they never despoiled the dead. That was a trait of only the most inhuman and depraved. It was a sad commentary on the human race that such brutality was still so common in some parts of the world.

Aaron Kurtzman shuddered and finally turned away from the monitor. He couldn't watch it any longer.

Barbara Price was made of sterner stuff, but she, too, had tears in her eyes by the time the video clip ended.

"I'll never understand man's inhumanity toward

his fellow man,'' Yakov Katzenelenbogen commented. In his long career, he had witnessed more bloodshed than most and was beyond shock. But even he had to agree that this was a particularly nauseating performance. "I hope that the bleeding hearts of the world who think that all men are brothers are watching this carefully."

"Unfortunately," Kurtzman said, "they'll never get the chance."

"The man responsible for that seriously needs to be killed." Price bit out the words. Since she was a woman who marked men for death as part of her daily routine, her words carried a finality few could give them.

"We can only hope," Katz fully agreed. But whether Stony Man would be called upon to deliver justice in this case was still undecided. Phoenix Force and Able Team usually worked in the world of clandestine warfare. It was no less dangerous— in fact it was usually more so—but it was conducted out of the public eye. This outrage had been broadcast all over the world, and a public response would be necessary to satisfy the American people.

He knew well, however, the problems of sending conventional forces in to deal with a situation like that. Taibu's Simbas had no homeland and not even a base camp. They were living off the land, looting both food and needed military supplies as they went. There was no place to bomb, and sending ground troops to try to chase them through the jungle would be a fruitless exercise and would raise a firestorm in the United Nations.

Even though they hadn't been invited to spearhead the American response yet, that didn't mean that he couldn't start working on a solution to this situation. As the Farm's tactical adviser, it was his job to evaluate situations and plan solutions to them. His plans, of course, would involve the practical application of the commandos known as Phoenix Force.

Congo

CHARLES TAIBU WAS QUICK to take advantage of the CNN news team's presence. As soon as they wrapped up shooting the street scene, he invited them to stay and film a news conference the next day. Considering what they had just witnessed, they had no choice but to agree.

THE NEXT MORNING Taibu wore his pressed colonel's uniform and faced the battery of CNN cameras calmly. In Moscow, he and the other Third World students had often made propaganda films, so this wasn't the first time that he had been in front of the lights. Plus, as a proved African leader, he was experienced at speaking to his intended audience. The populations of Africa and the so-called Third World nations were the targets of his performance today. And for that reason, he would conduct the press conference in English, the international language.

Much of his message, though, had already been delivered for him by CNN. There was hardly a non-Western country that didn't enjoy seeing dead Americans being dragged in the dirt. He had gained great stature with that broadcast, and that was only the beginning. The statements he would make today and the exhibits he would reveal would only make him that much more powerful.

His first exhibit was the material he had captured at the Donner's Station medical-research site—in particular, the heavy metal box with the red biohazard markings on all four sides and the top. Backing it up were the copies of research protocols in English and French, and the lists of experiments filling several cardboard boxes. When these were shown to the world, he would be seen as a savior.

When he got his cue from the cameraman, he stepped up to the microphone. "My name is Charles Taibu," he began, "and I represent the people of the Congo region of Central Africa in their rightful struggle for self-determination and freedom from the Western powers and their puppet governments."

Since Taibu had made it very clear that no interruptions would be allowed, no one questioned his self-proclaimed leadership or his view of Africa.

"In the conduct of my struggle, I started hearing stories of inhuman experiments being conducted at a UN medical facility at Donner's Station, experiments involving the Ebola virus. When I went there to investigate these rumors, my followers were attacked by UN troops and we were forced to fight for our lives. When the battle was over, we examined this so-called United Nations facility and discovered that it was actually financed by the infamous CIA."

He paused for a reaction, but there was none. This wasn't the first time the journalists had heard charges like this against everyone's favorite whipping boy, the CIA. It was the modern equivalent of blaming the Devil.

"I learned that they were manufacturing these viruses at this facility so they could be loosed on the nonwhite populations of the world. The Yankee capitalists plan to depopulate what they call the Third World so they can enslave the survivors and exploit the resources of these nations in a new form of colonialism.

"This box—" Taibu pointed to the biohazard container "—contains the results of their experiments, the Ebola virus grown to specifically attack Africans. And—" he swept out his arm to point at the wreckage of the crashed Spectre "—the aggressive response of the United States military is only further proof that this so-called medical-research station was working to create diseases, not to eliminate them. Had it not been, there would have been no need to try to keep me from exposing what I found there.''

He drew himself erect. ''I call upon all of the peace-loving peoples of all the world to protest this violation of international law and to punish the criminals behind this unthinkable activity.''

He smiled. ''You may ask questions now.''

''Mr. Taibu?'' one of the CNN journalists cautiously asked.

''It is Colonel Taibu,'' the Simba leader replied. ''What is your question?''

''What do you plan to do with the hostages you took at Donner's Station?''

''They are not hostages,'' Taibu said sternly. ''They are capitalist war criminals and they will go on trial before a people's court to answer for their infamous crimes against humanity.''

Hearing the Marxist buzzwords, the journalists' ears pricked up. It had been a long time since an African leader had played that tune; African communism had been dead for years. If Taibu was reviving Marxism, as well as the Simba cult, the world was in for a nasty surprise. African Marxism had always taken a particularly brutal turn.

''Colonel Taibu,'' the journalist asked, ''would it be fair to say that you are a Marxist?''

Taibu smiled. ''I do not follow any one political doctrine,'' he said smoothly. ''I do know, however, that the Western powers have raped Africa and her resources for over a century, and the time has come

for that to end. Africa belongs to the African people, not to greedy imperialistic capitalists backed by
their military puppets. I intend to insure that the
peoples of Africa are no longer exploited by outsiders and can enjoy the wealth of their nations
themselves.''

The journalist wasn't naive enough to believe a
word Taibu was saying, but he did know that the
Simba leader was a man to be watched. If he was
planning to create a new Marxist state in the Congo,
blood would flow like a river.

United States

TAIBU'S ACCUSATIONS were taken at face value at
the United Nations, and no amount of expert testi-
mony from either the WHO or the CDC could calm
the storm raging in the General Assembly. As usual,
the Third World coalition, egged on by the militant
Islamic nations, used the Ebola crisis, as it was being called by the media, to heap abuse on the Great
Satan of America. In particular, Pakistan, India and
the Sudan were raising the issue of the United
States censuring them for having tested weapons of
mass destruction when America was working on
even more deadly biological weapons.

Even the Security Council got caught up in the
turmoil. As had happened one too many times in
the past, they hadn't been informed in advance of
the American hostage-rescue attempt. France and

Russia joined with China and made much of the debacle. They weren't buying the story that the CIA had gotten into the bioweapon business, but expressed their concern that the United States was flexing its imperialistic muscle in Africa. In particular, France considered Africa to be part of her traditional sphere of influence and didn't welcome Uncle Sam's new interest in the Congo region. A censure vote passed easily. When it was vetoed by the American ambassador, the French and Russian delegates walked out of the Security Council.

To make matters worse, Congress decided to take a dim view of the President's use of the War Powers Act this time. Had the mission been a success, they would have applauded him, but the dice had rolled against him and made him a target of political sniping. As the old saying went, every success had a thousand fathers, but a failure was always a bastard.

With the votes against him in both the UN and in Congress, the President had no choice but to publicly state that no further U.S. military action would be taken against Charles Taibu and his Simbas.

Even though the President had been forced to back down, he had no intention of leaving American citizens in Taibu's hands. He had absolutely no faith in the scheduled UN hostage-release negotiations and knew better than to expect anything to come from them. The UN's track record on that sort of thing could only be described as abysmal. He also knew that the longer the hostages were held captive, the less likely they were to survive the ordeal. The images of Simbas hacking at the AC-130 crash victims was indelibly burned into his brain.

Fortunately, there was always more than one string in the President's bow—there was the Stony Man option. It wouldn't be the public response he so badly wanted to send that butcher Taibu, but he couldn't sit on his hands and do nothing. Reaching for the secure phone, he punched in the speed-dial code for Hal Brognola.

The phone was picked up on the second ring.

CHAPTER FIVE

Stony Man Farm, Virginia

Hal Brognola's trip to the Oval Office didn't take long, and he called from Washington to alert the Stony Man crew to the pending mission. Barbara Price and Yakov Katzenelenbogen were both waiting at the landing pad when he stepped out of his chopper. They had long ago learned to judge the seriousness of any situation by the set of their boss's jaw, and it was clenched tightly this time.

"None of this needed to have happened, Hal," Katz growled. "If the President had turned us loose in the beginning, we could've easily whacked Taibu, and his movement would have fallen apart. Cults like the Simbas are always externally, not internally, driven. Without him yelling at them, they'd be nothing."

"But he didn't," Brognola stated bluntly.

After enduring years of Capitol Hill wrangling and infighting, Brognola had been forced to take a harshly pragmatic approach to his job. When everything turned sour, it didn't do any good to complain about what might have been if something had been done differently. To keep from going crazy, a person just had to pick up the pieces and try to do something useful with them.

"Has Striker arrived yet?" Brognola asked.

"He got in last night," Price said.

Mack Bolan wasn't officially a member of the Stony Man action teams, but more often than not, he took part in their operations. Next to the Phoenix Force commander, David McCarter, he had more time working in Africa than anyone in Phoenix Force, and he would be a welcome addition to the team this time.

"Ask him to please join us in the War Room."

BROGNOLA STARTED with the bad news. "We've lost all international support on this one," he announced. "Even the British are lukewarm about taking any further measures against Taibu. They're still fighting the bad karma left over from their old African empire."

"Bloody bastards," David McCarter muttered. "What good are allies if they won't stand by you?"

"The risk of Ebola getting loose has shocked them into immobility."

"And they think that if they just sit on their thumbs, everything will go away?" Katz asked. "They think that Taibu will 'do the right thing' and we'll all live happily ever after? Not likely!"

As a veteran of the Israeli wars, Katz knew the futility of wishful thinking. His nation had survived only by taking a proactive view of politics and never expecting the other guy to be anything other than a heartless, treacherous bastard—which was why he was called the enemy.

"You're stealing my lines." McCarter grinned.

"What does the Man want us to do?" Mack Bolan cut to the chase. Like Brognola, he knew they had to play the hand they had been dealt.

"To be honest with you," Brognola said, "he doesn't know what we *can* do at this point in time. He's asking for suggestions."

"We can make a surgical strike with a small nuke," Aaron Kurtzman suggested. "That will take out the man and the virus at the same time."

Brognola shook his head. "The Joint Chiefs already brought up that idea, and he turned it down flat. The biggest problem with that solution is that Taibu reportedly is keeping the hostages with him at all times. The other thing, of course, is trying to get the international support that would be necessary for a nuke strike. With the President's problems in both Congress and the UN, that's pretty much impossible unless we can show a direct threat to the United States."

"We can always try our luck on the ground," Bolan said. "Jump in, try to rescue the hostages and get them to safety before they can catch up with us."

"I think that's what he wants to hear," Brognola admitted. "But considering the difficulties of the situation on that particular piece of ground, I wanted to talk to you before I made a commitment."

"It's not a particularly good scenario," Katz readily agreed. "We all know that. But it might be the only card we have to play."

"How soon could you launch?"

"That's up to the Air Force, since they're going to have to drive us there. The other part, of course, is how fast we can get a fix on where Taibu is holding those people and what kind of opposition we'll be facing."

"We might have that covered," Kurtzman said. "The last information I have is that the Simbas are heading for a small town, and chances are good that they might stay there for a while. Every few days, they stop and hole up to rest and replenish their supplies."

"Let's take a look at it," Bolan asked.

Kurtzman used the keyboard on his wheelchair tray to call up a digital satellite photograph on the big-screen monitor. As he zoomed in, a small town appeared. Many of the buildings were of typical African construction, but a cluster of structures in the center of the town had the unmistakable look of European colonial architecture. The paved plaza in front of the largest of the buildings was a dead giveaway.

"If they keep on the route they're taking now," he said, "they're going to run into this place."

"Keep an eye on the approaches to it," Brognola stated, "and let me know as soon as you can confirm their movement toward it."

"Can do."

"And in the meantime, David—" Brognola turned to McCarter "—you and Striker get the men ready."

The Briton stood. "Piece of cake, boss."

EVEN THOUGH they didn't have an exact target yet, the Phoenix Force warriors knew the drill, and the mission prep went into high gear. McCarter and Bolan made up an equipment list, and the commandos started filling it. While Bolan worked with them, McCarter went down to the Computer Room to start the map-and-photo recon of the area they'd most likely be dropping into in a day or two.

As they worked together, Katzenelenbogen noticed that McCarter was considerably less than his usual self. Katz had been the leader of Phoenix Force before moving into the tactical adviser job at the Farm, and he easily caught the mood of his old teammate.

"You look a little pensive, David," he said as McCarter went over the satellite shots of the tentative landing zone again. "What's on your mind?"

"It's that bloody Ebola," McCarter answered. "I don't like messing around with it. It's nasty stuff."

Katz instantly understood where the ex-SAS commando was coming from, but there was little he could say to reassure him this time. A good burst from an H&K would kill any man, but a person couldn't get a sight picture on a virus. The mission was going to be dangerous enough without the added threat of an invisible foe.

"And I don't like bloody Simbas," McCarter added. "I thought we'd seen the last of those bastards years ago. They're right nasty buggers, too."

"That they are," Katz agreed.

No one knew exactly when or where the Simba warrior cult had originated, but it had been resurrected several times during the African colonial wars of the sixties and seventies. Each time, warriors who believed that they were invulnerable to bullets had savaged large regions of the continent. Unlike their cousins, the Mau Mau, the Simbas had ravaged both the African and European populations equally, and this time was no different.

The news from Africa was grim. It was almost as if their leader had taken a page from the playbook of Chaka, the great king of the Zulus. The Simbas were making their way through the Congo Basin, leaving nothing behind them but death and total destruction.

Even grimmer than the devastation the Simba army was leaving in its wake was the fact that none of the national governments in the region were in any shape to even try to confront them. For the first time, the chance of a Simba government, if such a thing could exist, controlling a large part of the Congo Basin was a distinct possibility. That wasn't a Stony Man concern, however. Their mission was much more focused.

Taking out the Simba's leader, Charles Taibu, was always a possibility, but that task would be better assigned to a Tomahawk cruise missile. There was no way that Bolan and Phoenix Force could take on an army of fanatics. Any assassin trying to go through the Simbas to get at their leader wouldn't make it three steps.

"This isn't going to be a walk in the park, David," Katz told his old friend. "But with a little bit of luck, you'll only be on the ground a little over twenty-four hours."

"As far as I'm concerned," McCarter said, "that's twenty-four hours too bloody many.

"And—" he tapped the satellite photo "—this pickup zone doesn't do much for me, either."

"Remember," Katz said. "That's just a tentative PZ for planning purposes. We won't make the final decision until you're in the air."

Since the Simbas were always on the move, finding a place to hit them wasn't going to be easy. They stopped each night and camped, but in the mornings, they usually moved on again—except when they ran across a sizeable town as they had done now.

"If they go into that town and spend a few days

looting and pillaging like they've done before, you'll be able to make your move there.''

''And if they don't,'' McCarter argued, ''we'll be bloody well strung out all over half of the Congo trying to chase the bastards down.''

''They'll stop sooner or later,'' Katz said confidently. ''Even an army of marauding butchers has to rest and regroup every now and then.''

IN THE ARMORY, Bolan and the rest of Phoenix Force were preparing the weapons and equipment they would take on the mission. As always, John ''Cowboy'' Kissinger, the Farm's armorer, was on hand to fill their requests and make last-minute checks and repairs.

Gary Manning prepared their weapons, the standard assault mission mix. Manning and Calvin James would take the 5.56 mm Heckler & Koch assault rifles, while the rest of the team would carry the MP-5 submachine guns. Since they were going up against fanatics who attacked en masse, the fast firing subguns would go a long way to blasting them out of trouble if they needed them. Plus, since the 9 mm ammunition was lighter than the 5.56 mm, they could pack considerably more of it.

''You want me to carry demo?'' Manning, the team's blaster, asked Bolan.

''I don't see that we'll need too much, but take a minimum load in case we need to get into that building.''

T. J. Hawkins, ex-Ranger, was Phoenix Force's jump master, and he always saw to the preparation of the equipment for airborne operations. Since their jump this time would be made from a C-141 Starlifter at ten thousand feet, he chose to use the standard thirty-two-foot steerable parachutes. Since the low-altitude jump wouldn't require the use of oxygen equipment, the weight saved could be reassigned to extra ammunition and medical supplies.

Calvin James doubled as the team's medic, and he gathered the medical supplies they might need to take care of mistreated hostages. Since they didn't expect to be on the ground for much more than twenty-four hours, they would go light on rations so they could take even more medical gear than normal. One day's worth of MREs and two days' emergency rations should cover any emergencies.

Rafael Encizo prepped the communications gear, both the com links that connected them in the field and the satellite communications radio they would need to keep in contact with the Farm. Extra batteries and a spare com link were set out, as well. This was one mission where they couldn't afford to be out of communication with base.

NOW THAT THE LAST of the stumps in the Annex had been hauled away, Buck Greene felt that he could relax a little. That part of the project had been contracted to a local logging outfit, and the wood was being sold to a furniture-making company in the next county. It sounded harmless enough, a PR gesture to the local community, but Greene had seen it as the greatest threat of the whole Annex program, as none of the loggers had been backgrounded. But that was finished now, and all those uncleared people were back where they belonged— outside of his perimeter.

The next thing on the schedule was the excavation phase and it would be done by the cleared contractors, Belmont Construction, and Three Sons. Lyons and his team had completed the new background checks on all of their employees, and everyone had come out clean. That didn't mean that he would trust them any further than he could spit backward, but it should mean that they would be a little more trustworthy than the uncleared local loggers.

The Belmont trucks would start rolling in the morning, but tonight the old perimeter of the Farm would be fully activated again. He wouldn't shift the perimeter defenses to cover the Annex until there was something there worth guarding. After checking on the deployment of the blacksuit night guard, he headed for the dining room. Katz's goulash was on the menu, and he loved goulash.

CHAPTER SIX

Stony Man Farm, Virginia

The man driving the Belmont Construction flatbed
truck loaded with the backhoe didn't miss a beat
when he turned into the main gate of Stony Man
Farm and braked to a stop. He raised a hand in
greeting to the two farmhands at the gate without
worrying that they would recognize him. It hadn't
been that long since he had been one of them, but
he wasn't wearing the same face he had worn back
then. The name he was using now wasn't going to
set off any alarm bells with anyone, either. It had
originally belonged to a Belmont Construction
worker in California.

The driver had been born Dimitri Spatkin in a
little town outside of Leningrad, the son of a KGB
officer and a Bolshoi ballerina. At six years of age,
he had been sent to a special KGB school outside
of Moscow known as "Little Amerika." There he
learned to be as American as the proverbial apple
pie and the boy next door. Growing up, he had

chewed Juicy Fruit gum, watched American TV and movies, played baseball and football, joined the Boy Scouts, ate Big Macs, went trick-or-treating each Halloween and spoke American English all day long.

When he graduated from the Little Amerika High School, he saw his mother and father one last time before taking a flight to Canada. Once there, he crossed the border in British Columbia, and drove south to Eugene, Oregon, where he stepped into the life of a young American named James Gordon. What happened to the real Jim Gordon after he showed up, Spatkin never found out.

That fall, he went to college in Portland, where he had majored in law enforcement. Little Amerika agents were encouraged to get into jobs of trust and responsibility.

After college, he became a federal marshal and waited patiently to be activated by the KGB. Instead of getting his chance to go into action for Mother Russia, though, he watched in utter dismay as the Soviet Union collapsed and all of America rejoiced in the fall of the Evil Empire of communism. With the demise of the KGB, as well, Spatkin had resigned himself to never being able to strike back at the nation that had brought down the government of his homeland. Rather than try to return to a new Russia in turmoil, though, he stayed in the States.

He was in his tenth year of federal service when

he was tapped to apply for a highly-classified federal job at a place called Stony Man Farm. He had never heard of the place, but the level of clearance involved meant that it had to be something important and he accepted the offer. He easily passed the interview process and was hired on as a probationary security guard at the facility, a blacksuit.

When he realized what kind of organization he was working for, he saw that he had finally found a way that he could strike a blow for his Mother Russia. He learned that Stony Man Farm had played a big role in the demise of the Soviet Union, that their so-called action teams had been responsible for hundreds, if not thousands, of Russian defeats on the world stage. He started testing the Farm's defenses and gathering information for a strike.

Before he could finish the job, though, something went wrong. It was actually a series of somethings, all small, but revealing to the professional paranoids who ran the security apparatus at Stony Man. He had been forced to shoot his way out to keep from being captured, but had made good his escape.

Rather than flee the country, though, Spatkin went to California and took up one of the active identities he had in reserve for emergencies and started to look for a way to link up with other ex-Soviet agents who had been left behind. The biggest part of the problem was that as a Little Amerika agent, he had never had a handler to check in with. When he was to be activated, someone would contact him and he didn't know who this person was or even if he still existed. He had only known that such a man should have existed and, that if he did, someone would know who and where he was.

The man he had sought would be an old KGB spymaster, but not one of the New York or Washington, D.C., diplomatic corps spy crowd. He would be another man who had been secreted into the United States as a deep-cover agent, and he, too, would have been in limbo since the destruction of the Soviet Union. If this man was still in the States, he would have contacts with what was left of the Russian Communist Party back in the Mother Country, the diehards who hadn't turned their coats and were only pretending to be good little capitalists.

Spatkin knew that he wasn't the only Little Amerika agent who had been cut off when the Soviet Union collapsed, and he suspected that they would have gravitated to the so-called Russian Mafia. Being a deep-cover agent required skills that only an organization like the Russian Mafia could use to the fullest.

Linking up with the local Russian gang had been easy enough. He just found the nearest stolen-car chop shop and convinced the men running it that he wasn't a cop. From there, he quickly worked his way up the chain of command until he reached a man named Anatoly Dubchek, late of Riga, and the leader of the largest Russian Mafia gang on the

West Coast. As he had expected, Dubchek had been a KGB operative and was currently also the owner of a string of "gentlemen's clubs" on the West Coast.

Dubchek hadn't been as interested in what Spatkin had to say about Stony Man Farm as he was in putting the young Russian to work in his organization. His extensive federal law-enforcement experience would help Dubchek keep out of trouble. Spatkin took up his old name and the cover of a recent immigrant, complete with Green Card, and went to work. As the months passed, he didn't forget his plan to make Stony Man Farm pay for what they had done to his country, but he'd had to file it under unfinished business.

It had been a pure fluke that had brought Stony Man Farm back into his sights.

Spatkin was at one of Dubchek's strip clubs in Stockton, California, one evening. The girls in this club were some of the finest women he had ever seen in his life and why not? Dubchek could take his pick from the finest young women Mother Russia could produce, and getting them to the States was no trick at all.

The girls saw ads in Russian newspapers promising high-paying jobs in the West, particularly in America and Canada, for outgoing young women who wanted to travel. Hoping to improve their lives, hundreds of them flocked to sign up for interviews. The interview process weeded out all but the youngest and best looking of the candidates, and they were sent to a two-week prep school in basic English and the ways of the West. After that, they were flown to the eastern United States or Canada before being brought to California. When they arrived, eager to pursue their new careers, they were told that they were to be "exotic dancers" at exclusive clubs to pay off the expenses of being flown to the West.

Most modern young Russian women, particularly those from the big cities, weren't as sexually prudish as their American counterparts, so this wasn't a big deal. The girls were sent to a school to be taught how to wear their hair and makeup in the latest American styles and how to "dance." After a week's training, they went to one of the clubs to start working off their airfare by flaunting their bodies.

Once a girl had settled down to the routine at her club, she would meet a nice young Russian man who would befriend her. Early in this friendship, the man would take the girl to his apartment and seduce her. Spatkin often enjoyed playing this role himself as a perk of his job. After their tryst, he would give the girl a little money, supposedly to go to help buy her out of the club. The girl would freely accept the money, not knowing that the entire procedure from start to finish, including the payoff, had been videotaped.

Once the club's owner had the videos in hand,

the girl was told that since she had started whoring, she would whore for him, as well. Some of the girls shrugged their shoulders and agreed. Those who refused were threatened with being turned over to the police and charged with prostitution. Faced with that, most of the girls immediately capitulated. Since they were Russians, being turned over to the police was unthinkable. Occasionally, a girl got stubborn and was raped into submission. Rarely did it take more than a day or two for that process to work. Any girl who didn't submit, no matter what was done to her, was driven out into the desert at night, shot and buried.

As a result of the Russian pipeline, Dubchek's clubs had the finest selection of girls to be found anywhere in America. They weren't cheap, but they were exclusive and well worth the money. Since Spatkin had risen high in Dubchek's organization, he had free run of the clubs and made the most of the privilege.

One night, Spatkin was at the bar of the club and the man sitting next to him was well on his way to getting drunk. As the man knocked them back, he muttered to himself about his troubles. Though Spatkin wasn't particularly interested in hearing what he had to say, he couldn't help but overhear much of the drunken monologue. It was the usual tale of work and women problems. But when Spatkin heard the man mutter something about "Stony Man Farm," he couldn't believe his ears.

"Excuse me, mister," he said, "I don't mean to be butting into your business, but I thought I heard you say something about a place called Stony Man Farm in Virginia. I've got a friend who lives around there, Jed Monroe, and I've been thinking about visiting him."

"You can have it, pal." The man looked at the stage again. "That fuckin' farm, whatever it is, and the whole fuckin' state of Virginia. I've never been there in my life and I sure as hell don't want to go there now. All I want to do is stay right here."

"Why don't you, then?" Spatkin asked.

"It's the damned company I work for," the man said. "They provide workers for classified government construction jobs all over the damned place. And they have these stupid work rules that say I can't turn down two bids in a row without losing my ticket with them. I turned down the last one a month and a half ago and the one before it so I could stay here."

His eyes flicked back up to the stage "And if I don't take this one, I'll get fired."

The man shook his head and downed the last of his beer in one gulp.

"Damn! They pay real good money, travel expenses and per diem, as well, so I can't complain about that. But I want to stay in California so I can see Katrina on the weekends. There's no fuckin' use in me making all this damned money if I can't spend it on someone when I want. And Katrina sure as hell needs it more than I do, the poor kid. She's Russian, you know, and she's got family back home she wants to bring over here. Her little sister is real sick, and you know how backward Russian medicine is.''

He shook his head. ''You know, those bastards over there are still…''

Spatkin listened to the man's concern for a girlfriend in trouble and couldn't believe his luck. The story he was hearing was one of a dozen different scripts the whores were taught to give their customers in hopes of getting bigger ''tips.'' The house took seventy-five percent of each girl's wages for selling her body, but she got to keep half of the tips. The girls were encouraged to collect special friends they could see on their day off, and this guy had fallen for it big time.

As he listened, Spatkin started working out a plan. This guy wanted to stay in California, and he wanted to get back to Stony Man Farm. That could be arranged.

IT HAD BEEN EASY to convince the lovesick Mel Bradley to brief Spatkin about the details of working for his specialized company, Belmont Construction. A few dollars and some extra time off for Katrina got him to turn over his ID and security-clearance papers. It was another happy coincidence that his FBI background check had just been updated and would be valid for another two years. For what Spatkin planned, that was more than enough time. He should only need a month or so to do what he wanted to do—find a way to destroy Stony Man Farm once and for all.

To make this plan work, Spatkin submitted to some basic plastic surgery, dyed his hair and grew a mustache. When he was done, he wasn't an exact twin of Mel Bradley, but the resemblance was close enough.

One night, the real Mel Bradley received a panicked call from Katrina to come to her place quickly. He was never seen again. The next day, a different Mel Bradley flew east to join up with the Belmont Construction crew in Virginia. Since he was a driver, his first task was to deliver the backhoe on his truck to the construction site.

"You with Belmont Construction?" one of the farmhands asked as he stepped up on the running board and leaned in the open window of the truck.

"Yep. " Spatkin tapped the photo-ID badge clipped to his left shirt pocket. "That's me."

"Name?"

"Mel Bradley."

The blacksuit ran down his list and checked off his name. "Okay." He waved him through.

Spatkin wisely kept the smile off of his face as he shifted into first gear and let out the clutch. Once again, he was inside Stony Man Farm, and this time he wouldn't fail.

As Spatkin slowly maneuvered his flatbed truck past the vehicle shed and gas pumps, he took in everything he could see without being too obvious about it. Since he knew the Farm's secrets, he could look past the pastoral serenity of the place and see the hidden teeth. He also saw that Buck Greene had extra men working the boots-and-jeans detail. Opening up the Farm for this construction job had to be giving him screaming nightmares. The Farm's security chief was professionally paranoid, and this would be punching all of his buttons.

Considering the serious risks that it entailed, Spatkin still wasn't sure why he'd felt so strongly that he had to come back to the Farm. Maybe it was because he had blown it so badly the first time and wanted a chance to try to rectify his failure. Now that he was here, though, he was very glad he had come.

He didn't know what this construction job entailed, but it was obvious that America's premier terrorist command center was expanding its operational base. And that could only mean that they would be able to cause more trouble than before for the rest of the world. Now that the capitalists in Mother Russia were thoroughly ruining the country, the Communists were poised to take control again, and he would be a hero of the new revolution if he could help their cause by shutting down this viper's nest.

While he was glad that he had come, now that

he was seeing the Farm again he wasn't sure what, if anything, he might be able to do to damage Stony Man. With the blacksuits on extra alert, his job was going to be even more difficult. But, if nothing else, he could make a detailed recon of these improvements and try to get it to someone who could use the information to plan future operations against the enemy.

ON HIS SECOND TRIP of the day, this time carrying a load of steel rebar, Spatkin saw Barbara Price walk out of the farmhouse on her way to Cowboy Kissinger's armory. He hadn't forgotten how stunning she was, but seeing her anew was a bit of a shock.

During his life as a Little Amerika agent, he had spent most of his time alone. Having a permanent girlfriend wasn't a good thing for an agent. Since getting tied in with the Russian Mafia, however, he hadn't spent many of his nights alone. He'd had his pick of dozens of women, each of them Slavic beauties. Every time he had taken a long-haired Russian blonde into his bed, he remembered an American blonde who had worn her beauty as unconsciously as an angel wore its wings.

There was something about Barbara Price that had gotten under his skin like no other woman he'd ever known. The funny thing was that he couldn't say that he really even knew her. He had seen her from a distance a few times and had spoken to her twice, but it had been enough.

He knew he was acting like a schoolboy about her, but he couldn't help himself. And he decided that when he brought vengeance to the Farm, he'd do everything he could to keep her safe from it.

CHAPTER SEVEN

Over the Congo

The C-141 Starlifter cruising at twelve thousand feet over the Congo was transmitting the identification of an unscheduled Air France commuter flight. It had taken off from Morocco and, after it dropped off its Phoenix Force cargo, it would turn off its transponder and disappear from radar. As the jet transport approached the drop zone over the Congo Basin, it descended to ten thousand feet and slowed to 175 miles per hour.

"Coming up on the drop zone in ten mikes," the pilot called back over the intercom.

"Roger, ten mikes," T. J. Hawkins said as he stood and walked to the front of the cabin.

As the team's jump master, he ran the drop but would be the last one out the door. Since only the six of them would be jumping this night, he opened only one of the Starlifter's side doors and extended the blast shield. With the blast shield breaking the slipstream, exiting from the aircraft at 175 miles per hour wasn't much worse than jumping from a turboprop Hercules at 125.

"Okay, guys," Hawkins called out. "Let's do it. Secure equipment and stand at the door."

Hearing the traditional Airborne command, Bolan and the Phoenix Force commandos lined up single file in front of the open door. Since they would free-fall for most of the ten thousand feet to the ground, they didn't clip their static-line hooks to the cable running the length of the cabin.

The jump light above the open door was showing red. At the thirty-second mark, it started to blink, and when the light turned green, Hawkins shouted, "Go! Go! Go!"

David McCarter led the team out the door by diving into the night sky and assumed the spread-eagle free-fall position. He was quickly followed by the others at three-second intervals. Hawkins leaped into the dark after everyone else had cleared the door. Above him, the Starlifter throttled up and started to climb for altitude again.

The fall through the night sky went fast at terminal velocity. Even at that altitude, Hawkins could smell the jungle and feel the reflected humid heat of the vegetation below. Soon, he would be in the middle of that heat.

"Coming up on deployment in one zero," Hawkins called over the com link as he watched his altimeter wind down. "Five...four...three...two... one... Deploy!"

The sudden shock of the parachute opening drove the crotch straps of the harness into his groin, but that was a small price to pay for having a good canopy above him. With five more good canopies visible under him, Hawkins's jump master duties were over.

Any parachute jump that ended with a good canopy was a successful jump, but the landing was always another matter. Since they had pulled their rip cords at only one thousand feet, the ground was coming up fast. Through his night-vision goggles, Hawkins saw that for once the drop zone was as advertised—clear of major obstacles—so their landing should be good, as well.

They might do two for two on this night jump, a good start for the mission.

Stony Man Farm, Virginia

"THEY'RE DOWN," Yakov Katzenelenbogen announced in the Farm's Computer Room. "And the DZ is secure."

"What's the latest on the hostages?" Hal Brognola asked.

"It still looks like they're headed for Molani, that town we spotted," Aaron Kurtzman replied. "Taibu sent some of his Simbas ahead this afternoon, so they might be staying there for a while."

"Send that to Striker."

"It's on the way."

Congo

THE STONY MAN TEAM moved out at first light the following morning, and the dawn brought them a vision of hell on Earth. Their DZ had been on the edge of the swath the marauding Simbas had cut through the countryside. When they emerged from the jungle, they ran right into the aftermath. The path the lion warriors had made ran straight toward a nearby village. The destruction was total.

What could be burned had been set alight, and tendrils of smoke from the ashes of huts and corrals still stained the morning sky. Crops and gardens had been trampled into the earth or burned, and the corpses of livestock littered the area. It was scorched earth at its finest and would have impressed even Genghis Khan.

When they got closer to the burned homesteads, they saw the debris of looting—broken pottery, household goods and clothing—scattered on the ground. The debris of rape and killing was also evident. Hacked, bloated bodies lay in the grotesque postures of death. They had been there long enough that it was no longer easy to tell how much of the damage had been inflicted by the Simbas' machetes and what was from the carrion eaters that were following in their wake like hyenas following a lion pride.

McCarter's eyes flicked over the bodies of three women lying beside a well. From the condition they were in, he couldn't tell what had caused their deaths. Nonetheless, he gave them a wide berth. Disease always followed war, and nowhere was that more true than in Africa.

McCarter was no cherry when it came to working in Africa. From Cape Town to Tangier, from Angola to the Red Sea, there was hardly a spot on the continent that hadn't felt his boots at one time or another. The devastation they had jumped into this time wasn't new to him. The only thing that was different about it was having the Ebola virus on the loose.

Anyone who had been a soldier as long as he had been had encountered the world's more exotic diseases more than once. Disease followed war like dawn followed the night. If you were lucky, it passed you by. If you weren't, Western medicine could usually take care of you. That wasn't the case, however, with many of the new diseases that had cropped up in Central Africa over the past few decades. By far, Ebola was the worst.

He adjusted his load harness and continued on, knowing he couldn't outwalk a virus.

BY THE TIME the Simbas reached the town of Molani, Dr. Frank Bullis was staggering, barely able to put one foot in front of the other. On any other occasion, he would have collapsed several hours earlier, but he had witnessed what had happened to those who dropped out of the column. The Simbas hadn't even tried to get them back on their feet, but had simply butchered them where they lay. It was a powerful incentive for him to keep walking.

This was the third long march he had made since he had been captured, and he wasn't sure that he'd be able to make another one unless he got food and a chance to recover. None of them would.

As the prisoners were herded into an animal corral in the center of the town, Bullis smelled the fetid water in the wooden troughs. He knew that drinking from them was a sure ticket to any number of African maladies, but his cells screamed for moisture and he knew that if he didn't drink, he would die.

The Simbas laughed as the prisoners fought to get at the muddy, stinking water. They did, however, let them drink their fill before herding them into a nearby building, the largest in town. At one time, the building had been a combination colonial administrative office and jail. The Simbas had taken over the offices in the front of the building and were making use of the cells, as well.

The holding area was two open cells with the traditional iron bars for walls. Each cell had only four beds, but twice that many people were being packed into each of them. Bullis was surprised to see a couple of other whites already in the cells. Taibu's people had to have swept the surrounding area and added any Westerners they found to their catch.

The white man in Bullis's cell was overweight

and dressed in what had once been one of the expensive tropical suits often seen in movies. When the man realized that Bullis wasn't a local, he walked up to him with a smile on his face and his hand out. "I'm Bill Jordan, director of the World Children's Foundation."

Bullis took his hand. "Frank Bullis."

"You're an American, right?"

When Bullis nodded, Jordan continued. "What are you doing here, getting back to your roots?"

Bullis ignored the jab, realizing that black Americans making pilgrimages to Africa had become a well-worn cliché. "I've been working at a World Health Organization research station here."

"Can you talk to these people?" Jordan glanced over at the Simba guards. "I've been trying to tell them who I am, but none of them speak English. Even their leader doesn't seem to understand."

"I don't speak any African languages, no," Bullis replied. "But their leader, Colonel Taibu, speaks French, as do many of his men. I also know that he speaks very good English whenever he wants to."

"I'll be damned. You speak Frog, then?"

Bullis simply nodded. This self-important, insensitive asshole wasn't the first ugly American he had run into in Africa, or back in the States for that matter. While men like him could be found in all walks of life, they seemed to be very commonly found overseas.

"Great." Jordan beamed. "Maybe you can tell them who I am and see if they can get in contact with my office for me. My wife is a big contributor in Washington, and she sits on the boards of several major charities. If I can get word to her about where I am, I'll be out of here in no time. My wife doesn't mess around, I can tell you that.

"Oh, yes," Jordan added when Bullis didn't automatically respond. "I'll also do what I can to try to get you out of here along with me. You know what they say, one hand washes the other."

"I wouldn't count too much on Taibu caring about who you are back in the States." Bullis wanted to get this guy calmed down before he got himself in big trouble. "I'm a doctor with the CDC, and that doesn't seem to impress him much."

Jordan got a blank look on his face. "What's the CDC?"

"The Centers for Disease Control and Prevention in Atlanta," Bullis replied dryly. "It's an arm of the federal government."

"Oh, yeah, that," Jordan said. "But I'm a big political contributor and I met the President. If they don't let me go, there's going to be real trouble for them, I can tell you that."

Bullis decided not to waste any more of his time trying to get through to Jordan. Some lessons were best learned alone.

"I'll do what I can."

"I won't forget it," Jordan said. "I promise you,

and I'm a man who never forgets a favor. You know, my brother runs a big Cadillac dealership in Maryland. Maybe I can get him to give you a break on a new car.''

"Thank you," Bullis said, trying to keep a straight face. "But I have a Mercedes in storage back in Atlanta."

"Oh."

Stony Man Farm, Virginia

AARON KURTZMAN HAD BEEN blessed with a cloudless day over the Congo Basin. It had been fortuitous that an NRO Keyhole 12 satellite had been parked in orbit over the region earlier because of the general level of unrest. When the mission was laid on, he had been able to assume control of the spy bird and zero it in on the operational area. With Hunt Wethers assisting him, they were able to keep a close eye from space on the Stony Man team's movements.

"How are they doing?" Barbara Price asked.

"Not too badly," Kurtzman said. "They're keeping well behind the main body, and the Simbas aren't much for watching their back trail. In fact, they aren't much on anything that might be called tactics."

"What's the latest on the hostages?"

"It looks like a couple more of them dropped out along the way, but there were still a dozen of them on their feet when they were crowded into that building at Molani."

"Are you going to be able to keep a night watch on that place?"

"Not as well as I'd like," he admitted. "I'd sure as hell like to have one of the new Blackbirds orbiting over the area, but..." He shrugged.

It was ironic that now that the United States had their SR-71 Blackbird fleet back in the air, they had been forbidden from using one of them to cover this mission. The refurbished spy planes had the most sophisticated sensors and cameras that had ever been flown, but the President had expressly denied their use this time. Until the hostages had been freed and were waiting for pickup at the pickup zone, Taibu's threat was being taken seriously.

"As long as the weather stays clear," Wethers interjected, "we should continue to have adequate coverage."

"Tell Striker to try for the rescue tonight."

"He's already planning for it."

CHAPTER EIGHT

Molani, Congo

Dusk found the Stony Man team roughly one-quarter mile outside the town of Molani. Littered as it was with debris and the occasional hacked-to-death body, the Simbas' trail hadn't been difficult to follow. But then, Taibu had no reason to try to hide his army's movements. He had the largest cohesive force in the region, and no one dared to try to confront him. He was the lion king, and lesser men were well advised to keep out of his way.

Once they were within sight of the town, the commandos went into a defensive circle, rested and checked over their weapons as they waited for the night. Lions weren't the only ones who knew how to hunt.

As soon as it was dark, the team got ready to move in on Molani. Before they left, Bolan put in a satcom radio call back to Stony Man Farm.

"The Simbas look like they're planning to stay

awhile," Yakov Katzenelenbogen said, giving him the latest report. "They've settled in, and it looks like they're throwing one of their famous parties, bonfires and all. We'll keep an eye on them with the infrared and let you know if they look like they're going to go out for a midnight snack."

Bolan chuckled.

"The hostages are still being held in the main building," Katz continued. "So that's still your primary target."

"Roger," Bolan said. "We'll be moving on it immediately."

"We'll be standing by here. Good luck."

T. J. Hawkins joined Calvin James on point for the movement into the outskirts of Molani. Gary Manning and Rafael Encizo took the flank guard positions, while Mack Bolan and David McCarter brought up the rear. Even before they approached the first of the houses, they heard pounding drums and chanting. Katz had said that Taibu was having a big party, and that would make their work much easier. Simbas liked their beer, and drunken warriors wouldn't be as alert as they should be.

It was nice when the enemy made the job easier. The Stony Man team was well aware that they were only six men going up against almost a thousand, and they needed all the help they could get, as well as a little luck. But they also knew that a man made most of his own luck.

As they reached the edge of town, they saw no

signs of the inhabitants. No one wanted to stick around when the Simbas were coming through the area. From the looks of the household furnishings scattered around the dwellings, they had been looted of everything of any value. That, too, was a standard Simba practice.

"We have bodies," James whispered over the com link.

"Roger."

A minute later, James came back. "Disregard, they're drunken Simbas, not dead ones. But be on the lookout for them."

Closer to the center of town, drunken Simbas littered the ground like the dead. The commandos let them live as long as they didn't wake as they passed. Those who stirred were silently dispatched with a fighting knife.

Kurtzman's Keyhole satellite images had showed the hostages being herded into the biggest building facing the central square in town. They couldn't be positively IDed from space, but that building would be a good place to start looking for them.

"The plaza's dead ahead," James reported. "And I think I've spotted our target."

From its position in front of the central plaza, it was obvious that the building had once housed the colonial administration offices. It was the most massive structure they had seen so far, and it had that "official" look to it. There were no guards walking their posts around it, though—only two Simbas by the front entrance, and both of them looked to be drunk or asleep.

"James, T.J.," Bolan said over the com link, "check around the back."

When Hawkins and James reached the rear of the building, they found the entrance unguarded and the door unlocked, as well. "It's completely clear back here," James reported.

Now that they had located the building, Bolan, McCarter and Encizo split off to take up blocking positions around it. If they were discovered before they could get the hostages out, they would try to fight a rearguard action to give the others time to make their escape.

Once the security was in place, James, Hawkins and Manning slipped into the building. Inside, only one Simba was awake, but he was drunk and singing to himself instead of watching his prisoners. Hawkins slipped in behind him like a dark green shadow, reached out to slap a hand over his mouth and drove his fighting knife into the hollow of his neck. The Simba stiffened and died without making a sound.

While Hawkins was taking care of him, Manning and James went through the building behind him, dispatching the other sleeping Simbas where they lay.

"All clear," James called over the com link.

"I found the cells," Hawkins called back to

James. "You and Gary watch the back door while I get the people ready to move out."

Rifling the body of the guard, Hawkins didn't find any keys, but when he tried the cell doors, he found that they weren't locked.

"Okay, people," he called out softly as he swung the doors open. "Time to go home."

Most of the hostages started to talk at once when they woke to see Hawkins in a camouflage uniform and face paint. The cavalry had arrived

"Silence!" he hissed, trying not to raise his voice. "Dammit! Shut up!"

When the hostages fell silent, he asked, "Is there anyone here who speaks English. We've come to get you out of here."

When several hands were raised, he pointed to the man closest to him, a black wearing what had once been Western-style clothing. "I want you to be in charge of these people until we're clear of the town."

"What do you want me to do?" Frank Bullis asked.

"Just make sure that you all stay together," Hawkins said. "Anyone who gets lost on the way out of town will be on their own. We won't be able to go looking for you. We'll be taking you out through the Simba camp, and it's essential that you stay absolutely quiet. Most of them are drunk, but we can't count on that. If they spot us, we won't be able to fight them off."

Bullis nodded his understanding.

"What about me?" Bill Jordan pushed his way through the crowd to the front.

"What about you?" Hawkins frowned. "If you want to get out of here, mister, just follow everyone else and keep your mouth shut."

The rebuff was so unexpected that Jordan slunk back and kept his mouth shut.

"First," Hawkins said as he turned back to Bullis, "can everyone here walk on their own?"

Bullis translated that into French for the few non-English speakers. When no one raised a hand, Hawkins keyed his com link. "We're ready in here."

"It's clear back here," James radioed from the back door of the building. "Bring them on."

"Okay, people," Hawkins said, "let's go, single file and for God's sake keep quiet."

The hostages left the cells and fearfully followed their rescuer past the Simba bodies, swinging wide around the pools of fresh blood on the floor.

THIS TIME, Hawkins was alone on point while the other commandos rode herd on the ex-hostages and watched their rear. Rather than lead them directly to the south and their planned extraction point, Hawkins took them back out the way the team had entered the town. From there, they picked up the trail the Simba army had taken into the town and followed it in reverse. The footprints of hundreds of feet would hide their tracks from the teams Taibu would put on them as soon as he discovered that the hostages were gone.

As soon as they were well clear of the town, Bolan called in the flank and rear security. James joined Hawkins on point again, and they moved out to the east at a faster pace. The hostages were having difficulties keeping up, but this was no time to go easy on them. The next few hours could make the difference between their escaping and being recaptured. They realized that and didn't complain.

Two miles farther on, Hawkins found a hard patch of ground that wouldn't show footprints very well and turned off to the south. So far, the march had been hard enough on the ex-hostages, but once they reached the jungle, the going really got rough.

The two pointmen had found an established game trail and were following it. But following a trail in the Congolese jungle at night was like breaking a fresh trail in any other jungle in the world. More than once, one of the ex-hostages had to be helped back on his or her feet after stumbling and falling. The only plus was that it wasn't hot and humid. Instead, it was chilly and damp, but their exertion kept the hostages from feeling it.

BY THE TIME the commandos halted, their charges were near collapse. Several of the ex-hostages were leaning on one another, and Encizo was supporting the one woman in the group. They were still trying, but they just weren't able to give more.

The first thing the commandos did was break out their emergency rations and hand them out to the exhausted people. They weren't very tasty, but if a person was hungry, it didn't matter. The ration bars were high in calories and would provide them with badly needed energy.

Water was more of a problem than food. A person could go for days without eating, but dehydration could put him down quickly. For the past several days, none of the hostages had had enough water, and they were on the verge of collapse. The commandos carried only four quarts of water each, and it would have to last until they were flown out.

Some of the civilians had instantly fallen asleep and had to be woken to get their share of the food and water. After they drank, Manning talked to them long enough to get their names and nationalities so they could be radioed back to the Farm. No matter what the outcome of this mission, at least the hostages' families would be notified that they had been rescued.

"These people are in real bad shape, Striker," Encizo said, stating the obvious. "Do you think we're going to be able to move them fast enough tomorrow to keep ahead of those bastards?"

"We have no choice," Bolan said. "We sure as hell can't stand and fight them."

"Let's hope they get a lot of rest tonight."

HAL BROGNOLA WAS in the Stony Man Computer Room when the call came in that the escape had been successful. They had been scanning the town with the space-borne IR sensors, but with all the Simbas in Molani, it was difficult to pick out who was sending the heat signatures.

"We're well clear now," Bolan reported, "and we halted to give the prisoners a little rest. They're in pretty bad shape and haven't been fed much recently."

"Good work, Striker," Brognola replied. "We'll be keeping watch over you, so you should be able to let them get as much rest as they can before you have to move out again."

"Watch well," Bolan said. "This jungle is thick. We'll need all the early warning we can get if they start after us tonight."

"We will."

"Is the extraction still laid on?"

"I have a CH-47 standing by ready to fly in as soon as you reach the pickup zone."

"I'll give you a tentative ETA after we get moving again in the morning."

"Good luck."

IT WAS WELL PAST DAWN before Charles Taibu learned that his hostages had escaped in the night. And from the dead Simbas in and around the administrative building, it was obvious that they'd had help getting away. His reaction to this setback to his plans was well studied.

Taibu was half-white, he had a Western first name, he spoke three Western languages and he had attended a Western university. He had learned to function well in the Western social milieu, but it was all a well-practiced facade. In his heart he was all African, and that was the only reason he had been able to weld the Simbas into the force that they were. Like the lions whose name they had taken, the Simbas would follow only the strongest and most fearless, and he always met their expectations

It was at times like this that he had to make sure that he didn't show weakness in any form.

Intruders had sneaked into the lion's den and had stolen what was his. It didn't matter that it had been men and a woman who had been taken from him instead of gold. He was the lion, and the hostages had been his to do with what he wanted. Now they were gone, and someone would have to answer to him for that outrage.

Taibu was rational enough to know that the rescue had been pulled off by professional soldiers, most likely Americans, and his men hadn't stood a chance against troops like that. But the lion never showed mercy. He led the Simbas only by imposing unwavering discipline, and to excuse this failure would be the first crack in his leadership. Before he sent his Simbas in pursuit of these intruders, he first had to punish those who had failed him.

This failure was too serious to simply allow the

miscreants to dig their own graves and then stand in them while they were shot in the head. He also couldn't spare the time to give them the grand punishment, setting them loose in the jungle and sending his men out to hunt them down.

He could, though, put them in the ring of death to play the role of the lion's prey. It wasn't as satisfying as a full hunt, but it would serve to again remind the Simbas of his power.

At his command, a hundred Simbas in full regalia formed a ring in the plaza in front of the old administrative building. The half-dozen survivors of the enemy attack were pushed into the ring. They had been stripped naked, but had been given machetes to try to defend themselves. They were Simbas, and the lion didn't go down without a fight.

One of the men simply threw himself against the ring and was quickly hacked to death. The others tried to defend themselves, but in vain. Even when they landed a good blow at one of their attackers, a fresh one moved in to continue the fight. Even so, it took almost ten minutes before the last man went down. When his body stopped twitching, the Simbas started roaring their hunting cry.

"After them!" Taibu roared, and pointed toward the jungle. Screaming their hunting cries, the hundred Simbas raced for the edge of the trees.

After watching his warriors head off in pursuit, Taibu went back inside the administrative building. Even when he was on the move, the Simba leader wasn't out of touch with the rest of the world. He had a powerful radio in his baggage train that he used to keep in contact with his main base. The Yankees had defied him, but he had a way to make sure that it didn't happen again.

The Ebola virus samples he had taken from the WHO research station at Donner's Station were with him. They were a source of power greater than anything he would ever get his hands on, and he hadn't trusted them out of his sight. The Westerners quaked at the mere name of the virus, and now he would give them something to worry about.

The main reason that Ebola wasn't a greater killer than it was was that it hadn't been introduced to the crowded cities of the West. When it flared up in remote African villages, it was relatively easy enough to isolate the infected and let the virus burn itself out. Were it to get loose in a major Western city, hundreds of thousands of people would die.

Keying the radio microphone, Taibu issued a set of orders to the cadre he had left behind. The CNN TV news crew was with them as his "guests," and he would use them again to get his message to the American government.

Once his message had been delivered, he could take his time tracking down his prisoners and those who had taken them from him. And he would let the jungle do most of his work for him. The lion didn't fight the jungle; he owned it.

CHAPTER NINE

Stony Man Farm, Virginia

Dimitri Spatkin knew how observant the blacksuits could be, and he tried not to be too obvious as he looked around each time he drove through the Farm to the job site. With the exception of the work that was being done on the new project, he didn't see that much had changed since he had last been there. The blacksuits had a couple of new pickups, the vehicle shed had been painted and the old gas pumps looked to have been replaced, but that was about it.

All of the camouflage that allowed the Farm to exist out in the open was still in place, but camouflage only worked on someone who didn't know what he was looking for behind it. He didn't buy the peaceful-farm facade because he knew where the teeth were hidden. But as he had proved before, the teeth weren't enough to defend against an enemy who was inside the perimeter.

He hadn't spotted Buck Greene yet, but he was

in no great hurry to do so, either. Even though Spatkin looked very little like the probationary blacksuit who had called himself Jim Gordon, he wasn't ready to look the security chief in the eye and see if he was recognized. He hadn't forgotten the man's eyes and how they hadn't missed anything. Even something as small as "Gordon's" cheating at cards so he could lose to his fellow guards.

He also hadn't forgotten the ever present video cameras that had been his downfall first time around, and he was fully aware that he was being watched every minute he was inside the perimeter. Even though most of the cameras were well camouflaged, he knew where to look, and spotted them. He knew that Greene would be working overtime checking the tapes, so he would have to be careful not to do anything that any other Belmont employee wouldn't do.

Spatkin also hadn't missed the extra security guards at the work site itself. Having worked on the boots-and-jeans detail himself, he knew who the blacksuits were. He also knew that they were wearing their com links and had their weapons close at hand. He was still casting around, trying to find the weak link he could exploit, but not just any weak link.

He owed it to his country and to himself to find something that would inflict maximum damage on this place and put it out of operation. He knew that the American government would never stop interfering with the internal affairs of Mother Russia, but maybe taking out Stony Man Farm would make it more difficult for them to cause trouble in the future. When a socialist Russia was born again, she would need all the help she could get to become strong.

BELMONT CONSTRUCTION HAD rented an entire motel in the nearby small town of Wilsonburg to house their workers for the duration of the job. It was right next door to a tavern and across the street from a steak house, a perfect location for their work crew. Spatkin hung out in the bar, playing pool and keeping his ears open. It didn't take long before he started to pick up on the local buzz.

"You're one of the guys working out there at Stony Man Farm, aren't you?" the barmaid asked as she brought him a refill on his draft.

"Yeah, I am," Spatkin answered.

"You don't happen to know when they're planning to have that chipping mill up and running, do you?"

When he looked blank, she said. "You're building a wood-chipping mill out there, aren't you?"

"I guess we are." He laughed. "I wasn't listening to that part of it. You know how it is, the foreman's always jacking his jaw about something, and all I want to know is where they want me to drop my load."

"You're a driver?"

Spatkin nodded. "Yep, all that construction material's got to get out there somehow."

The woman frowned. "I still don't understand why some of our local companies couldn't bid on that job instead of bringing in all of you outsiders.

"No offense," she added quickly. "But we really need the work around here. My sister's oldest has been out of work for months now, and his wife is expecting again."

She shook her head. "They're nice enough people out there at Stony Man, but they can sure be strange at times."

"I'm afraid I really don't know anything about them," Spatkin said. "Like you say, I'm from out of state."

Spatkin listened with half his mind while the barmaid went on and on about people he didn't know and would never meet. If this woman's sentiments were common among the local population, the Stony Man operation wasn't making many friends lately. What Chairman Mao had written in his Little Red Book about running guerrilla operations applied equally to secret organizations. You needed to have the locals on your side so you could hide among them. Maybe he could use this dissatisfaction to his advantage somehow.

When the barmaid stopped for breath, Spatkin quickly dived into the one-sided conversation. "I'll tell you what," he said. "If I hear anything about their future plans, I'll let you know, okay?"

"Thanks, mister."

Though the woman was well beyond the cutoff age of anyone he would ever consider having anything to do with and was ugly to boot, it never hurt to keep the locals on your side. Barbara Price might have forgotten that critical factor, but he sure as hell hadn't.

"I'm Mel," he said, flashing her a winning smile. "Mel Bradley."

The barmaid almost blushed as she ran a hand through her hair. "I'm Mabel Windam. Pleased to meet you, Mel."

After finishing his beer, Spatkin left the bar and headed back to the motel. He was a working man now and had to keep working man's hours.

THE ANNEX PROJECT WAS GOING so smoothly that Carl Lyons and Able Team were starting to get seriously bored. The first round of background checks had all come in, and except for the barroom dustups, nonsupport beefs and speeding tickets one could expect from construction workers, nothing significant had turned up with any of them. It was almost as if Belmont Construction were a Boy Scout troop for adults.

They were running the information on the Three Sons Construction workers right now, but they didn't expect it to be any different than the Belmont results. These companies had a long history of working on federal contracts, and they couldn't afford to hire anyone with a shady past. In fact, even getting a DUI while on a job was grounds to be terminated.

Schwarz and Blancanales were suiting up in work clothes each day and were acting as the Farm's liaison to the work crews. They hung around the trailer that served as Belmont's on-site office, drank coffee with the foremen and toured the work site several times a day. A crew of the blacksuits from the boots-and-jeans detail was also on hand, preparing the acreage for the planting of the poplar trees.

All told, there was one set of Stony Man eyes for every two Belmont workers. Nothing was going to happen that someone didn't see. Even so, Buck Greene knew that human eyes could blink, so he'd had several extra video cameras installed to cover the new area. If anything happened, he was going to have a tape of it.

Since its inception, the Farm's security had depended in large part on a series of surveillance cameras that covered almost every square foot of the grounds both inside and outside of the perimeter. They were controlled by computers, and the programming included having the computer sound an alarm if it saw anything that was on its list of things to be on the lookout for. The list was long and the tapes were even longer, but the computer scanned them at the speed of electrons, making short work of them.

This time, though, Greene wasn't satisfied to let the computer do the detective work for him. After each day's surveillance tapes were electronically scanned, he was going over them again himself, watching every last minute of video from start to finish.

Carl Lyons had offered to help Greene go over the tapes each night. It was a complete waste of time, but if it got Greene calmed down a bit, it was well worth it. The other two members of Able Team had the actual site covered, so there was little for him to do except give Greene a hand with whatever needed doing.

"I didn't see anything unusual today, Buck." Lyons rubbed his eyes as he clicked off the monitor. Even running the tapes at three times their normal speed, he had been at it for hours.

Greene's eyes were fixed on his monitor, and he only grunted in reply.

"Buck, what do you say we get a beer and kick back as soon as you're done with that."

"Thanks, Carl, but I need to talk to Cowboy about moving that number-twelve camera to give us a little better coverage. The Belmont trailer's blocking it on the far left sweep."

"For God's sake, Buck," Lyons said, sighing. "Just call Cowboy, tell him what you want and come have a beer with me. You're not going to be any good to anyone if you don't take a break here."

"Go ahead," the security chief said. "I'll catch up with you later."

Shaking his head, Lyons went to look for his two partners. Maybe one of them would have a beer with him.

SPATKIN HAD Saturday afternoon off, and after grabbing lunch in the tavern, he drifted down to the local open-air flea market. This was a typical rural Southern event with everything from genuine Civil War–era antiques to homemade quilts and honey being offered for sale alongside the usual range of garage-sale garbage tarted up as "collectibles."

Down at the end of the lot, a couple of good old boys were hawking hunting supplies, including ammunition and a few weapons. Most of the guns were shotguns or scoped bolt-action rifles, but there were a few handguns. When Spatkin walked up, he spotted a 9 mm Smith & Wesson Model 59 pistol. The weapon was still in its original box and had the spare magazine. He had carried one of them for several years with the Marshal Service and knew it like he knew his own hand.

"What do you want for the Smith?" he asked the old codger behind the table.

The man looked him up and down for a moment. "You ain't from around here," he stated.

"No, I'm not," Spatkin admitted. "I'm working out at Stony Man Farm."

"The pistol's $350." The man paused. "Cash. I don't like to take checks."

Spatkin grinned. "How much would it be if I was from somewhere around here?"

The old man didn't change expression. "Three hundred."

"You throw in that ammo—" Spatkin pointed to the box of commercial 9 mm hollowpoint bullets lying next to the pistol "—and you got a deal."

"You drive a hard bargain, mister."

A little farther on, Spatkin found another box of 9 mm ammunition and bought it, as well. That gave him a hundred rounds, which was more than enough for anything he might have to go up against. Any plan he came up with that required more firepower than that wasn't going to be workable for one man alone.

When he got back in his pickup truck, Spatkin decided to make a thorough recon of the town and the surrounding area. He had only come to Wilsonburg once as a blacksuit, and then had only visited the tire shop and farm-vehicle parts store. When he made his escape from Stony Man Farm this time, he didn't want to have to depend on blind luck as he had done the first time.

After cruising through town and making mental notes of routes and landmarks, he headed out into the countryside. This being farming country, he wasn't surprised to see that the big feed-and-seed store a mile out of town was open on Saturday.

Farmers didn't keep city hours. What really caught his eye, however, were the two tall steel cylinders standing at the edge of the lot.

When he saw the red No Smoking and Danger— Explosives signs on the ammonium-nitrate fertilizer silos, he smiled. He had just found his way to destroy Stony Man Farm. Rather than stop, though, he drove past.

LATER THAT NIGHT, Spatkin visited the feed-and-seed store again. This time, though, he was dressed in black and left his truck a quarter of a mile down the road. After walking in through the fields behind the store, he carefully checked the grounds before closing in on the fertilizer silos. Using a shielded penlight, he checked the locks on the delivery chutes and saw that they were common hardware padlocks that could be picked or cut with bolt cutters. It would be best, though, to try to pick the locks rather than cut them. Since the Oklahoma City bombing, everyone was a little jumpy about missing ammonium nitrate.

To make a proper fertilizer bomb, he would need powdered aluminum and high-octane aviation gas to add to it, and a mixing machine to get an even mix. Considering where he was, though, it wasn't likely that he would be able to find those ingredients, and he knew enough not to ask about them. But that didn't mean that he couldn't make a powerful bomb. He would just make a simpler, but still effective cratering explosive often used in construction—ammonium nitrate soaked in diesel fuel.

Pound for pound, it wouldn't pack the punch of the bomb that had taken out the federal building in Oklahoma City, but he wouldn't need anything that powerful. The Stony Man farmhouse could be completely eradicated with only five hundred pounds of the cratering mixture. He could easily carry that in the back of his truck.

NOW THAT HE HAD A PLAN, Spatkin went about gathering the rest of the material he would need for his bomb. The diesel fuel was easy; almost every Belmont Construction vehicle ran on diesel. If he could score a fifty-five gallon drum, no one would think twice about seeing it in the back of his pickup.

The hardest part was going to be finding a foolproof way to detonate the bomb. Before the Oklahoma City bombing, buying blasting caps hadn't been a big deal. Sure, you'd had to sign for them, but didn't need a user's certificate from the local authorities. That was something he wasn't going to be able to get in Virginia, and wouldn't try even if he could.

There was more than one way to make an explosive detonate, however, and he was good with explosives. He bought large rifle primers from the reloading supplies at the local gun store and a one-pound can of black powder. With those, he could make a crude but effective fuse train and initiator.

Getting the bomb inside the Stony Man perimeter wasn't going to be easy, either. To limit the vehicle traffic in and out, Buck Greene had leased a bus and asked the construction company to use it to transport their people to and from the work site. It and all the other Belmont vehicles were equipped with transponders that let the blacksuits on the main gate know who they were as they approached. Even so, one of the blacksuits still checked the ID of each man before waving the vehicle through.

If he was going to drive the bomb in, Spatkin was going to have to acquire one of those transponders and put it on his truck. Getting it shouldn't be too difficult. He could switch the unit over from his company truck to his pickup for the run in.

As he ran the details of the plan through his mind, he kept thinking about Barbara Price. It was true that she was one of the enemy, but he didn't want to see her blown to bloody fragments by the bomb or buried in the rubble of the destroyed farmhouse. If it was at all possible, he would try to find a way to get her safely away.

He knew that would increase his risks, but he had to at least try to protect her.

CHAPTER TEN

Wilsonburg, Virginia

Spatkin was stretched back on the bed in his motel room with a can of beer, watching TV before going across the street to get his dinner at the bar. He now had his method to attack Stony Man Farm, but he was trying to figure out how to increase his chances of success and survival. As it was now, he could probably get the bomb in, but it was going to be dicey for him to get out alive before the thing went off.

He was going over scenarios in his mind when his attention was drawn to the woman reporter on the newscast. The perky blonde looked like a cross between a young Kathie Lee Gifford and an animated Barbie doll. Her voice, though, was throaty and pure silk.

"…and now that Mayor Bud Dilworth's scheme to sell the city's only park to developers has been exposed, the citizens of Woodland can continue to have a place to take their families for an outing.

This is Sylvia Thompson-Bracket for Channel 7's *Virginia Undercover.*''

Spatkin was a TV news junkie, but he usually watched it as background noise. He'd caught this woman's act before, but it hadn't really connected with him. Perky, big-breasted blondes were nothing special on TV news shows today; every channel had at least one of them on staff. This one, though, was different. She obviously enjoyed making trouble and was good at it. That could be a useful asset for a man in his profession.

He downed the last of his beer, put on his boots and headed across the street.

MABEL WINDAM WAS behind the bar again. She started to talk before she took his order for a chicken-fried steak with home fries and creamed corn.

"I haven't been able to find anything out," he said when she stopped to catch her breath. "But, you know, there might be a way you can find out something yourself."

"How's that?"

"Well, you know that woman reporter for Channel 7 in Richmond? Sylvia what's-her-name?"

Windam sniffed. "You mean the one who's always sticking her nose into other people's business?"

"That's the one." Spatkin grinned. Mabel wasn't the kind of woman to have anything good to say about a younger one and certainly not a woman who looked like the reporter did.

Sylvia Thompson-Bracket fancied herself an investigative reporter in the journalistic tradition of Woodward and Bernstein. In reality, she was a Jerry Springer wanna-be and her bag was exposing petty scandal, not journalism. She went into the smaller communities of Virginia with her camera crew sniffing out trouble. When she found it, she raked the muck until she came up with a hot, steaming morsel and held it up for all to see. Anything from illegal after-hours clubs, speed traps, small-town cops on the take or a popular preacher's mistress were all fair game for her program, *Virginia Undercover.*

"But, she's a bitch, pardon my language." Windam didn't even bother to blush. "And all she does is cause trouble for folks. Why, I can remember just last year when she went down to Hunter's Gap and—"

"But," he said, cutting her off abruptly, "she might be useful this time."

"How do you mean?"

"Why don't you give her a call and tell her what you know about the work that's being done out at Stony Man Farm? Tell her about your nephew being out of a job and them bringing in guys like me from out of state to work. I'm sure she could get you the information you want."

Spatkin saw the light come on behind her eyes as she digested what he had said. It wasn't that

Mabel was as stupid as she sounded. It was that most of the time she talked without clicking on her brain before she opened her mouth. If she took the time to think this one out, she might be able to get the ball rolling for something Stony Man Farm absolutely didn't want—publicity. He could see Buck Greene going ballistic at the first sight of a TV news chopper overhead.

"You know," Windam said, "I think I will call her. Someone needs to know what's going on around here. It just ain't right that my sister's oldest—"

"I have her number," he cut in.

She wrote it on a napkin as he recited it, then she headed for the phone at the end of the bar, leaving Spatkin to his dinner.

Congo

THE STONY MAN TEAM had taken turns keeping watch over their charges all night. There was no doubt in Bolan's mind that Taibu's Simbas would be after them and they needed to leave at first light. The planned chopper rendezvous was several hours away, and he wanted the hostages at the pickup zone as soon as possible. He knew they were in bad shape, but they could rest there while they waited for the choppers.

After another meal of emergency rations and a carefully allotted drink of water, the Stony Man warriors got their charges on their feet again and moved them out.

Stony Man Farm, Virginia

FOR THREE HOURS, Kurtzman kept watch from afar as the Stony Man team herded the ex-hostages through the jungle. When they reached the small clearing that had been designated as the pickup zone, Hal Brognola went to relay that information to the President and to get clearance for the choppers to take off to pick them up. When he returned to the Computer Room his face was ashen.

Barbara Price didn't wait for the ax to fall. "Okay, Hal, what did the Man say this time?"

"Well," Brognola replied, "when Taibu discovered that his hostages were missing this morning, he sent a message to that TV crew he's holding on to and had them transmit it. This time he threatened direct retaliation against the United States and the Western nations with the Ebola virus if we interfere again in what he is calling 'his' affairs. That includes any Western aircraft overflying what he calls his territory, most of the Congo Basin."

"And?"

"The 'and' is that the President has canceled the planned extraction of the team and the hostages."

While Price didn't agree with a great deal that the current chief executive did, she saw this decision as a difficult, but necessary call. The good of the many always outweighed the good of the few, and when you started adding up the butcher's bill this time, the math wasn't with Stony Man. The threat of widespread Ebola contamination simply weighed more than the lives of the six Stony Man warriors and their eighteen hostages.

It was a harsh math lesson, but it was realistic.

"Okay," she said, turning to Katzenelenbogen, "how do we get them out of there?"

Congo

THE FORCED MARCH to the pickup point had been brutal but necessary, and the ex-hostages seemed to understand without being told. No one fell out along the way, but several of them were on their last legs when Bolan finally called a halt.

While the rest of the commandos set up a security perimeter, Calvin James went from one hostage to the next, checking them out and dispensing salt tablets and their ration of water with another round of emergency rations. A few of them needed blisters bandaged, but there had been no major medical problems so far.

Gary Manning was on radio watch when the call came in from the Farm. "Mack," he called over the com link, "Katz wants to talk to you."

"When's the extraction time?" Bolan asked.

"That's what we need to talk about," Katz said. "I'm afraid that I've got bad news for you."

"Is there any other kind?" Bolan replied. "Send it."

"Taibu just went on the air on a CNN hookup ranting and raving again. In short, he's royally upset that you snatched his hostages from under his nose and he's threatening reprisals. The kicker this time is that he's threatening to release the Ebola virus he has in major Western cities, including the States, if any further action is taken against him. And he specifically mentioned aircraft flying into what he calls 'his airspace.'"

"What's the bottom line?" Bolan asked.

"The bottom line is that both the Security Council and the President are in a state of panic. No one is prepared for an Ebola attack."

"So you're saying that we're going to have to walk out, right?"

"I'm afraid so, old friend. At least walk to someplace where we can get an aircraft in without being spotted by Taibu's followers."

The Executioner didn't skip a beat at hearing the bad news. Wanting things to be different than they were was a waste of time, and they had no time to waste. "How does that look?"

"Well," Katz said, "Aaron's working on a three-day route that shouldn't be too bad."

"Remember that I have walking wounded here, and they're all civilians."

"I know," Katz replied. "We're taking that into consideration."

"Consider it carefully," Bolan said, "and give us an easy route. We're not equipped for that kind of trek. We don't have enough rations and canteens to support eighteen more people, and if we don't find supplies, we'll all be living off the land by tomorrow."

"We're working on that aspect, too," Katz replied. "Aaron has spotted a UN outpost half a day along the planned route that appears not to have been ransacked. The troops took off when the Simbas got too close, but it looks like they bypassed it. He's betting that you'll be able to find rations there and other gear your hostages might be able to use."

"He'd better be right, or they won't be making it."

"I do have some good news, though," Katz said. "Aaron has secured exclusive use of both a Vortex and a Keyhole satellite. They'll be parked overhead until we can get you out of there, so we'll be able to provide real-time warning of Simba movements. That might make the difference."

Bolan knew that it would help, but they were going to need more than an eye in the sky to see them through this.

"Let me talk to the people and I'll get back to you after that."

"Good luck with them."

BOLAN WAS VERY MUCH AWARE that everyone's eyes were on him as he walked up to the cluster of hostages and he saw the shock, fear and exhaustion in the faces. Every one of these people had been through an ordeal that few Westerners had ever known. They had come this far on sheer guts and now were ready to fly home to safety. Telling them that the nightmare wasn't yet over wouldn't be easy.

"Captain," one of the American men called out, "I need to use your radio to let my family know that I'm safe and when they can expect me home. I asked the sergeant and he told me that we couldn't make calls."

There hadn't been time to make introductions the previous night, nor was it really advisable in this case. But the hostages had noticed the two commandos who seemed to be in charge—him and McCarter.

"I'm sorry," Bolan said bluntly, "but there will be no unofficial use of the radios."

"But, Captain—"

"But nothing," Bolan said. "A list of your names has been radioed in, and notification will be made to your next of kin. And since this has come up, I want to mention something else before we go any further. This isn't a democracy we have here. We have come to try to take you home, but to do that, we have to have your complete cooperation without argument. It is in your own best interests to do exactly as you're told, when you're told to do it. Any questions?"

When there was none, he continued. "There has been a problem back in the States. The aircraft I was expecting won't be coming to get us. We'll be walking out to a place where an aircraft can get in to fly us out."

As expected, that announcement created pandemonium. Several of the hostages fell to their knees and started to cry. Others stood and sobbed silently while their neighbors shouted questions. Bolan gave them a mere sixty seconds of that before cutting it off.

"That 's enough!" he snapped. "You're wasting valuable time, and we don't have any time to waste."

"But why?" someone asked. "What happened?"

"It doesn't really matter why the plane isn't coming," Bolan said. "It just isn't, and you're going to have to live with that. When you get back to the States, you can bitch about politics and fix blame then."

Bolan's blue eyes went from one face to the next. "Right now, if you want to live, you have to deal with the situation as it is. And the situation requires that we walk out of here."

"When are we leaving," Frank Bullis asked, "and how far do we have to go?"

Those were the first intelligent questions anyone had raised, but Bolan knew they weren't going to like the answers. "We're leaving right now, and it looks like we'll have a three-day walk."

That brought gasps and moans from people who had already pushed themselves beyond anything they had ever done before. They couldn't imagine another three days of it.

"I understand the situation," Bullis said, "but we aren't equipped for a long walk in the jungle. As you can see, we don't have adequate clothing or any way to carry food and water. Is there any chance that we might find supplies along the way?"

"That's a rational question, Doctor." Bolan was more than thankful to find a natural leader among the hostages. It would make the ordeal ahead of them that much easier. "And there's a good possibility that we will. My intelligence says that there's a deserted UN outpost half a day away. We'll go there and see what we can salvage from it. Hopefully, there'll be something there we can use.

"If not—" he shrugged "—we'll all just have to live off the land."

Bullis nodded.

After answering a few more questions from the stunned hostages, Bolan took Bullis out of earshot of the rest for a private conversation.

"I'd like to deputize you, so to speak," he said, "to be the leader of your group. That way we won't have to tell everyone individually what has to be done. This isn't going to be easy, and my men aren't going to have much time to waste on hand-holding.''

''I understand,'' Bullis said. Some of the hostages had just arrived in Africa and weren't familiar with the realities of life there. Even those who had been in-country for a while had never been exposed to this particular kind of African reality. They were prey now and had to remember that at all times.

''And, since we're going to be working together, Doctor,'' Bolan said, holding his hand out, ''I'm Mike Belasko.''

''I go by Frank,'' Bullis said.

''Okay , Frank. Let's get them moving again.''

CHAPTER ELEVEN

Stony Man Farm, Virginia

"They're on the move again," Aaron Kurtzman announced as he watched the monitors displaying his spy satellite feed. By superimposing the deep-space images from the Keyhole satellite's digital camera, the near infrared and the radar scanners, then zooming in on the result, his view was as good as if he were flying low over the jungle in a light plane.

After glancing at the close-up view, Yakov Katzenelenbogen studied the monitors showing the high-altitude view of the Congo Basin. "What's the extended weather forecast for the area?"

Hunt Wethers clicked on the scan from the deep-space weather satellite and read the data. "It should be pretty clear for at least the next two days."

That would make it easier for the satellites to keep the men and their charges in view, but it would also make tracking them on the ground much easier. Anyone could follow a group that large, particularly when most of them had no field-craft skills. A good rainstorm might blank the view of the satellites, as well as make the hostages miserable, but it would also erase their tracks. The weather, unfortunately, wasn't something that the Stony Man crew could call up to fit the mission.

"Keep on top of that," Katz said, "and let me know as soon as you see any changes."

"I'm on it."

Congo

IT TOOK AN HOUR and a half longer than Bolan had expected for the ragtag group to make the march to the UN outpost Kurtzman had spotted for them. The ex-hostages were still weak from the confinement and the escape march, and had few energy reserves. The Stony Man warriors had shared their rations with them, but one meal couldn't make up for several days of going hungry. If they didn't find adequate food soon, they would only grow weaker.

To complicate matters, they were in the Congo, and that meant that they were in some of the thickest jungle in the world. There was worse to be found in the Amazon, but this was a humid, green hell for the ex-hostages. Many of them had worked in Africa for years, but few of them had ever wandered off the beaten paths into the jungle they now found themselves in. Under other conditions, this would be a great learning experience. As it was, it was a grueling ordeal.

As the only black in Phoenix Force, Calvin James was the natural choice as the pointman for this stage of their march. A Simba spotting him wouldn't automatically fire on him. The camouflage pattern of his field uniform wasn't the same as that most of the Simbas wore. But since Taibu had taken in deserters from so many of the local national armies, seeing a strange uniform wouldn't be too unusual.

It was only when they got close enough to talk to him that James would be in trouble.

WHEN THEY FINALLY REACHED the edge of the clearing around the UN camp, Bolan had the hostages stay well out of sight behind the tree line while the commandos went forward to recon. With Manning and Hawkins backing him up, James carefully crossed the open ground around the outpost. The compound looked to be completely deserted, but a person couldn't take any chances with the Simbas. Like their lion namesakes, they were good at concealed ambushes and could have left a stay-behind team.

When he reached the open gate and hadn't tripped an ambush, James felt sure that the camp was abandoned. Nonetheless, he quickly looked through all of the buildings. When they turned out to be deserted, he clicked in his com link. "It's clear," he said.

The hostages emerged slowly from the jungle,

but started hurrying toward what they saw as hope or at least a place to rest for a while. The first place James led them to was the water tank beside the kitchen area. A person could live a long time without food, but water was mandatory.

While the ex-hostages drank their fill and collapsed to the ground, the commandos quickly searched the camp to see what the UN troops had left behind when they evacuated. A great deal of material remained, but they had taken all of their weapons and ammunition with them. Not even as much as a smoke grenade had been overlooked. David McCarter wasn't pleased to hear that. He had hoped to supplement their meager firepower by arming some of the hostages at UN expense. Now they would have to wait until they made contact and could salvage Simba weapons from their first firefight.

Gary Manning made the big find of the day in the storage rooms of the main barracks building. Stacked neatly in a corner were cardboard boxes labeled in English, and they were a welcome sight. Each box contained twelve MREs, the U.S. Army–issue Meals Ready to Eat field rations. If carefully rationed, the MREs would last the planned three-to four-day trip.

Just as important as finding the food was the fact that the outpost's water tank was full. Since this was a UN camp, they could count on it being potable, which would cut the risk of weakened people getting sick from drinking what water they came across in the jungle. Before they left, they would have to find something to carry as much water with them as they could.

"We're not in too bad a shape right now," Hawkins said, reporting the results of his search to McCarter. "I found eight plastic two-quart canteens and half a dozen pistol belts to hang them on. There's also several pairs of boots and some uniform clothing, as well. Most of it's in larger men's sizes, but I don't think our woman's going to be too fashion conscious right about now."

"How about load bearing gear, assault harnesses or rucks?" McCarter asked.

"I found some butt packs and ammo pouches, but that's about it. We can take some of the extra uniform shirts and rig makeshift carrying slings from them."

"That ought to work," the Briton said.

BOLAN GAVE the hostages time to have a meal of MREs and drink their fill again from the water tank. While they were resting, James checked them over and saw to their minor injuries. So far, none of them had anything wrong with them that couldn't be cured with a week's rest and adequate food. With luck, they'd have that in the near future.

"Captain?" The man who had insisted on using their radio approached Bolan.

"Yeah?"

"These meals aren't a hell of a lot to eat, Captain. I think you should give us another one."

"What's your name?" Bolan asked. As could almost be guaranteed, the man was overweight, and his brief stay in Simba custody hadn't been long enough to slim him down much. His kind could be depended upon to complain about the rations no matter where he was.

"Bill Jordan." The man puffed up like a balloon with self-importance. "I'm the executive director of the World Children's Foundation. I'm sure you've heard of our work with deserving children?"

Bolan hadn't. Charity wasn't his line of work, but he passed on telling Jordan so.

"Well, Mr. Jordan, that meal you were given contained eighteen hundred calories, and you'll get another one tonight. That's thirty-two hundred calories a day, enough food for a fighting man carrying a load. You aren't laden down, so it should be more than enough for you."

Jordan's face got red. "That 'food,' as you like to call it, was shit. I couldn't eat it. I gave it to one of the blacks."

Bolan's ice blue eyes drilled into Jordan's florid face. "If you fall behind because you won't eat what you are given, mister, you'll be left where you fall. None of us will carry you a single step. You got that?"

Something in the depths of Jordan's brain warned him not to get too aggressive with this soldier. That didn't mean, however, that he wouldn't put him in his place when he got home. No one messed with Bill Jordan and got away with it, and this tin soldier was no exception.

"I have friends on Capitol Hill, Captain, good friends," he said ominously. "And I'm going to have your job when we get back to the States."

Bolan smiled slowly. "Mister, I'll tell you what. When we get back to the States, you can tell anyone you like, anything you want about me, I don't care. First, though, we have to get back, so I recommend that you stop making empty threats and get your ass in gear like the rest of us."

It was the smile more than anything else that sent Jordan packing.

After Jordan left, Bolan took Frank Bullis aside. "Look, Doctor, I have two choices with the rations we found. I can divide them up and expect everyone to watch their own consumption or I can have you keep track of them and issue them on my orders. Which do you think will work best here?"

"In the best of all possible worlds, which this sure as hell isn't, I'd let everyone keep track of their own food. But I'm not sure that'll work this time. Even though I was caged up with these people for entirely too long, I really don't know them well enough to know if they can be trusted to do the right thing."

"Okay." Bolan took the doctor's honest assessment at face value. "I'll issue two meals apiece to them right now, and I want you to pick responsible men to carry the other boxes. But," he cautioned, "make sure that Bill Jordan isn't one of them."

Bullis didn't smile. "He's been pretty much a problem all along. He claims to be politically connected back home and thinks that he should get special treatment because of who he says he knows. The Simbas didn't buy it, but I'm not surprised that he's trying it on you."

"This is no place for a man to try to throw his political weight around," Bolan warned. "If he becomes a problem out here, he's going to end up dead."

Bullis smiled thinly. "I'll try to impress that point on him."

"You'll be doing him a favor."

"Unfortunately."

THE SUN WAS LOW in the sky by the time the Stony Man team left the UN outpost. Bolan didn't want to march the ex-hostages through the night, but they had to get far enough away from the camp to be well out of the way from any roving Simba patrols. From his experience, he knew that Simbas traditionally didn't have the discipline and training to work at night. But Taibu might have pumped them up enough to have overcome their natural reluctance.

When they halted again, the commandos took up a defensive perimeter around the cluster of ex-hostages. The MREs were doled out, but eaten cold this time. As the ex-hostages ate, Frank Bullis walked among them answering questions as best he could. Most of the questions were things that not even Belasko could answer, and Bullis didn't even bother taking them to the soldier. He did, however, pass on to them Belasko's latest cautions.

"If I can get your attention," he said. "The captain wanted me to remind you that we have to keep completely silent at night," he said. "And no fires at all. Not even a little one."

As he had almost expected, Bill Jordan walked up to him. "Who put you in charge here, Bullis?" he asked. "I sure as hell don't remember voting for you."

"The captain asked me to be his point of contact with all of us," Bullis explained. "And since he's the man of the hour, I guess that puts me in charge. And he wanted me to remind you that until we get out of here, this isn't a democracy."

"When I get back," Jordan threatened, "I'm going to have your job, too. No one treats Bill Jordan this way."

"I'll be glad to listen to any suggestions you might have and pass them on," Bullis said firmly. "But until we get out of here safely, the decisions will be made by Belasko and his men."

"I'm going to get him, too, buddy," Jordan snarled. "You just wait and see if I don't."

Bullis wanted to smile at the empty threat, but

refrained. From what he had seen, Belasko looked like a man who knew how to take care of himself, even on Capitol Hill. Jordan had best watch his mouth around him, or he'd end up having his fat face being fed to him one bite at a time.

"You'd better bring your lunch, Jordan, 'cause I think it's going to be an all-day job."

Jordan snarled something unintelligible and stalked off to sulk. Bullis didn't bother to report the exchange to Belasko. The captain had enough to worry about.

WHILE CHARLES TAIBU had adequate communication with the outside world, his Simba army lacked enough radios to allow all of the smaller units to keep in contact with him or with one another. That particularly hurt him when he sent out the trackers and scout teams to look for escaping Yankees. Unless it was one of the few tracking teams with a radio who first found them, they would have to send a runner back before he would know where they were.

Thus it was late afternoon before he learned where the Yankees had fled. A runner came back and reported that he had tracked them to a clearing ten miles away that showed signs of their having camped there overnight. It was apparent that the Yankees had gone to that clearing because they had expected to be picked up by a helicopter.

It was too late for him to send new teams after

them, as his Simba warriors weren't good at night operations. Like all Africans, they liked to keep close to the fire at night because the dark held danger. He didn't fear, however, that the Yankees would escape from him overnight. In the condition they were in, they wouldn't be moving too fast.

At least he no longer had to fear that the Americans would try to sneak a helicopter in to fly these people out. The United Nations General Assembly resolution to close Congolese airspace to all foreign aircraft had passed with few dissenting votes.

Once more, the great international debating society had proved to be a hollow drum that sounded with the slightest wind. He remembered his classes on how the Soviets and Maoist Chinese had used the United Nations to promote the spread of international communism. Had it not been for the unwitting help of the UN, the Communists wouldn't have been even half as successful as they had been. With the exception of the intervention in Korea, the UN had proved impotent and totally ineffectual when it came to stopping the march of international communism.

The UN had, however, worked hard to create the chaos that now engulfed most of Africa, particularly the Congo Basin. Thanks in great part to them, there wasn't a single viable government in the entire region. There was, though, mass hunger, never-ending warfare, collapsed economies and millions of people who were desperate for someone to tell them that he had a plan to alleviate their miseries. And that's where he came in.

Marxism had been tried before in Africa, but it had never quite caught on. One of the biggest reasons was that back in the sixties and seventies when it had been introduced, the United States had been more than ready to put down Communist-sponsored insurgencies no matter where they took place. Even as late as the eighties, they had supported the anti-Communist forces fighting in the Angolan civil war. Today, though, American foreign policy had been neutralized by its blind obedience to the impotent UN and fear of the liberal cowards in Congress. Regardless of the provocation, any attempt they made to interfere in Africa would now be denounced as racism.

Even more important than that was what he had learned from studying the failures of the earlier attempts to impose Marxist regimes in Africa. They had failed miserably because they had all depended too strongly on Russian, East German and Cuban military and political advisers telling the African rulers how they should rule their people.

Taibu had no intention of calling on foreigners to tell him how to control Africans, particularly not white foreigners. Regardless of their politics, they simply didn't understand the realities of Africa.

His version of a Marxist society would be solely for Africans, those who followed him, and by Africans, namely him, and it wouldn't fail.

CHAPTER TWELVE

Stony Man Farm, Virginia

Even a place locked down as tightly as Stony Man Farm was had to have some kind of accessible link to the outside world. In their case, it was a normal phone listed in the local white pages as S.M. Farm. Even so, the number was given out to very few, and the line terminated only in Barbara Price's office. Usually, she ignored it and let the answering machine catch it, but when it rang this time, she picked it up and answered.

"This is Barbara," she said.

"Is this Stony Man Farm?" a woman's voice on the other end asked.

"Who is this, please?" Price asked politely.

"Is this Stony Man Farm?" The woman was insistent.

"If I don't know who you are," Price said, "you don't need to know where this is."

"This is Sylvia," the woman replied.

"Sylvia who?"

There was a long pause. "Sylvia Thompson-Bracket."

The name only vaguely registered in Price's mind. "Okay, Sylvia, what can I do for you?"

"I need to know if this is the number for Stony Man Farm."

"It is."

There was another long pause as if the woman was at a loss for words. "Ah, do you have a construction project going on right now?"

Now Price remembered where she had heard the woman's name. Sylvia Thompson-Bracket was a muckraking reporter for Channel 7 out of Richmond. Her specialty was creating tempests in local teapots and milking them for all they were worth. "I'm not sure that's any of your business, Sylvia."

"I have a report that you are doing construction on your farm and aren't letting local firms bid for the work."

"Why is this of interest to you, Sylvia?"

Again the reporter was put off her stride. She was used to doing the questioning herself, not being questioned.

"Well, I don't understand why you aren't hiring locals to do this work. I have a report of families in your area who are out of work and—"

"Are you with a social-services agency, Sylvia?"

"Why, no," she sputtered, "I'm a reporter."

"Then I'll ask you for the last time—" Price put

an edge into her voice "—how is this of any possible interest to you?"

"I am always interested in injustice, and this clearly is a case of—"

Price cut the connection and immediately hit the intercom button for both Hal Brognola and Buck Greene. "Buck, Hal," she said, "I just got a call from that female reporter for Channel 7 in Richmond. I think you both need to come up here and listen to the tape."

"On the way," Brognola said.

"DAMN," GREENE SAID after hearing the tape. "I knew something like this was going to happen. We've never drawn this much attention to ourselves."

"I'm afraid that woman's not going to let this drop." Price said. "She sounded determined."

"That she did," Brognola agreed.

"That BS about 'social injustice,'" she snorted. "That's just liberal media shorthand for 'we don't like what you're doing and we're going to shut you down.' Can you get some agents to look into her sources on this? It's got to be someone in town."

"That's real tricky," Brognola said. "Freedom of the press and all that."

"How about national security?" she shot back. "Obviously, someone's running an operation against us and using her as the front man."

"Even so, it's got to be a little more serious than

her asking uncomfortable questions before the Man will let me sic the dogs on a reporter.''

She turned to Greene. "Are you finished with Carl and Pol?"

"Ah, I guess," he answered. "They've finished the background checks on the Three Sons personnel, and they're just helping me keep an eye on things around the job site."

"Hal, I want to let Buck cut those two loose and have them start tracking this down. The last thing we need is a news chopper circling overhead. This is supposed to be a low-profile operation, and if someone gets tapes of what we're doing here, we're finished. We might as well shut the Annex down and forget about it."

Brognola decided that he didn't need to check in with the Oval Office on this one. If Stony Man was being threatened, they were authorized to protect themselves. "Call them in," he said. "We'll go over it in the War Room."

Wilsonburg, Virginia

CARL LYONS WAS MORE than glad to hear that Price had a real job for him to do. Hanging around the Computer Room waiting for background-check confirmations to come in wasn't the kind of thing that got his blood pumping. Chasing down whoever was causing trouble for the Farm was much more to his liking. Even though the primary suspect was a woman, maybe she had a male sidekick he could shake down.

Stony Man Farm had an unofficial relationship with the police chief in Wilsonburg. Chief Ed Baumann had been cleared to be told that the Farm had an association with the federal government. He didn't know exactly what that association was, and he was smart enough to know that he didn't have a need to know. All he needed to know was that the people at the Farm were good neighbors and could always be depended on to pitch in and help in any community emergency. More than that, he didn't really want to know.

"Carl!" Baumann said when he saw Lyons walk into his office. "Long time no see. What brings you here?"

"We have a serious problem at the Farm," Lyons said, getting right to the point, "and we think it's coming from someone in town."

"How's that?"

"Someone has sicced that Sylvia Thompson-Bracket from Channel 7 on us. She called and started asking questions about that construction job we have going."

"That woman," Baumann said. "I don't know why the hell that station keeps her around. She's a real troublemaker. What kind of questions did she ask?"

"She wanted to know why we were bringing in an outside company to do the job instead of hiring needy locals. She sounded like a candidate on the campaign tour talking about 'social injustice' and all that politically correct touchy-feely crap.''

"Damn!'' Baumann said. "I've been hearing a little bitching now and then about that, but I didn't know it had gotten that far yet.''

"What do you mean?''

"Well, Carl,'' the chief said, "we have a bunch of people out of work around here, and some of them think that you should be hiring more of them to do that job for you.''

"But we've never hired the locals,'' Lyons said. "You know that.''

"I know that, and I think I understand why. But when you gave that land-clearing job to some of the loggers around here, that got people to thinking that if some of us could do that, why not the rest?''

"Can you find out who's talking the most about this? We have to get that reporter off our asses.''

Baumann looked out the window for a moment. "You know, Carl, a man's got the right to speak his mind.''

"I know that, Ed,'' Lyons replied. "But I need to know why this person decided to call in an outside agitator to cause trouble for us. That's a sensitive job we have going out there, and the last thing we need is a so-called investigative reporter shining a spotlight on us.''

Lyons shook his head. "As you know, we try to keep a low profile, and we don't want to have to shut that job down. And I can tell you that it's not going to be good for the town if we have to do that.

"That's not a threat, Ed," Lyons said when he saw the look come over Baumann's face. Stony Man had never had to lean on Baumann before, but something like this had never come up, either.

"It's simply the way things'll be if my bosses decide that we're being threatened by the townspeople. We buy a lot of our supplies here, and even if we don't hire locally, there's a lot of people here who depended on us for a large part of their livelihood."

Baumann sighed. "I'll look into it."

"Please do it quickly. We don't have much time."

"I'll get on it."

"Thanks."

SYLVIA THOMPSON-BRACKET knew that she was onto something big this time. Most of the time, her exposés were little more than the rankest tabloid tales exploiting the petty jealousies, greed and stupidity of small-minded people. If television was the "vast wasteland" of America, her program was a public toilet in that wasteland and a toilet badly in need of a thorough cleaning. But it brought in the ratings, and that was the name of the game in TV journalism.

If people wanted to rat out their friends and neighbors, that was fine with her and it kept her in business. This small-town muckraking actually had a greater purpose, though. She was looking for the one story that would carry her to the national spotlight.

Finding this Stony Man Farm thing in her own backyard was like winning the lottery without even buying a ticket. Something told her that there was a real story in this, and it wasn't the sniveling tale that whining barmaid had given her about her nephew needing a job.

As soon as she'd gotten the call, she'd had her staff start doing the background work on this farm, and it was coming up strange. For one thing, they'd not been able to find out who owned the place. The taxes were up-to-date, but they were being paid by a corporation and the deed was in its name. In the days of corporate farming dominating the rural landscape, that wasn't all that unusual. But she'd hit a brick wall when she tried to learn anything about the company. It existed, but it was some kind of front organization. Exactly what kind, though, she couldn't tell.

Thompson-Bracket was well-acquainted with front companies, most of them involved with the drug trade. Her father had been a hotshot L.A. lawyer who had specialized in cartel business. He had made a lot of money from men with Latin family names, but L.A. bred greed like sewage bred cholera. He had stupidly decided to go into business for himself and had gotten caught.

Had he been caught by the LAPD or the DEA, a young girl named Tracy Woods wouldn't have become an investigative reporter named Sylvia Thompson-Bracket. But Vince Woods, L.A. lawyer, had been caught by the people he worked for when his daughter was only seventeen. In order to keep himself from being brutally executed, Woods offered his daughter in exchange for his life. Since Tracy Woods had been a typical California blond teenager, the offer had been eagerly accepted and she started on a quick trip into hell.

It had taken almost two years for her to find a way to escape. In those long months, she had been a sex toy for cartel dignitaries visiting their distributors in the L.A. region. Though she hadn't been a virgin when she was handed over to her new "owners," she quickly learned that sex came in many varieties and not all of them were fun.

It had been the death of her father from a cocaine overdose that started her on the road to freedom. In the confusion surrounding his death, she managed to sneak away from her keepers and head east.

Now that her new persona was well-established, she was ready to move on to greater things. Her two years with the cartel had taught her things that most people didn't even know existed outside of movies and TV shows. For one thing, she knew that situations were rarely what they seemed to be on the surface, and that went from the President of the United States to the small-town mayor.

Everything she had learned about clandestine operations told her that this Stony Man Farm operation was more than a peaceful Virginia farm. Exactly what it was, she had no idea yet, but it wasn't an agricultural operation. The first step to finding out exactly what it was would be for her to descend on the little town of Wilsonburg and start raking through the muck.

Somewhere in the small-town dung heap she would find the jewel that would make her a princess, maybe even a queen, the queen of medialand. It was time for Barbara Walters and Diane Sawyer to move over and make way for a real talent.

WHILE LYONS WAS KEEPING close to home, Rosario Blancanales went to Richmond to dig into the background of Sylvia Thompson-Bracket. He had always liked the onetime capital of the short-lived Confederate States of America and didn't mind the trip. Though the city had been ravaged in the last year of the Civil War, much had survived of its storied history. This time, though, he wasn't there to take in the atmosphere.

At first, it had looked as if it would be easy for him to do a background on Ms. Thompson-Bracket. The TV station's publicity department had been more than willing to fax him an information packet on their most famous reporter. However, before he left the Farm, he'd had Akira Tokaido check the information against the data banks, and what he found there didn't match what the PR packet said about her.

To start, her birth name was Tracy Woods, and she wasn't a real Southerner. She was a native Californian who had gone to college in Atlanta. It was there that she had unofficially changed her name and picked up her generic Southern accent. Her Steel Magnolia act was tempered with a lot of California attitudes, but most people thought that was just because of her age. She was a "modern" woman.

Tokaido had also found that Ms. Thompson-Bracket didn't live in one of the stately old houses the city was so famous for. She lived in a California-style condo in a suburb under yet a third name, Donna Morgan. The Virginia Motor Vehicles Department said that Thompson-Bracket was driving a red Pontiac Grand Prix. However, Donna Moore was the registered owner of a gray Lexus coupe. A woman who changed names like most women did hairstyles and really needed looking into.

All of that information was interesting, but it wasn't helping him find out who or what had put her onto Stony Man Farm. To get a handle on that, he had to get closer to her, which meant a face-to-face. His cover, that of a journalist for a trade publication, was a bit thin, but anyone as publicity hungry as she was should open her door to anyone who wanted to do a story about her and her program.

CHANNEL 7's production offices were in a modern chrome-and-glass tower in downtown Richmond. Getting through to the station's managers had been a piece of cake. They had fallen all over themselves at the thought of their station being the lead story in *Southern Television Magazine*. The program manager himself escorted Blancanales to Thompson-Bracket's office to make the introductions.

Blancanales had reviewed several clips of the woman's work before leaving the Farm, but the small screen hadn't shown Thompson-Bracket to her best advantage. She was gorgeous in a cross between a Southern belle and a classic California beauty. But beyond the blond hair and green eyes, there was something about her that no camera could catch. There was a steel-trap mind behind those eyes.

As soon as the program manager excused himself, Blancanales found himself on the wrong end of that mind.

"Mr. Blancanales—" she read his name off of the card he had offered "—what have I read of yours?"

"Well, nothing in *Southern Television*, because I just started working for them. But I've done a few pieces for *Variety* and—"

"Why did you leave California for Georgia?" she asked, shifting topics suddenly.

Blancanales had to remember that the magazine's headquarters was in Atlanta. "Leaving California has almost become an American tradition. It's not what it used to be."

"But nothing is, is it?" she said. "Now, what can I do for you, Mr. Blancanales?"

"Well, I admire your work and thought that I might tag along with you on a story and watch you put it together. You know, start with the tip-off, so to speak, and watch you as you develop it. I think our readers would love to get a behind-the-scenes look at Sylvia Thompson-Bracket."

She studied him for a long moment. "I don't think that will be possible, Mr. Blancanales. Part of what makes my programs so effective is that people don't know how I develop my investigations. If I let you in, you would expose that and I can't afford that."

"It would get you a great deal of publicity in the industry."

She switched on the charm. "I think I have just about all the publicity I can use right now, Mr. Blancanales. Thank you for stopping by."

He stood and held out his hand. "I don't know what I'm going to tell my editor. He's going to really be disappointed. He's a real fan of yours."

She took his hand. "I'm sure you'll think of something to tell him. You seem to be a resourceful man."

It had been a long time since Blancanales had struck out that badly, but he knew to hold it in. "I like to think so." He smiled.

She didn't smile back.

CHAPTER THIRTEEN

Congo

Calvin James was glad that they were up against Simbas this time and not a disciplined national army. It was true that if they stumbled into a nest of the bastards, it would be all over. But the Simbas usually won their fights by sheer numbers and the berserker-like frenzy they worked themselves into. Most of them had little or no military training beyond that needed to operate an AK-47. And since you could train anyone to fire an AK in an hour or so, that wasn't saying much. If they could keep from running into large formations of the Simbas, they should be okay.

One on one, a Simba was an easy kill. They weren't used to fighting against one opponent and were likely to run rather than to stand their ground against someone who wasn't afraid to get down and dirty with them. It was only when they got together in large groups that they were dangerous.

Even so, walking point for a slow-moving group

of refugees wasn't a cakewalk. And since they were moving so slowly, James was staying several hundred yards ahead, clearing a zone, then stopping and waiting for the others to catch up. He was leap-frogging forward again when he caught a flash of movement in front of him.

Sending a click alert on the com link to warn the others, he silently made his way through the dense vegetation. It took several minutes for him to get to a position where he could see what had alerted him. Slowly parting the vegetation, he saw two Simbas straddling the trail, cooking something over a small fire. Over the heavy jungle odors, he smelled roasting meat. Considering some of the things they had seen along the way, he didn't want to think about its origins.

After backing off far enough that the Simbas couldn't spot him, James double clicked his com link twice to signal for Hawkins to come up from his slack position and join him. A few moments later, the ex-Ranger silently slipped up beside him. After a whispered conference, the two commandos faded into the jungle. Hawkins swung out to the right and crossed the trail so they could attack from both sides at once.

The Simbas were so intent upon their meal that they were oblivious as the two commandos slipped up behind them. Their AKs were lying on the ground, and even their ever present machetes had been laid aside. Apparently, they had no idea that the Yankees they were looking for were in the vicinity. And by the time they figured it out, it would be too late.

James and Hawkins burst from the jungle at the same time, their fighting knives in hand. The two Simbas were startled by the intrusion and hesitated a moment before jumping to their feet. That hesitation cost them any chance they might have had to defend themselves. The commandos' blades sunk deep into their bodies and slashed the life out of them before they could react.

"We're secure," James sent over the com link. "You can move out again."

"Roger," McCarter sent back.

WHEN BOLAN and McCarter reached Hawkins and James, the bodies of the dead Simbas had been dragged off the trail, but the blood on the ground told the story.

"They didn't have much with them except their AKs and ammo," Hawkins reported.

"Did they have a radio?"

The ex-Ranger shook his head. "We lucked out this time."

Bolan called Bullis forward. "Find out if any of your people have had military experience. We have two AK-47s now and some ammunition, and we need all the guns we can get."

"I can take one of them," the doctor said. "I've

fired an AR-15, and they can't be all that different.''

Hawkins took one of the AKs, cracked the bolt to make sure that the chamber was clear and handed it to him along with a full four-magazine ammo pouch.

"The magazines hold thirty rounds each," he said. "So that's 120 shots. If you're careful, they should last you until we're out of here."

Bullis knew that was a best-scenario estimate and didn't ask how long they would last if they got in trouble.

Hawkins quickly showed him how to put in the magazine and explained the three positions of the selector switch. "If you have to fire, keep it on single shot and you'll do a lot better, as well as conserve ammunition. If you're not used to automatic fire, you'll waste most of it."

"How do the sights work?"

Hawkins slid the sight ramp down to the one-hundred-meter notch. "That's the battle-sight zero setting. Just leave it there and you'll be okay. For anything beyond a football field, just aim a little high—for anything under the fifty-yard line, aim a little low."

Bullis nodded and took the assault rifle from Hawkins. He was supposed to be a man of science, not violence, but he now felt a little more in command of his fate. The reassuring feel of cold steel in his hands felt good. Now he wouldn't end up in a Simba cooking pot without a fight.

Because they had made contact, when they moved out again Manning joined Hawkins on slack and the flank security moved out farther to the sides.

BILL JORDAN WAS NOT happy, and early in life, he had learned that being unhappy was a good way of getting things his way. It had worked every time with his parents as well as it did in the schoolyard. Since he had been strong, as well as fat, he had been able to back up his temper with his fists.

When he went to college, he'd had to modify his tactics and use his force of mind and his bulk to practice his tactics of intimidation. Those around him usually gave into his wishes rather than face down his imposing personality. In the work place, though, he soon learned that he again had to change his modus operandi. Bosses usually didn't care if one of their employees was unhappy, and he hadn't been able to stay in any one job long enough to become a boss. Then he married into money and finally found a place to exercise his ability of using his unhappiness to get things done.

His wife's family fortune had created a job for him that gave him hundreds of people to intimidate. As the director of the World Children's Foundation, he had perfected his tactics of making himself happy by making others miserable. In the charity business, well-meaning, but somewhat simple-minded, people fell all over themselves trying to make him happy so he would smile while he treated them like scum. It gave him a secret pleasure to see these people, many of them wealthy and influential in their own right, fawning on him so he would let them do "good works."

For the first time in his adult life, though, his well-tested system wasn't giving him the results he wanted. That he hadn't been able to get through to the Simbas came as no big surprise. They were savages, and he hadn't really expected them to understand how important he was. But leaving their custody hadn't improved his situation, either. That tin soldier in charge of this fiasco was so dense that he wouldn't listen, and that so-called doctor he had chosen to be his mouthpiece was being so imperious that there was just no use talking to him either.

What made it worse was that the other people in this group had witnessed his humiliation at the hands of the soldier, and he knew they were laughing at him behind his back. They weren't the kind of people he would ever associate with and he would never see them again, but he hated to be laughed at by anyone.

He tried to tell himself that he didn't mind their laughter, and he knew that he'd get the last laugh as he always did. No one crossed Bill Jordan and got away with it. With his connections in Washington, it would be no problem to put both that soldier and the doctor in their places. They would regret ever having crossed him.

What rankled him more than that, though, was this wandering aimlessly around in the jungle. It was keeping him from getting out of this mess. He thought of slipping away into the jungle and trying to make his own way to the nearest town with a phone. But he wasn't a woodsman and knew that he would only get lost.

His best chance of survival was to stay with these people until they ran into more Simbas. Then he was going to surrender to them and get this fiasco over with. The Simba leader couldn't be so dense that he couldn't be made to understand how valuable he was. Even if it cost him a few thousand dollars to buy his way out of this mess, it would be worth it.

He was unhappy, and that wasn't an acceptable situation.

RAFAEL ENCIZO WAS taking his turn on drag at the rear of the group, watching over their back trail. That was always a consideration in any tactical situation, but since they were moving so slowly this time, it was an absolute must. For the second time in as many minutes, he thought he had spotted movement in the jungle behind them.

"Striker," he said over his com link, "I think we have some ankle biters on our trail. I've spotted something moving back there twice now."

"T.J.," Bolan called back to Hawkins and James, "you and Calvin drop back and see if you can peel them off us."

Hawkins double clicked his com link and motioned for James to move out. The two commandos split off from their positions and cloverleafed out to each side of their back trail. With their com links, they kept in contact as they moved out far enough to let the Simba trackers bypass them without being spotted. Once they had passed, the two moved in on their rear to recon their targets.

The three Simbas following the group acted as if they were the only predators in the jungle. The fact that the Americans they were following were also warriors simply hadn't occurred to them. They had completely bought into Taibu's talk of invincibility.

The Simba in the drag position was content to let his two buddies break trail for him. With them twenty yards in front, he had no reason to do more than follow their tracks. He wasn't keeping an eye out for anything else around him, but then, why should he? They were tracking ignorant Westerners who were herding a bunch of prisoners, and that wasn't a threat that a lion warrior needed to be concerned about.

Not knowing if anyone was following behind the tracker team, the two commandos opted for silent kills again. James took on the Simba in the drag position, and it was almost too easy.

Matching his steps to those of his intended target,

but taking longer strides, James strode up behind the unsuspecting Simba. When he was within striking range, his left hand flashed out, clamped over the man's mouth and pulled him off balance backward. At the same time, his right fist hammered his heavy fighting knife into his kidneys, once, twice. Then the long blade reached deep inside his unprotected torso, far enough to sever his aorta.

The Simba went limp in an instant from the loss of blood pressure. James eased him down and click signaled Hawkins to join him.

The two commandos carefully moved in on the two remaining Simbas. Again, they stalked them like panthers and when they were close enough, took them out with cold steel.

WHEN THE REPORTS from his tracking teams started to come in, Taibu finally had the information he needed. One of his teams in the east had come upon the bodies of two of his men hidden in the bush off a main trail through the area. The men had been sent out as a trail-watch team and had apparently been caught off guard. The kills had been clearly professional. Dragging the bodies out of sight off the trail and covering the blood spill was a dead giveaway.

The invaders had passed that way, and now he knew where they were going. They were trying to escape to the east to get out of his territory so they could call an airplane in to pick them up. He had to admit that it was a good plan; his forces were the thinnest to the east. But as he would show them, it wasn't quite good enough.

He issued orders, and his runners disappeared into the jungle to deliver them.

Stony Man Farm, Virginia

HUNT WETHERS HAD his academic face on when he walked over to Yakov Katzenelenbogen's work area. While Katz and Aaron Kurtzman had been focusing on the immediate vicinity that the team and the ex-hostages were moving through, Wethers had been looking farther afield, watching the approaches to the greater area.

"I think I've spotted some Simba units moving in to create a blocking position along their planned route of march."

"Show me," Katz said.

Wethers slid a stack of photos taken by the Keyhole satellite's digital cameras onto his desk.

"Here and here," he said, pointing out two roads twenty miles or so apart that led generally eastwest. "You can see the truck convoys full of troops. And here—" he flipped to the last photo in the stack "—you can see where they're headed if they continue along those roads."

You didn't have to be a tactical genius to see where the two roads led. They terminated at a fairsized town straddling the route he and Kurtzman had plotted for Bolan and his people. If they continued on as planned, or if the Simbas started to sweep the jungle, the two groups were sure to encounter one another. The result of that encounter could only go one way. A quick head count showed at least fifty Simbas in each convoy.

If the Stony Man team was on its own, there was any number of things they could do to bypass and evade the waiting Simbas. But none of them were practical to even think about with the eighteen ex-hostages in tow. He had to find a way to get them out of the area quickly.

"Aaron," Katz called across the room, "it's time for us to go to Plan B."

"What's that," Kurtzman asked, "an act of God?"

"That's about what it's going to take this time," Katz said.

Kurtzman wheeled his chair around. "Show me."

CHAPTER FOURTEEN

Katzenelenbogen and Kurtzman studied the maps and the satellite photos of the operational area for half an hour, but it appeared that there was only one viable option for the team and the ex-hostages. Their planned route was taking them close to a bend in the great Congo River. There were a couple of small towns along that stretch of the river, the kind of stops along the way that served as market towns and water-transport hubs.

The satellite photos showed boats of all sizes in the towns tied up at docks along the river. If they could requisition a boat and head upstream, they might be able to bypass the Simbas lying in wait for them and get clear. The latest intelligence reports were indicating that Taibu's army controlled many of the waterways in the area, so being on the water would have risks they hadn't had to deal with yet. But staying in the jungle gave them no chance at all.

And when it came down to choosing between slim and none, slim won out every single time.

"I'll call Mack," Katz volunteered. No one contested his right to announce the bad news.

Congo

WHEN THE CALL came in from Stony Man Farm, Bolan and David McCarter took the news calmly. Raging against the enemy's actions was a waste of time. The only way out of the trap the Simbas were setting was for them to take bold action, and moving to the river was about as bold a step as they could take.

The Congo was one of the world's great river transport systems. At almost three thousand miles long, it was one of the longest waterways in Africa, second only to the Nile. Its headwaters rose in mountains of southern Africa, and from there it slowly wandered westward through the Congo Basin to dump into the Atlantic. Catching a ride on that watery highway had its risks, but less than remaining in the jungle.

Checking the map, they saw that Karaha, the closer of the two towns Katz had mentioned, was only four miles' map distance away. With the condition their charges were in, that would be two hours by day, almost three by night, and night was falling.

"Let's take a rest break here and feed them now," Bolan said. "We might not be able to stop again until we've found us a boat."

AFTER AN HOUR rest break, the Stony Man team briefed the ex-hostages on the change in plans, got them on their feet and pressed on for the river. While they still weren't in good physical or mental condition, the food and medical attention had gone a long way toward bringing them back from the half-dead condition they had been in. Nonetheless, after the two-and-one-half-hour forced march to the river, they were ready to rest again.

Leaving Manning, Encizo and McCarter with the ex-hostages, Bolan, James and Hawkins went to recon the town and to look for some transportation. According to Kurtzman's satellite recon, a number of fairly large craft were tied up at the dock and, from space, one of them looked big enough to be some kind of military patrol boat. If that was the case, it would be the best break they'd had since the operation started. The gods of war hadn't exactly frowned on them yet, but they hadn't given them their blessings, either.

Karaha was a typical Congolese river town. It was situated along a straight stretch of the Congo where the river was slow and wide, and the land sloped gently down to the water. There, the people in the surrounding region could take a ferry to cross to the other side or they could catch a riverboat to travel up or down the river. As the largest town in the area for fifty miles, it was also the major regional market.

And as in every market town, there was a need

to feed, house and entertain those who came to sell their goods or to catch a boat. In Africa as everywhere else, that meant that Karaha had a string of beer joints, whorehouses and gambling dens flanking the docks. Sin City on the Congo River was no different than Sin City on any other river.

Karaha was too remote to have a central electrical power grid. That didn't mean, however, that the town was dark. Japanese-made portable generators hummed like a swarm of mosquitos powering the gaudy lights in front of the bars and brothels. There were even streetlights on poles every forty yards or so to keep the drunks from getting lost on their way to the next watering hole.

The three commandos kept close to the river as they approached Karaha, making their way past the fishing boats and skiffs pulled up onto the bank. The occasional fisherman was sleeping with his boat, but they managed to get to the pier without being noticed.

A guard shack stood at the head of a pier, and a man wearing what looked like uniform pants and combat boots was sitting in a chair in front of the shack with his head tilted back against the wall, asleep. An AK-47 was leaning against the wall beside him, so he wasn't likely to be a civilian.

The commandos could hear the hum of a nearby generator powering a series of lights hung along the length of the dock. At least one-third of the bulbs were burned out, but it was still too light to attempt to sneak a dozen people past without being seen. "We're going to need to kill the rest of those lights on that dock," Hawkins pointed out.

"Finding the generator will take care of that," James said.

"You want to take care of Sleeping Beauty," Hawkins asked, "while I see to the lights?"

James took the razor-sharp Tanto fighting knife from his assault harness. "Be glad to."

Keeping to the shadows, James worked his way around behind the guard. Since the man had his back to the shack, James had to come in on him from the side. The planks of the pier weren't stable, so he stepped lightly to limit the creaking. When he was within two feet of his target, he struck. Stabbing the knife into the hollow of the man's neck, he ripped it sideways, slicing through both the carotid and jugular.

The guard fell unconscious instantly from the sudden drop in blood pressure. He was dead in sixty seconds.

Grabbing him under the armpits, James dragged the body down under the pier so no one would stumble onto it and raise the alarm.

With the guard taken out, Hawkins moved to the generator. Ripping the ignition wire off the spark plug and throwing it away silenced its hum.

"That's better," he said as he snapped his night-vision goggles over his eyes. "Now I can see."

In the green glow, the ex-Ranger could clearly

make out the shapes of the boats tied up to the pier. Most of them were primitive sail or outboard motor-powered boats, far too small for what they needed. But at the end of the pier was the vessel Kurtzman had spotted from space. It looked to be a sixty-five footer, which was small, but the boat was still large enough for all of them to crowd onto.

MCCARTER KEPT AN EYE on the edge of the village. So far the natives didn't seem to be too restless, and that meant that the commandos hadn't been spotted. He grinned when he saw the lights on the pier wink out. Hearing someone approach, he turned and saw Frank Bullis. "What do you need, Doctor?" he asked.

"As you know," Bullis said, "Captain Belasko asked me to be in charge of the civilians, but I've got a problem I don't know how to handle."

"Let me guess," McCarter said. "Mr. Jordan doesn't want to go along with the program."

"How did you know?"

"His type never do."

"What should I do about it?"

"Leave him to me."

When McCarter walked up to the cluster of ex-hostages, it sounded as if Jordan was trying to talk them into surrendering to the first Simba they saw.

"There will be none of that talk, boyo," McCarter snapped. "No one surrenders, no one. Everyone is going to get out of this."

"I don't see why we just can't surrender," Jordan insisted, "and end this nonsense. We're tired of running through the jungle without enough to eat and sleeping on the ground. We're protected by UN charter, and these Simbas won't dare to do anything more than take us into custody until a release can be arranged."

McCarter had had about all he could take from this man and exploded. "Listen, you ignorant bloody Yank. If you want to get yourself killed, you are bloody well free to do it in any manner you desire. I personally don't think that being eaten alive is a good way to die, but to each his own. And, if you like, when we move out again, you can stay behind. I don't care."

The Briton moved right into Jordan's face. "You are not, and I say again not, however, going to take the rest of these people down with you. The next time I hear that you are trying to start a revolution, I'm going to bind and gag you.

"Unless, of course, you want to stay behind." McCarter grinned. "And, if that's the case, I'll leave your hands free so you can defend yourself."

Bill Jordan wasn't accustomed to being talked to that way. As the executive director of the World Children's Foundation, he was used to being respected and deferred to. His charity was the third largest in the States, and he intended to take it to number one. It was true that much of the respect came from his wife's family fortune, which had founded the organization, but it was still respect and a man of his stature deserved it.

He was certain that this group of mercenaries wasn't connected with the United States government. He had met the President at a White House Rose Garden Children's Day ceremony, and there was no way that he would have sent men like these to rescue American citizens. There was probably a force of U.S. Marines somewhere in the area looking for him right now. If he could get away from these madmen and find them, he would be treated as the VIP that he was.

LEAVING HAWKINS to cover them from the end of the dock, Bolan and James headed toward the boat. After clearing it and finding no one on board, they hurried to the bridge. With a shielded penlight, James quickly familiarized himself with the patrol boat's controls. Everything was as expected in a boat of that size, and he wouldn't have trouble piloting it.

The gauges indicated that it had full power in the batteries, but when he tried the starter, the engine turned over but didn't start.

"Come on, baby," James muttered as he worked the throttle. He hit the starter button again, and the engine refused to even cough.

"David," Bolan called over the com link, "send up Gary. We're having trouble with the engine and I need him to take a look at it."

"On the way," Manning radioed back.

Keeping to the shoreline, Manning sprinted the distance to the dock. When he reached the rickety pier, he walked so as not to make too much noise. "What's the problem?" he asked when he reached the boat."

"We have full battery power," James stated, "but the damned thing won't catch."

"You've got five minutes down there," Bolan said. "If you can't find the problem by that time, we'll have to try the next town."

It was less than two minutes before Manning called up from the engine compartment. "I think I found what was wrong," he said. "The fuel petcocks were shut down. Try it now."

This time, the engine sputtered and caught. James worked the throttle, gently trying to prompt the diesel to run smoothly. A few belches of oily smoke and flame later, it was throbbing powerfully.

"Thank God for German engineering," he muttered. Though the patrol boat and its engine had been made in Communist East Germany, the prayer still applied. Marxism hadn't completely ruined the Germans.

Clicking in the com link, Bolan radioed to McCarter. "Bring them on, David."

"We're on the way."

"OKAY, PEOPLE," McCarter said. "We have the dock and the boat secured. All we have to do is to move quietly and we'll be okay. If we get spotted, though, run for the dock and we'll cover you.''

Keeping to the shadows, the commandos moved their charges past the edge of town toward the river. They were two hundred yards from the end of the dock when a dozen Simbas came out of one of the taverns and started to walk down the street toward them.

''Quickly now,'' McCarter whispered as he shifted his H&K to cover them.

When Bill Jordan saw the Simbas, he decided to take his chances with them rather than risking himself any further with this foolishness. A man of his stature shouldn't have to endure that kind of treatment. Breaking out of the group, he ran toward the Simbas with his arms held high in the air.

''Don't shoot!'' he shouted. ''I surrender! Don't shoot! I'm an American!''

''Shit!'' McCarter said. The ex-hostages were frightened and exhausted, but there was no time to coddle them now. ''Run, you lot!'' he shouted. ''Goddammit, run!''

With a surge of adrenaline shooting through them, they found the energy to run for their lives.

A Simba raced toward Jordan, his AK leveled. ''You Yankee?''

''Yes, I'm an American,'' Jordan said. ''And I surren—''

In a flash, the Simba reversed the assault rifle and drove the buttstock deep into Jordan's belly. The

American bent over and collapsed on the ground. The rifle butt slammed down on his back several more times, driving him into the dirt.

Having a captive to play with seemed to temporarily satisfy the Simbas. They wasted several valuable moments tormenting Jordan before turning their attention back to the fleeing ex-hostages.

When the Simbas started after the group, they ran into a blaze of fire from Hawkins and Encizo. The ambush caught them completely off guard, and they fell back in confusion, leaving three lion warriors lying in the dirt.

"Run, people, run!" McCarter yelled over the fire.

There was nothing like the sound of gunfire to motivate people to move, and the ex-hostages sprinted the last hundred yards to the head of the dock. From there it was only a hundred feet to the waiting patrol boat.

Hawkins and Encizo fired another volley in the general direction of the Simbas and started to pull back, as well. When they reached the boat, they grabbed the last ex-hostage and swung him onto the deck.

"Move out!" Encizo shouted up to the bridge.

James slammed the throttle forward and, diesel exhausts bellowing, the patrol boat pulled away from the dock and headed for the middle of the river. In seconds, it was lost in the darkness.

The last thing the Stony Man commandos saw as

the stolen patrol boat pulled out into the river was that two dozen Simbas had gathered in a ring under one of the working streetlights. In the center of their circle was a man on his knees with his arms up, trying to protect his head as they slashed and stabbed at him with their machetes.

Once more, Bill Jordan was learning the hard way that his influential friends in Washington weren't much use to him in Africa. It was the last lesson he would ever learn.

Stony Man Farm, Virginia

THE SENSE OF RELIEF in the Stony Man Computer Room was palpable. For the first time since the mission started, there was optimism that it could actually be concluded successfully.

"What does the river look like?" Hal Brognola asked Aaron Kurtzman.

"It's pretty clear right now," Kurtzman replied as he studied his satellite scans. "But the locals don't go out much at night. Come dawn, it might turn into a real freeway down there. We'll just have to wait and see."

"A lot of it's going to depend on how much command-and-control capability Taibu has," Katz added. "We've spotted a couple of other patrol boats upstream, but we don't know who controls them. For planning purposes, though, we have to assume that they're his and that he can contact them.''

"How far east will they have to go before we can get an aircraft in?" Brognola asked.

"Well, if they can get to the eastern provinces, we should be able to get a special ops Herky in to take them out.''

"How far is it?"

"The Congo River isn't exactly straight," Katz reminded him, "so they'll be traveling almost a hundred more miles than if they'd stayed in the jungle. But since they can easily travel at night now, I'd say another day and a half should see them well clear of Simba-controlled territory.''

"I'll start working on getting that aircraft laid on.''

"With all this back patting that's going on," Kurtzman said, "I hate to be a party pooper, but is anyone working on what we're going to do about those Ebola samples? When we get the people out, Taibu just might take exception to our having spoiled his fun. And if he gets pissed, we're going to have a real problem.''

"Dammit, Aaron, one thing at a time," Katz said. "We have to get Striker's people out first. Then we'll worry about the damned virus.''

"Okay." Kurtzman shrugged. "I just wanted to make sure that we weren't forgetting something that we need to be keeping track of.''

"I won't forget," Brognola reassured him. "The Man won't let me.''

CHAPTER FIFTEEN

On the Congo River

As soon as the stolen patrol boat was in the middle of the half-mile-wide river and well out of the range of rifle fire, Mack Bolan joined Calvin James on the bridge. "How's she doing so far?"

"Say what you like about those wicked old East Germans," James replied, grinning, "but the bastards could sure as hell build fine machinery. I don't think she's had a hell of a lot of TLC lately, but she's still a Thoroughbred. If nothing major breaks down, we should be okay."

According to the data plate riveted on the steel bulkhead, the boat they had liberated was an ex–East German Navy Osprey Class coastal patrol boat that had been built in Rostock in 1968. How it had ended up on the Congo River was anyone's guess. But along with the Cubans, the East German Communists had been the major Soviet surrogates and arms suppliers to the region during the cold war.

"How's the fuel?"

"If the gauges are functioning," James replied, "we should have more than enough."

"Is she armed?" Bolan asked.

"I ran into some kind of aft gun mount when we boarded, but I didn't see a weapon on it. And—" he squinted into the darkness "—I think there's another gun mount forward, but it looks empty, too."

"You'd better go to NV mode before you run into someone," Bolan said. With the moon down, the stars were bright, but not bright enough to navigate with naked eyes.

James snapped his night-vision goggles in place, and the darkness turned into glowing shades of green. "That's much better."

BELOW DECKS, the Stony Man team was trying to get the ex-hostages settled down for what would hopefully be an uneventful trip. None of the civilians had been hurt in the mad dash to safety, but that had been the last straw for many of them. The strains of captivity and the run through the jungle had drained them. They would need a long rest before they would be up for much more than just resting.

While the people were getting settled down, Hawkins went about investigating their new boat. In the galley, he found several mostly full crates of bottled African beer and a few bottles of the overly sweet orange soda that was so popular with the locals. He'd pass on the soda, but a beer sounded real good right about now. Digging into the food lockers, he found half a dozen tins of canned fish and a bag of ground maize meal that would supplement their meager stocks of MREs. Plus, now that they were on the river, they could try to fish, as well.

More important to their survival than the food was the contents of the arms lockers. He found two more AK-47s and several Chinese-style chest-pack magazine carriers full of loaded magazines. That gave them four extra assault rifles and enough ammunition to be useful if it came down to a major firefight.

"Try to find an RPD machine gun tucked away somewhere," McCarter said when Hawkins reported his find. "The gun mounts on this thing have been modified to take them in place of the original weapons."

"I'd sure like to find the East German 20 mms that used to be there stashed away somewhere," Hawkins said. "They'd go a long way to seeing that we get out of here in one piece."

"I'm sure they've been gone for years."

FRANK BULLIS WENT UP on deck and sought out Bolan to make his report on the condition of the ex-hostages. They had all been fed and had found places to sleep. They weren't necessarily comfortable accommodations, but it sure beat sleeping in the jungle.

"I think I can speak for all of us, Captain," he

said, "when I say that we're damned glad to be here right now. I'm not sure that we could have kept going very much longer in the jungle."

"We're covering distance faster, yes," Bolan explained. "But because the river loops back and forth, we're not moving toward our destination much faster than if we were still in the bush."

"What do you think our chances are?"

Bolan scanned the dark vegetation-covered banks of the river. "To be honest," he said bluntly, "I don't know. It's going to depend more on what Taibu does than on anything we might do. Even though this boat has a steel hull, it's not well armed. All we have to fight with are our small arms. If he can get heavy weapons in to block us, we'll have no chance at all.

"However," he added when he saw the look on Bullis's face, "if we just have to run a gauntlet of Simbas armed with AKs, we should make it."

Bullis kept himself from asking how likely that was. Any glimmer of hope was better than none at all.

"You'd better get some rest, Frank," Bolan told him. "We might need you in the morning."

Bullis didn't want to know why he might be needed. He just desperately wanted to sleep. "Okay, but call me if something comes up."

"Will do."

THE PATROL BOAT hadn't missed a beat all through the night. The six-cylinder German diesel had chugged along at 1,800 rpm, pushing the boat at a steady twelve knots. That was less than half its top speed, but it was too dangerous to try to run the river at night faster than that.

It was almost exactly at BMNT—Beginning Morning Nautical Twilight—when the diesel engine sputtered and died. Rafael Encizo had replaced Gary Manning on engine watch, and he instantly came awake.

McCarter was at the helm when the boat lost steerage. "What in the hell's going on down there, Rafe?" he asked over the com link.

"I don't know yet," the Cuban answered. "Better get Gary down here to help me."

"I'm on the way," the Canadian replied. Even asleep, he wore his com link and had automatically awakened at the sound of his name.

Bolan had also heard the call, and when he reached the bridge, Calvin James was already there. "Do you want me to throw out an anchor to stop the drift?" the ex-SEAL asked.

"No," McCarter replied. "I'm going to let her drift closer to the bank so we can abandon ship if we can't get the engine running again."

BMNT was defined as the time when it was light enough to barely distinguish between white and black. In the tropics, nautical twilight was brief. The sun rose above the horizon in minutes, and the mist would quickly burn off. When that happened, they would be exposed, dead in the water for all the world to see.

"Find Dr. Bullis," Bolan said over the radio to Hawkins, "and get him up on the bridge ASAP."

"On the way."

"The engine has stopped." Bullis stated the obvious when he was escorted up to the bridge. "What happened?"

"We don't know yet," Bolan replied, "but I need you to do something for us."

"What's that?"

"I need you to find the most steady African man from the ex-hostages to play Simba with you and Calvin up on deck. It's going to be light enough to spot us in a few minutes and we don't want anyone, military or civilian, to see white men on this boat. Strip down to what will pass for Simba dress, and Hawkins will give you both AKs."

James shook his head. "The next time you honkies decide to go to Africa," he mumbled as he stripped off his assault harness and jacket, "I think I'm going to stay home and shoot a few hoops. I seem to have gotten all of the choice assignments since we hit this damned place."

"We didn't leave you behind the last time we went to Russia," McCarter said, "and you got to skate that time because you stood out too much."

"That was different."

When Bullis came back, he had cut off his cotton pants at the knees and was wearing a ragged T-shirt.

The black man with him was wearing a faded pair of jungle-camouflage pants he'd found in the crew quarters, tied up with a rope belt. Both men wore chest-pack magazine carriers and had their AKs slung over their shoulders. Even up close, they both looked like real Simbas.

"This is Joseph Mimbali," Bullis said. "He doesn't have much English, but he speaks French."

Mimbali nodded to Bolan.

"Get up on deck, but don't look too alert."

In the hold, the ex-hostages woke to Hawkins's urgent call. "Okay, people, here's the score," he said. "As you might have noticed, the engine is shut down right now. It's light outside, and we're right in the middle of the river. We're expecting all kinds of traffic before too long, so we're going to have to keep quiet and not attract attention. And no one goes up on deck for any reason."

"WE FOUND THE PROBLEM," Manning called up from the engine compartment. "The fuel filters are clogged with years of crap. I can't even guess when they were last cleaned, and we were lucky to have gotten as far as we did on them."

"Are there any spares down there?"

"These are bronze-mesh filters, so you clean them instead of replacing them."

"How long will that take?"

"That's the problem," Manning explained. "We

don't have any solvent to clean them with, only more diesel fuel, so it's going to take a while.''

"Get on it."

"We are."

AS THE MORNING MIST BURNED off, several small boats could be seen on the river. Most of them carried fishermen, and they avoided getting too close to the gray patrol boat. The locals might have to live with Simbas, but they apparently went out of the way not to draw attention to themselves.

James thought that their ruse was working when he spotted a small fishing skiff headed downstream toward them. The boat carried two men, but from the AKs slung over their shoulders, they were Simbas, not fishermen.

"Oh, shit," James said when he saw the small craft turn in their direction. "Frank," he called to Bullis, "we have company."

When it was obvious that the boat was coming their way, Bullis called over to Mimbali, "Greet them, Joseph, and see what they want."

Mimbali spoke several of the local dialects, as well as French, so he had to be the pointman up on deck. After a brief exchange with the Simba, he spoke to Bullis in French, "He says he's a good engine man and he insists on helping his brothers with their boat."

"Tell him we don't need any help," Bullis said in the same language.

"He says that he's hungover and smelling the fuel will clear his head. He's still drunk if you ask me, and he insists on coming on board."

"Let him come," Manning called up from the engine room in English. "Have Mimbali lead him down here, and we'll deal with him."

"And get ready to help me take the other guy out, as well," James told Bullis. "I need you to keep his attention focused on you for two or three minutes after the first guy goes belowdecks."

Not trusting his voice, Bullis simply nodded.

Being an ex-SEAL, James wasn't afraid to use the underwater-attack option. Going to the other side of the boat, he silently lowered himself into the muddy water. After he sank below the surface, a few strokes of his powerful arms took him around to the stern of the boat. He surfaced enough to clear his eyes and nose so he could breathe while he listened. When he heard the first Simba go belowdecks and Bullis talking to the one in the boat, he made his move.

Though the water was muddy, the sun was bright enough to show him the shadow of the small boat's hull under the water. Surfacing by the stern, he filled his lungs and went back under. When he was behind the Simba, he erupted out of the water like a big crocodile. Grabbing the Simba around the neck, he pulled him backward into the water.

The African wasn't a swimmer and panicked as soon as he went under. Fear gave him strength, and

James had his hands full keeping him from fighting his way to the surface. The fight, though, was brief. With a last burst of air from his lungs, the Simba went limp in James's arms.

On his way to the surface, James released the Simba and let him settle to the depths of the river. To keep anyone from asking awkward questions, he pulled down the side of the small boat until it filled with muddy water and followed the Simba to the bottom.

As a LEADER OF AFRICANS, Charles Taibu knew that violent fits of rage went a long way to impress his followers with his concerns. He made sure that he didn't use them too often, but this was a circumstance that clearly warranted it. His orders hadn't been obeyed, and he couldn't allow his Simbas to think that they had any option but to instantly obey him at all times. To impress that fact on them again, rage was clearly called for this time.

"I ordered you to stop the Westerners," he roared, "but you let them walk right past you and take one of my boats. How did that happen?"

The unfortunate Simbas looked at one another and shrugged. The fact that they had been drunk wasn't going to work as an excuse, not with Taibu. He let them drink as much as they wanted, but he also expected them to do their duty drunk or sober.

"Dig your graves!" Taibu ordered.

As the unfortunate Simbas dug holes in the red

earth, the onlookers broke into the Simba hunting chant, but Taibu wasn't going to allow them to hack the guilty to death this time. He was in a hurry and a single shot to the head would have to suffice. Normally, he didn't play executioner himself, but this lapse called for it.

When the Simbas were standing in the shallow graves they had dug, he pulled the Makarov pistol from the holster on his belt. Standing in front of each man, he made the Simba look him in the eyes as he pulled the trigger. After each shot, the gathered Simbas howled their approval.

As soon as the executions were over, Taibu got back to the problem at hand. He was aware that to Western observers, his Simba army looked like a throwback to the days of Chaka and the Zulu wars of the previous century, rampaging African warriors destroying every living thing in their path. That was a calculated image he had carefully staged because he knew the effect it had on Westerners. His training in Moscow, however, had impressed upon him the need for a successful leader to be able to control his assets at all times. Though he had no fixed base, that didn't mean that he was out of communication with the various units he had left along his route.

The Westerners had surprised him again, but they wouldn't enjoy the fruits of that surprise for very long. Now that they were on the river, he would know where they were at all times. Many of his river observation posts had radios, as did all of his small fleet of patrol boats. The first thing he did was to call for the fastest of those boats to come to Karaha at top speed.

If the Westerners were on the river, he would be right behind them.

MANNING HAD JUST finished reinstalling the newly cleaned fuel filters. The gun-cleaning toothbrush from his assault pack had played a big role in busting up months of grime and crud enough that the diesel fuel could wash it away. In the best of all possible worlds, the filters would have been power washed to remove every last speck of contamination, but as it was, a good brushing would have to do.

"Give it a crank now," he called up to the bridge.

Encizo hit the starter button. The six-cylinder diesel cranked over, spit smoke a few times and started.

"Let's get this show back on the road," McCarter said.

Keeping the rpm down, Encizo piloted the patrol boat back out into the middle of the river and headed east. Up on deck, James, Bullis and Mimbali continued to play Simba deckhands well enough that the smaller craft gave them a wide berth.

Another day or two, and they should be in the clear.

CHAPTER SIXTEEN

Stony Man Farm, Virginia

When the intercom in Barbara Price's office buzzed, she clicked on. "Price."

"Barbara," Buck Greene said urgently, "we have incoming bandits."

To keep prying eyes in the sky from looking down on Stony Man Farm, the area over and around the farm was an FAA restricted flying zone. Those who wished to ignore the restriction were considered hostile and would be dealt with accordingly. To defend itself from aerial attack, the Farm offered a variety of options ranging from shoulder-fired Stinger missiles to a Phalanx 20 mm autocannon linked to radar. So far, these hadn't been called into action, but there was a first time for everything.

"Do you have ID yet?"

"It's rotary wing and flying low."

Price's mind clicked in on that information. "Track it, but check fire until you have an aggressive move. I need a flight number and N number on it ASAP. It might be that reporter who called here.''

''Barb, that leaves us wide-open,'' Greene said. ''It could be carrying a package.''

''Go to a silent second alert and warm up the Phalanx system, but don't fire. Give them the standard FAA air warning and see if they comply. I'll alert Hal.''

''I don't like it, Barb.''

''I know, I know,'' she replied. ''Just do it.''

''Yes, ma'am.''

THE SILENT ALERT flashed to every blacksuit, and the Farm went into action. Greene didn't call out the reinforcements, but had them standing by in the barracks. The men working outside stopped what they were doing and secured their weapons. The air-defense teams went to their positions and warmed up their Stinger missiles.

Inside the farmhouse itself, the blast doors were closed, the ventilation system went on filtration mode and the emergency generators were cut in. The innocent-looking farmhouse was built like a bunker and could withstand up to 750-pound bombs.

In the Computer Room, Aaron Kurtzman clicked onto the radar feed, and the big monitor lit up with the air-defense screen. If the bogey was a bandit, it wasn't going to escape being blasted out of the sky.

THE NEWS 7 HELICOPTER was flying low over the Shenandoah Valley. Up front, Sylvia Thompson-Bracket paid little attention as the scenery flew past her. Her attention was focused on Stony Man Farm and what the residents were going to do when the chopper sat down right in the middle of it. That smart-mouthed woman who had refused to talk to her would have no choice but to answer her questions then.

A faint smile crossed Thompson-Bracket's face. She wasn't the least hesitant to put herself in someone's face in an instant. As far as she was concerned, the traditional Southern-gentility crap was exactly that—crap. Regardless of the magnolia accent she had picked up, there was nothing she wouldn't do or say to get what she wanted. And she wanted to get this story. This was the one that was going to get her the hell out of this nickel-and-dime market into something worthy of her. She felt she had paid her dues and then some.

In the rear seat, the cameraman was taping anything of interest they passed. When they put the story together, the scenery shots would provide the lead-in for Thompson-Bracket's story of greed and corruption. For the life of him, he couldn't figure out what she was going after this time, but she didn't pay him to think. In fact, she actively discouraged it, and he had learned to keep his mouth shut around her.

Twenty miles out, the pilot's earphones kicked

in. "November Three Eight Seven," a man's voice said, "this is Richmond Control. Be advised that you are approaching a restricted airspace. Vector two-three-zero for ten miles. Acknowledge, over."

The pilot clicked on the intercom to his left seat passenger. "I just got an FAA warning that we're approaching restricted airspace. They want us to turn away."

The reporter smiled. Bingo! The average Virginia farm didn't have restricted airspace over it, so this proved her contention that all was not up-front about this Stony Man place. "Ignore it," she ordered.

"I can't do that," he said. "It's my ass on the line if I don't comply, not yours."

"Don't be a wimp," she shot back. "I'll pay your fine. Just fly this damned thing. We're only a few miles away from the farm."

The pilot was the third man in the past eight months who had been assigned to fly for Thompson-Bracket. The pay was good, but he now knew why his predecessors hadn't lasted on the job. It hadn't taken him long to learn that off camera the poised, glamorous Sylvia Thompson-Bracket was a world-class bitch, and a person had to be a masochist to work for her.

"I have to get out of here," he said. "It isn't worth losing my ticket over."

"We'll take it to court," she said. "Freedom of the Press and all that crap. Keep flying."

"November Three Eight Seven, this is Richmond Control. Vector two-three-zero immediately. You are in violation of restricted airspace and FAA flight regulations. Acknowledge, over."

"Roger, Richmond Control," the pilot replied. "Three Eight Seven turning to two-three-zero. Over."

"You fucking coward," she snapped, her face distorted with rage. "I told you to keep flying."

"November Three Eight Seven," the radio crackled again, "this is Richmond Control. You are ordered to land at Lynchburg and await FAA investigation of flight violation. Acknowledge, over."

"Shit!" the pilot muttered before clicking in his mike. "Roger, Richmond Control. Will comply."

"What in the hell are you doing?" Thompson-Bracket yelled at him as he banked the chopper back the way they had come.

"We've been ordered to land this chopper at Lynchburg, and I'm going to do exactly what they told me to do, Sylvia. This isn't one of your stupid sex scandals or corruption investigations where you can fuck around with state and local officials and get away with it. The Feds just told me to get my ass on the ground, and I'm going to do it. If I'm lucky, I might be able to keep my license."

"You sorry bastard! You're fired!"

"No, I'm not." He smiled. "I quit."

"THE CHOPPER VEERED OFF," Greene reported to Price, "and was ordered to land at Lynchburg to talk to the FAA about the airspace violation."

"Get someone over there and find out who's on board."

"They're already on the way."

Price knew that she didn't have to wait for that report to confirm who had been on that chopper. She'd bet her entire federal pension that it had been the reporter.

"And keep them on alert until we know what the hell's going on here."

"Yes, ma'am."

WHEN THE NEWS 7 chopper flared out and landed at Lynchburg, Sylvia Thompson-Bracket jumped out and motioned for the cameraman to join her. This was something she wanted a record of, and the tape was rolling when the car drove up and the FAA men stepped out.

"Shut off the camera," the lead Fed said.

"I'm a reporter," Thompson-Bracket shot back, "and I have a legal right to film federal employees in the conduct of their jobs."

The FAA man turned to the pilot. "Tell her to turn it off, mister."

The pilot shrugged. "I'm just the driver, and I just made my last flight for her."

The second FAA man walked over to the cameraman and simply said. "Turn it off or go into custody. Your choice."

The cameraman put his camera on the tarmac and backed up from it.

"Now, miss," the first FAA man said, "we can talk. This aircraft is being impounded until the flight violation can be investigated. I suggest that you find an alternate means of transportation."

"You can't do that," she said. "This chopper is the property of a television station."

"I don't care if it's the pope's personal helicopter, miss. In accordance with FAA regulations, until I can get this sorted out, it's grounded. Any attempt to fly it before the impound has been rescinded is a felony worth ten years in a federal prison and a fine of ten thousand dollars."

He smiled broadly. "Any questions?"

"I'm going to have your ass for this, mister," she snarled, dropping the TV persona. "And when I'm done with that, I'm going to ruin your life."

The FAA man laughed. "Communicating a threat to a federal official in the conduct of his official duties is also a felony, miss. But that one's worth twenty years. I'll see you in court."

Thompson-Bracket knew when she had to retreat and, motioning for her cameraman to follow her, she walked back to the chopper and took out her bags. The pilot got into the FAA car and went with them back to their office.

THOMPSON-BRACKET HAD her self-control back when her rented four-wheel-drive SUV pulled into the little town of Wilsonburg. With the defection of her pilot, she'd had no choice but to rent a car and drive the rest of the way. It had been either that or slink back to Richmond with her tail between her legs until they could hire a new pilot, and she wasn't going to wait that long to pursue the story.

Her informant had said that she worked in a tavern, so the reporter started at the one in the center of town. When she walked into the tavern, she was fully aware of the effect she had on the men drinking beer. It was too bad that she was meeting a woman informant. She was ready to do a number on the first man she met.

"Jesus," one of the drinkers said, "isn't that what's-her-face? The girl on Channel 7?"

"Sure looks like her," his companion said. "But what the hell would she be coming here for? There ain't nothing going on around here worth spit."

Thompson-Bracket walked up to the bar. "I'm looking for Mabel Windam."

Windam self-consciously patted the side of her hair before answering. "I'm Mabel Windam, and I'll bet that you're Miss Thompson-Bracket."

"I'm glad to meet you." The reporter put her hand out. "And please call me Sylvia."

"Okay, Sylvia. Can I get you anything?"

"Coffee, please—black," she replied as she took a seat on a stool.

"Coming right up."

WHEN THE BLACKSUIT at the Lynchburg airfield reported back in, Price called a meeting in the War Room. The meeting was missing a few of the usual players, but this wasn't the usual midmission meeting. The topic wasn't the situation Bolan and Phoenix Force were facing in Africa, but Sylvia Thompson-Bracket.

"We don't need this crap," Price said to no one in particular. "Not on top of the Annex job and the mission going sideways."

"I'll take care of the African situation," Hal Brognola told her. "So you, Buck and Ironman can concentrate on getting on top of this reporter. We can't afford to let her get the upper hand here."

"I can take her out of circulation for a month or so," Lyons offered. "We won't hurt her, but we can make sure that she doesn't hurt us, either."

"You know we can't do that, Carl," Brognola said. "There are lines that even we can't cross. She's a civilian, not a player, and until she attacks us directly or we find out that there's more behind her than there seems to be at this point, our hands are tied. If she moves on us, though, you have my prior permission to take any and all measures necessary to keep the Farm secure."

"But that leaves us only the reactive option," Buck Greene pointed out. "If we can't go proactive, we risk taking a hit before we can retaliate."

"I know," Brognola said, "and I don't like it

any more than you do, but for now, we're stuck with it.''

"Okay, then," Price said, "let's go over what we have on her so far, starting with the established fact that she revels in being a royal pain in the ass."

"What's new?" Lyons snorted. "That goes for damned near every reporter I ever met."

"But she's made a career of it."

"If she's more than that, though," Lyons stated flatly, "her career ends right here."

"But we need to tap into her modus operandi," Price said. "I have Akira going over tapes of her most recent 'exposés,' trying to see if there's a pattern in how she goes about her so-called investigations. She's already tried a flyover, and I want to know what she's going to try next."

"Her next move," Lyons replied, "will be to drive up to the front gate, drag out her cameraman and try to bully her way in by being from the 'media.' I've seen this shit a hundred times before, and it's carefully scripted. The chances are that she'll have a second camera far enough away that we don't notice it filming our reaction whatever it turns out to be."

"Is there a counter to that tactic?" Price asked.

Lyons grinned, and it wasn't a pretty thing to see. "We can deal with it on several levels, depending on how much of our hand we want to reveal and when."

"Lay it out."

"First off, we can go for the full monty right up front. Increase the gate guards and put spotters and a ready-reaction team outside the perimeter. We catch her second camera team moving in and put the hammer on them and then we mug her guy at the gate. We end up with both cameras and they have no proof of anything."

"Too risky," she said. "We do that, and we'll confirm her suspicions about us. I need subtle, Ironman, subtle."

Lyons laughed. "Okay, how about we keep the muscle well hidden and find a way to scramble the video cameras. She comes to the gate, we politely refuse her entrance. And while she's taping, we're using a Buck Rogers contraption to zap her cameras. Something magnetic maybe? She goes back and finds out that her tapes are blank."

"And what do we do for an encore?"

He shrugged. "More of the same?"

"That might work once," Greene interjected. "But a repeated video failure could also tip our hand. Not too many people have the know-how or the hardware to shut down a video camera."

"Speaking of the hardware, how do we do it at all?"

"I think that some kind of EM pulse should do it," Lyons said. "I'll have Gadgets get over to the armory and see what Cowboy has laying around. If nothing else, we can turn the air-defense radar on them. That should cook the cameras."

"How about cooking the media?"

Lyons shrugged and slowly grinned. "That's not my first concern."

"Only use the radar if it won't fry her, as well," she said. "Hal's not going to want to have to explain toasted reporters."

Lyons stood. "I'll see what Gadgets and Cowboy can come up with."

"Let me know."

"I need to go, too," Greene said. "I want to brief the blacksuits."

Price nodded. Like most problems, this was a situation that need never have happened. It didn't look to be an enemy action targeting the Farm, but one never knew. Some person jacking their jaws had been the catalyst for more than one disaster in history. Price would, however, do everything in her power to see that the Farm remained intact. If necessary, she would even turn Lyons loose on Miss Sylvia if all else failed.

The reporter might not fully realize what was going on, but she had declared war. Barbara Price had yet to lose a fight, and she wasn't going to start now.

CHAPTER SEVENTEEN

Part of the defensive strategy to protect the Farm against Sylvia Thompson-Bracket was to advise the foremen of Belmont Construction of the problem. His people had to be warned about what was going on. Frank Rose was Belmont's on-site supervisor, and Gadgets Schwarz had established a good rapport with him. He had made a point of taking his coffee breaks in the supervisor's trailer and generally making himself useful. When he walked into the trailer that morning, he stopped by the coffeepot and poured a cup before taking a seat in Rose's guest chair.

After exchanging their usual greetings, Schwarz got down to the topic of the day. "Frank," he said, "we've uncovered a security problem here, and we need you to talk to your boys about it."

Rose was an ex-Army combat engineer officer and he knew what a guard looked like when he saw one, even a guard wearing farm clothes and cowboy boots. He also knew enough not to ask questions about what the "farmhands" were guarding. He didn't want to know any more than was necessary for him to get the job done. But with all the guards and security measures he had spotted, he was surprised to hear that there was a problem.

"What's the story?"

"We have a TV reporter on our ass, and it looks like she's trying to infiltrate our operation. We're concerned that she might try to make contact with your workers and pump them for information."

"You said she. Who is she?"

"Sylvia Thompson-Bracket from Channel 7 out of Richmond. She's got a weekly sleaze-and-scandal show called *Virginia Undercover*."

"I've caught her act on the local station," Rose said, laughing, "and I think you guys may have your work cut out for you. She looks damned determined."

"Not as determined as we are to keep her ass out of here," Schwarz replied, dropping the good-old-boy act. "She has no idea of what she's messing with here and, if she finds out, she's going to be in a world of hurt."

"I know that it's none of my business," Rose said, "and I haven't forgotten that I signed a nondisclosure agreement, but I'm curious. Who the hell are you people working for, the Company?"

Schwarz grinned. "You know I can't say anything, Frank. But Sylvia Thompson-Bracket would be well advised not to mess with us too much, because we don't play by the same rules the CIA does."

"That's more than I want to know." Rose put up his hands. "What can I do for you?"

"Just tell the men that she's nosing around, and tell them that they're not to talk to her under any circumstances. We don't know if she's into offering cash or a quick screw to get what she needs. But if someone talks to her, losing his security clearance to work for you will be the least of his problems."

Schwarz leaned forward. "And make sure they understand that, Frank, and understand it good. I know that you guys do classified work all the time, but this is one of the most sensitive jobs you'll ever do. If this gets fucked up and we're compromised, all of you will be doing kitchen remodeling and deck work in the suburbs if you can even get that."

Rose swallowed hard. He didn't have the slightest idea what was at stake here, but the threat was clear. The money was very good on these hush-hush jobs, but messing with classified situations always carried risks. There was no way that he could make anywhere near the money he did with Belmont by doing completely civilian jobs.

"I'll tell them," he promised.

"It's not a threat, Frank," Schwarz said. "And I don't want you to think that I'm leaning on you. But if it goes wrong here, we won't have much input as to what happens in the aftermath. The shit will roll down from a great height, and they'll be no stopping it."

"I think I understand."

"I hope so, Frank. You're a good man, and I wish you nothing but the best when you leave here. It's what happens here that concerns me."

"I'll do everything I can."

"Good." Schwarz stood. "The cook did up a batch of doughnuts this morning, and I'll have one of the boys run some over for you."

"Thanks."

"No sweat."

BUCK GREENE HAD three blacksuits on duty covering the main gate. Two of them were working on the fence while the third was clearing the ditch, but their weapons were close at hand.

When Sylvia Thompson-Bracket's SUV drove up to the closed gate, the blacksuit leader keyed his com link. "We have visitors," he reported to Buck Greene.

"Keep your link hot."

"Can I help you, miss?" the blacksuit asked.

"Can you open the gate?" she replied. "I'd like to come in."

"I'm sorry, ma'am, but we can't let you come in without orders from the house."

"But I'm a reporter, Sylvia Thompson-Bracket."

"That doesn't change anything, ma'am. Our orders are firm."

"But what if I'm expected?"

"We would have been notified that you were expected," the blacksuit replied, smiling. "And then we would let you in."

"Can you check anyway and see if I can come in?"

"Sure." The blacksuit pulled a cell phone from his back pocket and dialed Barbara Price's emergency number.

"This is Hank at the gate," he said. "We have someone here who wants to see you, a Miss Thompson-Bracket... Yes, ma'am."

The blacksuit put his phone back in his pocket. "If you'll wait here, ma'am, someone will be down to talk to you."

"Can I wait inside the gate?"

"I'm afraid not."

BARBARA PRICE DECIDED to walk to the gate rather than having one of the blacksuits drive her in one of the Jeeps. For one thing, the walk would give her time to focus and get into combat mode.

Price walked quickly without hurrying and, as she had expected, she could feel the reporter's eyes on her every step of the way. At the gate, she stopped and took a long moment to assess her enemy.

The reporter was wearing light camera makeup, and her hair was in one of the traditional Southern "big hair" styles. It might work on camera, but looked rather stupid in rural Virginia. On top of that, her hairdo had been heavily sprayed to hold every hair in place and looked like a wig. Her low cut, tight-waisted dress with the full skirt was also totally inappropriate for visiting a farm.

Nonetheless, Price didn't make the mistake of underestimating her opponent. She looked like a caricature, but there was something behind the eyes. The reporter wasn't an enemy who could be taken lightly.

Price pulled off her mirrored sunglasses and tucked them into her shirt pocket. "What seems to be the problem here?" she asked the blacksuit.

Thompson-Bracket knew that she had just been assessed and put down as a worthy opponent. Before the guard could answer, she jumped in. "My name is Sylvia Thompson-Bracket, and I'm from Channel 7."

Price didn't show any signs of recognizing the name. "So, what can I do for you?"

"And you are…?" the reporter prompted.

"What business is it of yours who I am?"

Thompson-Bracket now knew that she was going to have to go all out. This was the same haughty bitch who had refused to talk to her on the phone.

"Barbara," she started out, "I want to talk to you about the construction job you currently have going on."

Price kept a straight face. "What business is it of yours what we do here?"

She glanced over to the cameraman for the first time. "Or of your station, either, for that matter."

"I have information—"

"I'm sure you do."

The reporter stopped and started again. "You have a job going on here that you have hired outsiders to do when there are families in Wilsonburg who need jobs."

"I'll ask you only one more time—how is this of any interest to you?"

"I'm always interested in injustice—"

Price laughed and turned to the blacksuits. "Boys, make sure this woman keeps on the outside of our fence. If she trespasses, arrest her and hold her for the country sheriff."

"But you can't do that," the reporter sputtered. "I'm—"

"Just watch me," Price said seriously. "You screw around with me, and you're going to get your teeth fed to you. Got that?"

"You can't threaten me!"

"I just did and, in case you missed it, have your boy rewind his tape. Now get your fat ass off my property. And my property line starts three feet from the edge of the roadway. If I look back and you're still here, I'm going to have you arrested for trespassing."

Price turned and walked back to the farmhouse. Her com link had been "hot," so Greene would have a recording of what had gone down.

"Okay, people," the blacksuit said, "you heard Miss Price. Get your asses off the farm."

"This isn't over," Thompson-Bracket warned.

"It is as far as I'm concerned." The blacksuit shrugged. "You've got thirty seconds to move it."

Being outnumbered, the reporter retreated again. Getting back in her rented vehicle, the cameraman backed out of the drive and turned down the road.

"She's clear," the blacksuit sent over his com link.

"Everyone keep a sharp eye out," Buck Greene ordered. "If either of them try to cross the fence, take them into custody immediately."

The blacksuit shift leaders rogered.

MABEL WINDAM WAS in a fine mood when Dimitri Spatkin walked into the tavern to get his dinner.

"You know that reporter woman," she said as soon as she laid eyes on him, "the one you had me call? Well, anyway she says that she's going to do everything she can to get my sister's youngest..."

Spatkin resisted the urge to reach across the bar and strangle the woman. If he ever heard anyone utter that phrase again, he was gong to kill them on the spot.

"Did she say exactly what she's going to do?"

"Well, not really," the barmaid said. "But she said that she'd do everything she could."

Without thinking about it, Spatkin slipped off the stool and headed for the door.

"Mel!" Mabel called out. "Where are you going? I was just telling you about what the lady said she'd do for my—"

The slamming door cut off Windam's nasal whine, and Spatkin headed across the street to the town's steak house. It was time for a change in diet anyway, and he couldn't afford to let that stupid, whining, neurotic bitch make him lose control. And, since her usefulness was over, he didn't need to talk to her ever again.

Now that Miss Sylvia Thompson-Bracket was in town, this was rapidly coming to a head. But the part he still had left to do would be the most difficult.

POLICE CHIEF BAUMANN'S deputy, Rudy Cullan, was in the tavern having a plate of ribs before he went on shift and he watched the exchange between Spatkin and Mabel Windam. He recognized Spatkin as being one of the guys from the Belmont Construction crew and wondered why he had left so abruptly. Since the chief was so hot on finding out who was spreading rumors about Stony Man Farm, he decided to talk to her.

As he got up and walked to the bar, he heard her say to no one in particular, "Well, I never. Here I was telling him the good news about my sister's boy when the man just up and walks out."

"Mabel," the cop said, taking a seat at the bar.

"Can I get you something, Rudy?"

"Who was that guy you were talking to?"

"Mel?" she said. "He's one of those out-of-towners working at Stony Man Farm. He's the one who told me that I might be able to get a job for my sister's boy by calling that reporter, Miss Sylvia. You know, she's got to be the nicest woman I ever did meet. You know I was wrong about her being a bitch, excuse my language. She really understands that—"

"You're the one who called that reporter?"

Windam smiled. "I sure did," she said proudly.

"And that guy told you to do it?"

"Well, not exactly," she said, trying to cover for Mel Bradley. "We were talking about my sister's boy not being able to find work around here because the folks out at Stony Man hired all those out-of-town people, and he said something about having seen Miss Sylvia on the TV. And—"

Cullan slid off of the bar stool and hurried outside to his car.

"CARL, ED BAUMANN," the Wilsonburg police chief said over the open line to the Farm. "I think we found who called Thompson-Bracket in on you guys."

"Let's have it," Lyons replied.

"She's a barmaid at the tavern. Mabel Windam."

"Why in the hell did she do something like that?

"Well," Baumann said, "Mabel's not exactly

the brightest citizen we have around here. One of her nephews is a completely shiftless, no-good son of a bitch, and she's always trying to find him a job. She's a persistent old biddy, but every time she talks someone into hiring him, he screws it up within a week and gets his ass fired. It's gotten to the point that no one around here will hire him, even to shovel shit."

Lyons shook his head in frustration. He had been looking for a sinister motive behind this attack, and all it turned out to be was a small-town busybody.

"Apparently," Chief Baumann continued, "she got to talking to one of the construction workers about her nephew being out of work again, and somehow Thompson-Bracket's name came up. She called her to bitch about you guys not hiring the town folks."

"Have you questioned her yet?"

"I don't have a reason to, Carl," Baumann said. "She hasn't committed a crime."

"Dammit, Ed," Lyons said. "We've got a problem here and we need to know what's behind it."

"Carl," Baumann replied, "look, I know that you guys are running some kind of hush-hush operation out there, but no laws have been broken here. And you only have a nosy reporter on your ass, not people with guns or bombs."

"Not yet," Lyons said.

CHAPTER EIGHTEEN

Wilsonburg, Virginia

After a great dinner at the steak house, a nice slab of beef, but grilled and not chicken-fried Southern style for a change, Dimitri Spatkin headed back across the street to his motel. With this situation rapidly coming to a head, it was time for him to load up the bed of his pickup so he would be ready for the grand finale. That would also put him at risk of being discovered for the first time, but he could no longer delay assembling his bomb.

He was putting the key in the door to his motel room when he saw a man and a woman walking toward him. When she passed under a light, he instantly recognized her and stood, arms at his sides, as she approached.

"Are you Mel Bradley?" the woman asked.

"I might be," he said. "Who wants to know?"

Spatkin knew full well who this puff-haired, big-chested blond was. Off camera she didn't have the impact she did on-screen, but there couldn't be two women like her in all of Wilsonburg.

"I'm Sylvia Thompson-Bracket from Channel 7," she announced, extending her hand.

Spatkin took her hand. "I'm Mel Bradley. What can I do for you, ma'am?"

"You're with the Belmont Construction crew that's working out at Stony Man Farm, right?"

Spatkin glanced over to make sure her companion didn't have a camera with him. "I can't talk on camera," he said. "My job's on the line here and I can't afford to lose it. I'm sure you understand."

"I understand all right, Mr. Bradley," she said. "But how does that make you feel? You have to be secretive to protect your job, but at the same time that job rightfully should have gone to someone here in town."

Spatkin shook his head. "I don't know anything about any of that," he said. "All I know is that the company I work for told me to get my butt down here to work, and here I am."

He shrugged. "And I don't know anything about why we were picked to work this job, either. Usually we work on bigger sites, so it's a bit unusual for us to be doing something as nickel-and-dime as a wood-chipping mill."

"What kind of bigger jobs?"

"Well," Spatkin said cautiously, "we usually work for the government building things like radar sites, prisons and other things I can't talk about."

Thompson-Bracket almost salivated as she jumped on that teaser like a pouncing tiger. "Why can't you talk about what you do?"

Bradley wanted to smile at her eagerness, but he didn't want her to get a hint of the fact that he was leading her around by the nose. Regardless of her appearance, he didn't discount her intelligence.

He shook his head. "I'd really like to help you, miss, but I just can't talk about our work."

"Are you saying that your company does classified work, then?"

"I guess that's what you'd call it. But it's not like we're a James Bond outfit or anything like that. We just do construction work for the government."

As far as Thompson-Bracket was concerned, that went a long way to explain the brick walls she had run into when she had tried to investigate Stony Man Farm. It was some kind of government operation and was under deep cover. She felt a sudden thrill when she realized how serious this might turn out to be. Once more her instincts for a story had paid off for her.

She thought back to the magazine writer who had wanted to follow her through a job so he could watch her in action. There had been something about him that had set off her alarm bells. She had seen his type before. He'd been a little too smooth and a little too unflappable when she'd turned him down cold. She had a feeling that if she checked his writing credits, she would draw a blank. But if her hunch was correct, if she called the magazine he had claimed to work for, she would be told that he was on their staff.

That was how a classified government operation would work, and that meant that she'd have to be even more careful than she had been so far. But now more than ever, she felt the risk would be worth the payoff she was sure to get.

"I don't know what else I can tell you about what we do, miss," Spatkin said.

"That's all right, Mr. Bradley," she replied, smiling like a Miss America contestant. "You've been a big help to me. I won't forget it."

"You'll remember that I can't have my name get out, won't you?"

"Don't worry," she said. "I keep all my sources completely confidential. You know, the First Amendment and freedom of the press."

If anyone in Wilsonburg knew how corrupt the American media really was, it was Dimitri Spatkin. He had lived through its campaign of disinformation against his motherland, and he had no illusions about the vaunted American press. That the average American citizen still thought that the media was anything other than totally corrupt was another sign of the people's political immaturity. This woman was motivated solely by self-seeking greed, instead of her stated ideals, but she might be useful to him.

"Do you mind if I ask what you're going to do

next?'' he asked. ''What are you going to do to get your story?''

''Can you keep a secret?'' she asked.

Spatkin laughed. ''I have to, remember? If my bosses find out that I've been talking to you, I'll get my butt canned for sure.''

''Well, Stony Man Farm's going to get a low-level visitor as soon as I can find a pilot with enough balls to fly me in there. There's some kind of bullshit FAA flight restriction over the place, and my regular pilot didn't have the guts to break it.''

Spatkin smiled to himself; that pilot was smarter than he knew. Unannounced aircraft attempting to fly over Stony Man risked getting blown out of the sky with little or no warning. But a small helicopter flying low to the ground just might make it.

''I'll keep my eyes open for you,'' he said.

She smiled. ''If you like. I'll let you know when I plan to go in. It might be worth watching.''

''Sure.'' He tried not to sound eager. ''It might be fun. Working a construction site can get a bit monotonous, you know. Every day is the same, so a little excitement might be welcome.''

She laughed. ''I think I'll be able to break up the routine for you.''

''I hope so.''

''And,'' she said, ''I might want to talk to you later, if I may.''

''Maybe,'' he said.

BARBARA PRICE CALLED another meeting in the War Room to go over the information Carl Lyons had received from the Wilsonburg police chief. "Just who is this Windam woman, anyway?" she asked.

"According to Chief Baumann," Lyons replied, "she's some busybody who has a nephew who's one of the town's more prominent drunks. Between stupidity and drink, he can't keep a job for more than a couple of days and everyone in town knows it. But somehow Mabel got it in her mind that by bringing in Belmont Construction we're purposefully cheating him out of a job and thereby taking food from his family's mouths."

Price shook her head. "I can't believe that we got into this mess over something as stupid as that. And we can't even put that guy on the payroll to make this go away."

"Not now we can't," Lyons agreed. "All that would do is cause us even more trouble."

"At least we now know this isn't an enemy probe against us," Buck Greene said.

"But it is," Price corrected him. "It didn't start out that way, granted, but it's not any less dangerous. If Miss Sylvia is half as smart as she's made out to be, it won't take her long to figure out that we're a little more than a garden-variety agricultural operation. If anyone looks close enough, this place screams 'covert operations.' It's only when you're used to seeing what we do around here that your eyes slide past the anomalies.''

Her face hardened. ''Thompson-Bracket's as dangerous as any enemy we've ever faced, and we can't let our guard down around her for an instant.''

''Do you think Hal's going to back down and let us put some pressure on her?'' Lyons asked.

''Not yet,'' she said. ''And as much as I hate to admit it, he's right. If we do anything less than outright termination, it's only going to make our problem worse. Short of that, I don't think that there's any way we can scare her off and insure that she keeps her mouth shut. I'm afraid that we're just going to have to try to ride this one out.''

''Until such time as the woman makes an overt move against us,'' Lyons growled. ''And then, reporter or not, she's dog meat.''

''If she does, yes.'' Price met his eyes as she gave the order. ''Take her down hard, and we'll worry about the fallout later.''

Lyons nodded. He knew that the fallout would get pretty deep over zeroing a ''member of the press,'' but he wasn't going to stand by and let some reporter take down Stony Man Farm.

''But,'' Price stated firmly, ''we have to wait till then, Ironman.''

''I just hope the waiting doesn't kill us.''

''I'll see to that,'' Buck Greene vowed. ''There's no way she's getting in here.''

''I'm counting on that,'' Price said.

Spatkin waited for a half an hour after talking to the reporter to make sure that she had left the area. The last thing he needed was for her to get it in her mind to follow him. He didn't bother to change out of his work clothes, but took a dark jacket out of his suitcase to go over his light-colored shirt. He tucked the 9 mm Smith & Wesson pistol in the back of his belt and pulled his jacket over it. He didn't think he'd need it, but he'd been a cop too long not to carry a piece on a job like this.

Getting in his pickup, he drove out of town at the speed limit, keeping a sharp eye on his rearview mirror. Law enforcement in Wilsonburg was a bit thin, just the chief and his two deputies, but caution always paid off. He drove past the feed store for a recon and saw that there was only one security light burning, and it was over the gas pumps on the opposite side of the building from the fertilizer silos.

Watching in his mirrors, Spatkin pulled off the road and waited to see if anyone had been following him. When the road was clear, he turned and headed back. Making sure to keep to the most heavily traveled part of the graveled parking lot, he drove around to the silos and stopped his truck under the delivery chute.

Getting out, he walked around to the back of the truck and knelt. Turning on his small flashlight, he shielded the beam and examined his tire marks. The lot was paved with gravel, and it didn't take tire impressions well at all. He wouldn't have to erase his tracks after he drove off.

As he had expected, the padlock on the silo's dump controls wasn't difficult to pick. There was a counter that registered the amount of fertilizer that was being delivered so it could be billed, but it was reset manually. The loss of a few hundred pounds of ammonium nitrate wouldn't be noticed. When he was done filling the truck, he'd reset the meter to zero and no one would be the wiser.

He filled the bed of his three-quarter-ton pickup to within a foot of the top. By the time he added the fifty-five gallons of diesel to the ammonium nitrate, his load would weigh about six or seven hundred pounds. That should be more than enough to take out the farmhouse.

Taking a blue plastic tarp from the truck's glove box, he stretched it over the bed and tied it in place. It wouldn't do to have someone ask him what he was doing with a truck load of fertilizer when he wasn't a farmer. If nothing else, the Oklahoma City bombing had made it a lot more difficult to be an agent saboteur in the good old United States.

Back out on the highway, he drove back to his motel, again keeping to the speed limit. He'd been parking his truck in back out of habit, so no one would question why he kept it out of sight back there.

Back in his room, he kicked off his boots, drank a beer and went to bed. Even if he had a bomb in the back of his truck, he was still a working man and needed his sleep.

Now THAT Sylvia Thompson-Bracket had confirmed her suspicions about the real nature of Stony Man Farm, she was more determined than ever to expose it. Exposing something that big was sure to make waves strong enough to carry her to the heights she craved. She wanted nothing in the world more than to drop the whining accent and lacquered hairdo and wear something that didn't look like it had come from the wardrobe of the *Hee Haw* set.

She didn't have a clue about what kind of government operation was going on out at the farm, but she didn't need to know to do the story. At a time when the average citizen distrusted the government more than at any other time in the nation's history, this story was a natural. It wouldn't even matter if the farm turned out to be something completely innocuous. The fact that the government was trying to keep the operation a secret from the American people would be enough.

Her next move, though, was going to have to be carefully planned and executed. She hadn't been fooled by the "farmhands" in their work clothes who had been guarding the gate at Stony Man Farm. She knew a hired thug when she saw one, and they had been thugs. She also knew without being told that there would be more of them covering every inch of that fence both day and night.

A ground approach simply wasn't going to work, so the only option left was an air assault.

A small chopper, flying fast and low to the ground, could get her across the fence in seconds and put her down right beside the farmhouse. Once she was on the ground with the tape rolling, there wouldn't be much that the bitch running the place could do about it. Any attempt to arrest or detain her would only make things worse for whoever they were and would give her story even more validity. And if they did hold her against her will, the court case alone would make her a superstar.

But to pull that off, she had to find a pilot with both the skill and the balls to fly her in. Someone who wasn't afraid to fly where he wasn't supposed to and who liked big paychecks. The station would have no problem with putting up the money for a story like this. The general manager trusted her nose for a story. She had never failed him yet, and she sure as hell wouldn't this time.

Taking her little black book out of her purse, she paged through her list of contacts on both sides of the law. In her line of work, she had made friends with hundreds of people who lived with one foot in the criminal world, men who liked the excitement and challenge of pushing the limits. Since that profile was similar to that of a hot-rock pilot, she knew several flyers who lived to fly against the odds.

Most of them were involved on some level with the drug trade, but she didn't have a problem with that. Her tour of duty as a cartel whore had given her an unusual outlook on that subject. As far as she was concerned, anyone who took drugs was too stupid to live, and drug dealers were doing them a favor by helping them kill themselves. The only thing wrong with the drug trade was that it was illegal. Her father would still be alive and she wouldn't have gone through two years of forced, unpaid prostitution had it been legal.

Finding the number of a small private airfield in rural southern Virginia, she dialed and got an answering machine. "This is Sylvia Thompson-Bracket," she said. "I met you when I was doing a story on the cops-in-the-sky traffic-ticket scam in your county, and I need a high-priced pilot for a risky job. You can reach me at the following number." She gave the number of her cell phone. "If I don't hear from you by noon tomorrow, I'll call someone else."

She got the call back in sixty seconds and arranged to meet the pilot. When she hung up, she started trying to figure out which big market she wanted to work in. California was out, but there was all the rest of the country.

CHAPTER NINETEEN

On the Congo River

The stolen patrol boat continued to cruise down the Congo River without attracting too much attention. For being in the middle of a war zone, there was a surprising amount of traffic on the waterway. Everything from ferries crowded with civilians to scores of fishing boats and polled skiffs came from both directions, but they all gave the patrol boat a wide berth. With Calvin James and his two ersatz Simbas on deck, no one wanted to get close enough to draw their attention.

Though they were confined belowdecks for their own protection, the ex-hostages were enjoying the trip, as well. The food stocks Hawkins had found in the galley were being put to good use, and two of the men had had good luck fishing off the fantail of the boat. They knew they weren't out of danger yet, but the relative comforts of the boat made the dangers seem further away for the moment.

The Stony Man commandos were also taking advantage of the slack time to catch up on their sleep by taking turns in the bridge and engine room. They had been running on catnaps for the past several days, and even hardened warriors had to rest every now and then.

FRANK BULLIS WAS AWAKE when Mack Bolan came down from the wheelhouse, and he followed him into the galley for a chance to talk alone.

"How are the passengers?" Bolan asked as he poured himself a cup of hot water to mix with the instant MRE ration-pack coffee.

"Much better now," the doctor replied. "The rest and food is doing wonders for them. Your medic has taken care of their miscellaneous cuts and blisters, so they're in pretty good shape considering what they've been through."

"Hopefully, we'll be able to keep them that way."

Bullis desperately wanted to ask Belasko if he thought that they were really going to get out of this alive. He wanted assurance from the professional that they weren't just running from one danger into another.

Instead, he asked a question that didn't sound quite so juvenile. "Where do you think they are?"

"I don't know," the soldier replied, "but I don't think that Taibu's given up on us yet. This is still his home turf, and he could have us under observation right as we're speaking. There's no way to tell. But every minute that we're under way is one more that we're not in the jungle."

It wasn't quite the reassurance he had wanted, but Bullis knew that it was an honest answer. Belasko and his men had been honest with them from the beginning. The fact that someone in Washington had aborted the original plan and left them on their own didn't reflect badly on the rescuers. They had put their lives on the line to save him and the others, and they were doing it still.

"How much longer do you think it'll be before we're out of Simba territory?"

"It's looking like two more days," Bolan replied. "As far as we know, Taibu doesn't have any troops in the eastern provinces, so as soon as we cross the border, we can call for the choppers."

Bullis looked out the porthole over the brown water. He didn't know where Belasko was getting his information from, but his calm confidence couldn't help but give him confidence, as well. When he got back to the States, he was going to insure that he and his men received the recognition they deserved for having pulled off this rescue.

If, of course, he could find out who they worked for.

CHARLES TAIBU WAS ALSO enjoying his cruise down the great river, and he, too, cruised unmolested. His flagship was another former East German patrol boat, and it was accompanied by two requisitioned river ferries crammed with almost four hundred Simba troops. The other water traffic took one look at the Simbas hanging off the ferries and headed for the riverbanks to let them pass.

The Simba leader had also radioed ahead to move his other units closer to the river so they could converge on the trap he was setting for the Westerners. No matter how good those commandos were, they weren't going to get away from him this time. In his march to the west, he had left as many men along the way as he had with him. Calling them all together created a second army even larger than his first.

With this incident coming to its conclusion, he had called for the case of Ebola virus samples to be put on board with him. He was still undecided if he should punish the Americans for sticking their imperialistic noses in his affairs. But since he had the vials with him, he could do that at any time. He didn't have to plan for it now.

It might be even better, though, for him to sell the vials back to the Yankees one at a time. He wouldn't, of course, sell all of them. That would be foolish, and he wasn't a foolish man.

The yellowish liquid in the vials looked innocent enough, but he knew the power they contained, the power of certain death. And he knew that as long as he had them in his possession, he was the most powerful man in Africa, maybe in all of the world. The power to cause death was the only power that really mattered, and he had millions of deaths contained in just one of those little glass vials.

Not even Stalin or Mao had ever controlled such a concentration of raw power. What they had done with their armies of millions backed by heavy industries that weren't found anywhere in Africa, he would do with a few thousand followers and a dozen small glass vials. He didn't need to have a huge army because he had the Ebola virus fighting for him.

EVEN THOUGH TAIBU didn't know that he was being watched from space, the Simba flotilla blocking the river wasn't even trying to hide. Over a dozen boats ranging from patrol boats to ferries and fishing skiffs were lined up almost gunwale to gunwale at a point where the Congo narrowed. There was no way that the Stony Man team was going to be able to get past them.

Aaron Kurtzman had spotted the first of the boats to reach the area and watched as the others joined it. When it was apparent what they were doing, he called Hal Brognola into the Computer Room.

"How soon will it take them to reach that blockade?" Brognola asked.

"At least an hour at their current speed," Katzenelenbogen replied. "Maybe a little more."

"If they didn't have those damned civilians with them," Kurtzman mumbled, "this wouldn't be a problem. They could take to the woods and bypass them.''

"But they do have them," Katz said, "and Mack's not going to abandon them."

When he turned to Brognola, the Israeli's face was hard. "This is one of those 'fish or cut bait' times that Hawkins is always talking about, Hal. The President is going to have to decide if he wants to risk sending in air support to clear an escape route for those people or simply write off our guys, as well as the civilians.

"And—" he glanced back to the satellite image on the monitor "—he's going to have to make up his mind about it real quick."

"Can they pull into shore and duck into that built-up area?" Brognola pointed to a town a quarter mile from the river about halfway between the team's current position and the waiting blockade.

Grenburgh had once been a colonial administrative center built by the European colonialists for the comfort of the European population. It was laid out on a square grid around a central plaza ringed with multiple-story masonry buildings. One prominent structure was a church large enough to be called a cathedral so the locals could see the power of the white man's God. In any Northern European country, Grenburgh would have only been a fair-sized town, but in the Congo, it had been a visible symbol of European might. After being ravaged during the colonial wars of the sixties and seventies, though, it had been abandoned and the jungle had worked on reclaiming the land it was built on.

"They can," Katz said, "but that's not going to be much better for them except that they'll be able to die on dry land instead of on the water. The Simbas won't have to move very far to surround them in there, and it'll be the Alamo scenario all over again."

Brognola's jaw was set. "I just want them to find a bolt-hole until I can get the President off his butt. This has gone on entirely long enough."

Katz knew that Brognola was sincere, but he also knew the hard political realities of the situation. Even though he knew that the big Fed had done everything in his power to rectify this situation, it was difficult to keep the sarcasm out of his voice.

"Why do you think it's going to be any different now than it was the last time you talked to him?"

"For one," Brognola said, "the list of the people they pulled out of that jail has turned up some interesting names. There are a couple of internationally known big names on that list, people who no one wants to see dead. Then there's the stories that captive CNN news team has been sending back about the activities of Taibu's Simbas. They aren't being broadcast on the evening news, but some of the people around the President are starting to realize that they can't let this go on much longer."

Brognola smiled thinly. "In other words, they're looking around to try to find the courage they misplaced when they heard the word *Ebola*. Even cowards hate to be blackmailed by butchers. They're politicians, and it's not going to look good next election day if they haven't done anything to stop Taibu's little reign of terror."

"In that case," Katz said, "I'll do what I can to get our people to a safe place in Grenburgh."

He turned back to Kurtzman. "Can you zoom in on that place so I can take a close look at it?"

Kurtzman shifted the image to center on the town and enlarged it.

"Give me a tight focus on the plaza."

Kurtzman tapped in a command, and the image enlarged to show only the plaza and the buildings around it. That close in, they could see the damage to the buildings done both by the passage of time, as well as the anticolonial revolutions that had swept central Africa for two decades.

Katz studied the partial ruins for a long moment. "That one," he said, stabbing a finger at a two-story building that looked to be completely intact. "It looks big enough to have a basement and thick walls. If they can get in there, they might be able to hold out long enough for the Man to pull his finger out and get some help in to them."

"You get them in there," Brognola promised, "and I'll see what I can do about getting them out."

"Better make it sooner rather than later," Katz said. "That looks like a good site to conduct a defense from here. But there's a lot of Simbas out there and they're not going to sit and wait for our guys to give themselves up. They're going to go in there after them.''

"You talk to Striker," Brognola said, "and tell him that I'm heading for Washington right now."

Price stuck her head around the corner. "The chopper's waiting,"

"I'm on the way."

"David," Katzenelenbogen called over the sat-com, "I need to talk to you and Striker. There's been a change of plans again."

"Send it," McCarter replied.

BOLAN CALLED Frank Bullis to the bridge to give him the latest bad news so he could pass it on to the ex-hostages. "Do you think you'll have any trouble with them on this?" Bolan asked. "When we get off, we'll need to move fast. It's not far to the town, but we want to limit our exposure on the ground, so we'll have to push them."

"I don't think you'll have any trouble with them," Bullis said. "Ever since Bill Jordan got chopped to bits, they've been paying extra attention to the realities of our situation. They'll do what they have to, even if it means leaving the boat."

"That's good," Bolan replied, "because this is where it's really going to get serious."

Bullis smiled grimly. "I thought this whole thing had been pretty serious right from the get-go."

"There's serious," Bolan explained, "and then there's the situation we're going to be in as soon as we leave this boat. Once we're in that town, we won't be able to run again. We'll have to stay where we are and fight it out until help can get through to us."

Bullis met the Executioner's eyes squarely. "Do you think whoever you work for in Washington will come through for us this time, or will they pull another last minute 'sorry about that, you're on your own.'"

"I wish I could say that I know what will happen," Bolan said honestly. "All I know is that the best people I know of are putting pressure on the President to do something concrete to get us out of here. The problem before was that Taibu threatened to loose that Ebola virus he got from your lab on major cities in Europe and the States if the planes came in to get us out. We didn't count for much against a threat of that magnitude."

"What's changed now?" Bullis asked skeptically. "We're still only a handful of people balanced against the lives of millions."

"One of the things is that I've asked for a long-range air strike this time, either cruise missiles or a stealth bomber, something that can get in here without whatever radars Taibu has spotting it. If they can, I'm counting on them doing enough destruction that we'll be able to break out and escape again."

"That still doesn't deal with the threat of the Ebola he has," Bullis said. "I can't even begin to tell you how dangerous that stuff is. It's not going to do much good for us to escape if he releases it. The contents of just one of those vials can kill hundreds of thousands of people."

"I know," Bolan said. "But my part in this is to get you people and my men out safely. Someone else can worry about the virus later."

"They'd better worry a lot."

"I think we can count on that."

WITH THE INFORMATION they had received from the Farm, Calvin James used their GPS system to bring the patrol boat to a spot Katz had picked along the north bank of the river. It was out of sight of the Simbas' river blockade, but still close to the town of Grenburgh, and the bank was shallow so the boat could be safely grounded.

Bullis had all of his charges get ready to move out when the boat's keel slid up onto the mud. They would carry all of the food and water, leaving the commandos free to fight if it came to that.

Keeping his rpm at a minimum, James carefully grounded the patrol boat against the riverbank. He nosed the boat straight in so the hostages would have an easier time disembarking.

"End of the line, folks," he said as he cut the fuel to the diesel.

Bullis had his people ready, and they started to

descend the rope ladder to the bank. The clock was running, and they could waste no time getting into the town.

"Time to leave, Rafe," McCarter called down to the engine room.

"Just a minute," Encizo replied. "I'm leaving a surprise for the bastards."

Since they were short of demo material, he had rigged a hand grenade to the fitting where the fuel line came out of one of the tanks. To make sure that a fire resulted from the explosion, he had packed the diesel-soaked rags from the filter-cleaning operation around the grenade. The flash of detonation should ignite them, and the burning rags would set off the diesel fuel pouring out of the punctured tank. It was a crude booby trap, but it should be effective.

Any Simba stumbling into the engine room would hopefully hit the trip wire and deprive Taibu of one of his better patrol boats, as well as a few of his men.

"Okay," he said as he backed out of the room and carefully stepped over the almost invisible trip wire. "Let the bastards come down here and snoop around now. It will be the last snooping they ever do."

CHAPTER TWENTY

Calvin James and T. J. Hawkins did the close-in recon of Grenburgh while the rest of the commandos held back in the jungle one thousand yards away with the ex-hostages. If the satellite information about the town being deserted was wrong, the pointmen would fight a rearguard action to try to hold the Simbas at bay while the others ran for cover in the jungle. What they would do after that was anyone's guess. This was their final option, and it had better be workable.

When the two commandos got in closer, it was apparent that not only was the town deserted, it had been deserted for some time. Since the dry season was in full swing, a thick layer of red dust covered everything. The tracks of animals showed clearly in the dusty streets, but they found no signs of human footprints, either new or old. Once more the superstitions of the locals had made the one-time European stronghold a place to be avoided.

Even so, the commandos covered one another as they leapfrogged deeper into the center of Grenburgh, clearing a zone to either side as they went. Not only was the town completely deserted, but it was also eerily silent. Unlike in the jungle, where the raucous sounds of life were a constant background noise, there were almost no sounds here beyond the soft calls of the few birds in residence in the deserted buildings.

As they entered the central plaza, they couldn't miss the building Katzenelenbogen had picked as their best defensive position. It dominated the empty square both from its position and with its sheer bulk.

The Belgians had known what they would be dealing with in the Congo when they built their towns, and they had built well. The stone and concrete of the massive building, though cracked and flaked, and pockmarked by shell fire, had endured and would be standing for several centuries yet to come. All of the exterior windows were covered with heavy wrought-iron grilles to keep invaders where they belonged—outside. Best of all, the thick mahogany double doors were still intact, and the last man to leave the building hadn't closed and locked them behind him.

It was a perfect place for a small group to defend as long as the Simbas didn't bring up artillery.

"I think it says Leopold II Bureau Of Civic Administration," Hawkins said when he noticed the French inscription carved in the stone over the main entrance.

"Wasn't he the king of Belgium?"

"That was a little before my time," Hawkins said, "but I think you're right."

"Let's check it out."

Though they had seen no footprints in the thick dust of the plaza, the commandos took no chances and continued to cover one another as they moved across the plaza and up the stone steps of the main entrance. They slipped through the massive wooden doors that had been left ajar.

Once their eyes adjusted to the dim light, it was apparent that the building had been thoroughly ransacked long ago. Even the scraps that had been left behind had decayed over the years in the humid climate. One thing that hadn't been carried away, though, was the massive steel beam that was used to secure the equally massive front doors.

"We're in," James told Bolan over the com link. "And Katz was right. This place was made to order for us. As David would say, it's a bloody fortress."

"Check the rest of it out," Bolan ordered.

James took the upper floors while Hawkins checked out the basement, and the two were back at the front door in a couple of minutes.

"It's perfect," James reported. "We have easy access to the roof, and there's a windowless basement for the civilians to take cover in. Part of it looks like it used to be a jail, but considering their circumstances, I guess that's fitting."

"Okay," Bolan sent back. "We're coming in."

"We'll cover you from the roof."

DAVID MCCARTER PUSHED the ex-hostages the last five hundred yards to the administration building at a run. "Come on, you lot!" he yelled. "The sooner you get there, the sooner you can put your feet up and relax."

Even though James and Hawkins had reported the town clear, Bolan and Encizo ran ahead, making sure that no one had slipped in after the pointmen had made their recon.

By the time the civilians had crossed the plaza, they were on their last legs again, physically and mentally. The commandos met them at the entrance and led them inside. "Get them down into the basement," McCarter told James. "Have Bullis get them sorted out and bedded down as best he can. We'll be getting this place ready to receive our expected visitors."

After James escorted the hostages into the basement rooms, he rejoined his comrades to do what they could to prepare their defense.

Along with the heavy doors and iron grilles on the windows, another great design feature of Congo colonial architecture was the flat roof with balustrades, which resembled the ramparts of castle walls and offered good cover while the commandos defended themselves. After surveying the building, McCarter decided to make their primary positions on the roof. That gave them better long-range fields of fire and better cover than fighting from the first-floor windows.

Manning went to the roof to find himself a good sniper's nest. Unfortunately, he didn't have his sniper's rifle with him this time, but the H&K assault rifle wasn't bad out to four hundred meters. If they had been carrying the 7.62 mm version of the rifles, he could have shot accurately as far as he could see. But they had only the lighter 5.56 mm versions, and the ballistics of that round weren't as good past a few hundred meters.

He found a good place that gave him a clear view of the plaza below and the streets leading into it. Setting the range on the sights, Manning got comfortable and waited for the Simbas to show up.

IT TOOK SOME TIME for the Simbas to realize that their prey wasn't going to motor up the river into the trap they had set. When the expected time had passed, they sent a small boat downriver with a radio to see what had happened to the Westerners. When they discovered the grounded patrol boat, they searched it and found it empty except for Encizo's booby trap, which killed two of them and set the boat on fire. They also found the trail the Stony Man team and their ex-hostages had left, heading directly for the deserted city.

It took some time for the boats from the blockade to reach the spot where the patrol boat still burned. From there it was no problem for them to follow the tracks. When they saw that the trail led into the town of Grenburgh, the lion warriors hesitated. The town was a place of bad omen. Simbas had massacred several hundred whites there back in the old days, including several of their priests and holy women.

It was said that as they were being slain, the holy men had placed a powerful curse on their killers. And when the Simbas moved on later that same day, they had been ambushed by a column of avenging French foreign legionnaires and slaughtered themselves. It was said that the death curse was still hanging over the town.

That was more than thirty years earlier, and these Simbas didn't fear the curses of long-dead white men, even priests. Taibu had shown them that the white God was helpless in the face of the lion, and they poured into the town by the dozens. When they spotted the Stony Man commandos at their rooftop positions, the hunting cry was raised and they charged.

"TAKE THEM UNDER FIRE," McCarter said calmly as soon as the Simbas reached the center of the plaza. If they had a single machine gun and unlimited ammunition for it, this would be a simple task. As it was, they were going to have to work to turn them back.

Manning took a good prone position and went to work. Leaving the Simbas leading the charge to the shorter-ranged subguns, he started picking off the lion warriors in the middle of the pack. He concentrated on anyone who looked like he knew what he was doing. As far as the Stony Man team knew, Taibu's army didn't have a formal organization of officers and sergeants, but even a mob needed leaders of some sort.

Every time he saw a man wave his arm as if ordering someone forward, Manning put a bullet in him. He didn't stop to see if he was getting clean kills with each shot, but quickly moved on to the next target.

The other commandos started out in single-shot mode. Steady fire started dropping the Simbas long before they crossed the plaza. Even so, the Simbas didn't falter, but pushed past their dead.

When they had closed to within fifty yards, the commandos switched their MP-5s to 3-round-burst mode. They hammered out a steady stream of fire that ripped into the lead ranks of the howling Simbas like steel rain.

As crowded as the attackers were, few of the bullets failed to find a worthwhile home. The warriors in the rear ranks were eager to get to the front and clambered over their fallen comrades until they, too, ran into the steel rain. It was too much for any man to face, even a frenzied lion warrior.

When the Phoenix Force warriors had torn the front ranks of Simbas to bleeding carcasses, they switched their fire to the middle of the mass. Now that they were taking fire, as well, the rear ranks stopped pushing so hard to get to the front. With Manning still taking out their leaders, the mob suddenly started falling apart.

A few grenades thrown down into the mass seemed to change the dynamics, and they finally broke and ran, leaving at least three dozen dead and wounded lion warriors behind.

"CHRIST!" Hawkins slapped a fresh magazine into his smoking subgun. "I thought those bastards were never going to figure it out."

"Some of them learned." Encizo's eyes swept the bodies littering the plaza.

"The hard way."

The Cuban shrugged expressively. "That's the only way some people learn."

Hawkins shook his head. "I'm taking bets that they'll be back for another lesson before too long."

"Not from me, T.J.," Encizo grinned. "That's a sucker's bet."

Beyond the outskirts of the town, the drumming started.

WHEN CHARLES TAIBU'S command flotilla arrived outside Grenburgh, he was glad to learn that the Westerners had beaten his lion warriors back. Now that he had them where he wanted them, he was in no big hurry to see them dead. In fact, they had played right into his hands. Had they been innocent, they wouldn't have run from him. They would have stayed for the trial he had planned and would have argued their innocence. Now that he had them trapped, he would still put them on trial and easily prove to the world that America was guilty of attempted viral genocide. At least all of the world that he cared about.

Even better, he would also capture the commandos who had stolen the prisoners from him. Putting them on trial alongside of the so-called medical workers would also be to his advantage. It would show the world that America was meddling in African affairs even after the President had promised that they wouldn't. Africans had to be shown that the Americans couldn't be trusted, but that he was as good as his word.

He was fully aware, though, that capturing these men alive was easier said than done. They had proved to be worthy adversaries. He knew that if he simply waited, he could starve them. They couldn't be carrying enough food and water to last them more than a couple of days. But if he tried to do that, he risked losing even more of his Simbas to desertion than he would if he just kept up the attacks.

He was the Lion, and he had to show the proper behavior at all times. Not to attack would make him look timid, and the Lion could never be seen as being weak. It would be better to keep throwing his men against that building with orders to take the enemy alive at all costs.

A series of attacks would also cause the commandos to waste their ammunition, and that was something else that had to be in short supply. No matter who they were, they could carry only so much weight, and it wouldn't all be in ammunition. From what had been reported to him, it was obvious that they had expected to fly out the day after they had raided his camp to free the prisoners. For a mission of that short a duration, they would have been traveling light and that meant little ammunition.

First, though, he would address his army and get them in the proper frame of mind to die for him. Since they had been repulsed in the first attack, he would have to restore their battle frenzy before sending them in again. When they were engulfed in their frenzy, they would gladly die. It was only when they had time to think about what they were doing that they faltered. So this time he wouldn't give them enough time to think about anything except his power.

He sent one of his runners back to his patrol boat to bring his most treasured possession to him, the visible sign of his power over the white men who were working to keep him from achieving his destiny. His mother had told him that only the sun could stop his greatness, and he knew that the sun wasn't going to come down from the sky.

A few Westerners weren't going to keep him from his destiny of being the greatest African of his day. Men everywhere, not just in Africa, would know his name and fear it.

CHAPTER TWENTY-ONE

Stony Man Farm, Virginia

Even with the threat of Sylvia Thompson-Bracket to contend with, the Annex project was proceeding according to schedule, if not a little ahead. The first stage of the excavation had been completed, and the concrete forms and rebar were in place, ready for the pour. Since the Farm was far from any large city, the concrete-mixing operation would take place on site. Belmont Construction had brought in a mobile mixer large enough to handle the job.

Even though things were going well, Buck Greene wasn't relaxing a bit. The threat of the woman reporter still had him on full mental alert. There was no doubt in his mind that they hadn't seen the last of her, and he couldn't relax his vigilance. To keep from giving the game away, though, he had reduced the day-shift patrols, but was running double shifts on the video monitors and the night patrols.

He also wasn't at all satisfied with the explanation he had been given about how Mabel Windam had gotten it in her mind to call in the reporter to investigate the Farm. There were other people in Wilsonburg who were out of work, as well, but they hadn't taken it upon themselves to make trouble about it. In fact, most of the town's people were well aware that Stony Man didn't hire locally. He was convinced that she had been put up to making the call by the Belmont Construction guy she had reportedly talked to, a driver named Mel Bradley.

Why Bradley would do something like that, though, was completely beyond him. According to the background information they had on him, he had been with the company for several years and was a good worker. The only anomaly in his file was that he had turned down the last two jobs he had been offered before accepting this one to come to the Farm. On the surface, that wasn't all that unusual, but Greene was taking nothing at face value.

The way companies like Belmont operated was that they required their people to work whenever a job came up or be dropped from their list. Most of the guys turned down a job every now and then, but few turned down two in a row. If you passed on three job offers, you were automatically released. The pressures of government contracts required that the companies have a work force they could depend upon month in and month out. With the security clearances that were required, they couldn't hire off the street corner if they were a couple guys short on a project.

So, he had a good worker who had suddenly started turning down jobs before he signed on for this one. There could be any number of reasons why Bradley had done that, but at this point in time, they were unknown and would stay that way until he dragged him for questioning.

Greene felt that he was missing something important, but for the life of him, he couldn't figure out what it was. He studied the face on the file copy of the photo ID Belmont had issued as if he were trying to get behind the man's eyes and see into his brain. Something about those eyes was tickling his memory, but he just couldn't get a handle on it. To the best of his recollection, he had never seen Bradley before in his life.

Hermann Schwarz put his head around the door to Greene's office. "You wanted to see me, Chief?"

Greene held out Bradley's photo. "Have you noticed this guy around the job site?"

"Mel Bradley," Schwarz said, reading the name. "I can't say that I have. What does he do for them?"

"He's one of their drivers, and he's the asshole who allegedly told that Windam woman to call the reporter in on us."

Schwarz studied the photo, but also didn't see anything unusual about the man.

Greene smiled. "You're a sneaky bastard, Gadgets, and I need you to try to put yourself into this guy's mind for me. You're good at that."

Schwarz grinned.

"Assuming," Greene continued, "that he actually did tell Mabel to call Thompson-Bracket, what would he gain from doing that?"

"That's a good question," Schwarz said. "If he in fact did purposefully set Miss Sylvia on us, it could only be to turn our attention away from something he's doing.

"But—" Schwarz held up his hand to keep Greene from racing out to put the guy under arrest "—do we know that it actually went down that way? Her program is shown in this area, and Bradley might have just casually mentioned it to Mabel and she took it from there. From what we know of her, she's a determined, devious old biddy all on her own. She might not have needed any prompting."

"If I had her in here," Greene growled, "I'd find out what the hell's going on in nothing flat."

"Brognola's never going to let you do that," Schwarz reminded him. "And even if this Bradley guy is bad, we don't want to bring him in, either."

"Why not?"

Greene was doggedly determined when it came to protecting the Farm, but subtlety wasn't one of his strong suits. In many ways, he was even worse than the Ironman when it came to bulling his way through a problem. Busting heads to get information was one of his favorite tools.

"Well," Schwarz explained, "we do that and we're tipping our hand that we're on to him. The best thing we can do is keep the guy under close surveillance and don't let him even take a leak without having two cameras recording how many times he shakes it. More than just grabbing him, we need to find out why he's doing this."

"You've got a point," Greene agreed. "I'll get the word out to the men."

"Also," Schwarz said, "I'll have a discreet little talk with Frank Rose and tell him that we're watching his guy. He might have some input we didn't pick up on during the backgrounding."

"Do that," Greene said.

"I REALLY DON'T KNOW much about him," Frank Rose said as he looked over the field file on his driver Mel Bradley. "He's never worked for me before."

Schwarz was surprised. "I thought that all of you guys stayed together on these jobs?"

"Most of the time that's true," Rose explained. "Belmont has over a hundred men on the books, and they work in several established teams. But one of my drivers couldn't make this job, so I got Bradley from one of the other teams to replace him."

"So you're saying that there's no one here who's ever worked with him before?"

Rose shrugged. "I don't have any way of knowing that without consulting the home office and having them go back through the assignment lists and check. Like I said, we're a big outfit. I know for a fact that we have three teams in the field right now, and I don't even know where two of them are working. All I know is that one of them scarfed up all the portable air-conditioning units they could find in our warehouse."

"Can you check on him for us?" Schwarz asked. "I'd like to know before sundown."

"Do you think he's bad?" Rose asked.

"All I know is that he talked to a barmaid in town who then called that reporter in on us. It might have been merely a casual comment, but we can't take a chance that he didn't do it on purpose."

"I can have him out of here and on a plane back to California in an hour," Rose offered. He was well aware that his job depended on handling this situation properly. Even though he didn't know what kind of operation Stony Man was running, it was something that needed to be protected. And if sending Bradley back would help, he would do it.

"I appreciate the offer," Schwarz said, "but if he's running a number on us, I want him close at hand where we can keep an eye on him."

"You've got a point there."

"Anyway," Schwarz said as he stood to leave, "talk to your home office and see if any of your crew has worked with him before. If they haven't, that makes this a different kind of problem entirely.''

''I understand.''

''And call me as soon as you get anything.''

''I will.''

BARBARA PRICE HADN'T forgotten Sylvia Thompson-Bracket, either. Since Rosario Blancanales had struck out when he tried for that interview with her, Price had put him to work on following up on what little they did know about the woman. Specifically, she had him digging into anything he could find about the reporter before she arrived in Atlanta.

Beyond her having been born and raised in California, they didn't have much on her yet, but she wanted him to keep digging. Most people in the country left some kind of trail behind them.

NOW THAT THE POUR was under way, the mixer was eating up a lot of cement. Spatkin was driving to the cement plant closest to Wilsonburg to pick up flatbed trailers full of bagged cement and sand. The gravel had come from a local quarry and had already been dumped on-site. Belmont's mobile mixing unit made short work of making concrete without having the trucks drive in.

When he brought a load up to the main gate, three blacksuits swarmed over the vehicle inspecting each and every bag visually and with a portable explosives sniffer. If they used that machine on every vehicle that showed up, he was going to have a difficult time bringing his pickup in. When he saw that they weren't checking the truck, however, he realized that it was just the trailer and its load they were interested in. It wasn't a Belmont vehicle and had originated somewhere else.

Before he made any final plans, though, he would wait to hear from Sylvia Thompson-Bracket. She had promised to warn him before she made her move, and he was still counting on her to provide a diversion for him. A speeding helicopter coming in low to the ground would push the blacksuits' buttons big time and take their attention away from everything else.

WHEN SYLVIA Thompson-Bracket reached the little airfield in rural central Virginia, the man she wanted to see was waiting for her outside the small hangar. She had met him one time before and had been impressed with his laid-back, but coldly professional attitude. He knew that he was good and hadn't needed to show off to prove it to anyone. That was the kind of no-nonsense pilot she needed for this venture.

To get the conversation going, she handed over the thick envelope containing twelve thousand dollars in one-hundred-dollar bills. It was an expensive airline ticket, but if the flight landed in the right place at the right time, it would be worth every last penny. And, with the flight schedule up to her, it would arrive exactly on time.

"Okay, lady," the pilot said with a grin as he thumbed through the bills. "You just bought yourself a high-speed ride in a helicopter flying about six feet off the ground. What the hell is this place you're trying to get into anyway, a prison?"

"Almost," she said as she handed him a map with the Stony Man farmhouse circled in red. "It's a large farm outside of Wilsonburg."

"I hope to hell they aren't growing pot or anything like that out there," he said. "Those damned dope growers are inclined to shoot at low-flying planes."

She smiled. "I give you my word that they aren't growing grass. I don't exactly know what they are growing, but I know it isn't dope."

"When do you want to go?"

"Sometime in the next twenty-four to forty-eight hours," she said. "And I'll need to be able to reach you around the clock."

He reached into the pocket of his flight jacket and pulled out a card. "This number's hot at all times, and you'll never get a busy signal."

The card had a drawing of some kind of armed helicopter on the front that bore a shark's mouth on the forward gun turret and a Maltese cross on the rotor tower. The word "Crusaders" was all it said, and under that was the name Rick Hansen and a cellular phone number.

"Okay, Mr. Hansen. I'll call you sometime within the next two days."

"Make sure you do," he said. "Like I told you, the ticket price is nonrefundable."

"I'll call." She locked eyes with him.

He smiled slowly behind the aviator sunglasses. "I'll be waiting."

AFTER WATCHING the woman drive away, Rick Hansen—one-time hot-stick Vietnam Loach pilot— went into the hangar to get his ship ready. This wouldn't be the biggest trip he'd ever made, but twelve large wasn't exactly chicken feed, and it beat the hell out of working the country fairs. Taking drunken assholes up for a look-see at the pigsty of a house trailer they called home wasn't exactly his idea of flying. Particularly when they puked in his bird. He always made them clean it up, often with their face, but it still pissed him off.

Every last dime Hansen had been able to get his hands on had gone into this machine. To say that he lived for flying wasn't exactly right; he lived to fly his Hughes Loach. He had it painted in a high-gloss dark green, almost black, with yellow trim and had painted a red-and-white Air Cav guidon on the nose.

When the Hughes Model 369 was being tested by the Army, it had been titled the LOH—Light Observation Helicopter, or Loach. By the time it got to Vietnam, the designation had been changed to OH-6 Cayuse, but the nickname had stuck. Even the Vietnam Loach's descendants, the modern Hughes 500 family, still carried the moniker.

Hansen's machine was technically a Hughes 500D, but it was lighter than the standard civilian 500 and possessed the 420-shaft-horsepower Allison turbine. What that meant was that the aircraft could easily carry him and three passengers at over 150 miles per hour. With only the reporter and her cameraman on board, he would be able to squeeze an extra ten miles per hour out of his bird.

While 160 miles per hour wasn't exactly supersonic speed, when you were flying only six feet off of the ground, it was blindingly fast. Almost too fast to track with handheld weapons. He had proved that more than once back in the good old days.

He had looked over the map the woman had provided him and had found an avenue of approach that would keep him out of sight for all but the last three-quarters of a mile. Even with the flare out and landing at the end, that would expose him for less than a minute. It would take thirty seconds for his passengers to exit the bird, and then another sixty seconds for him to accelerate and clear the area. Call it a hair under two and a half minutes.

In normal circumstances, two and a half minutes wasn't much time. But, as Einstein had said, time was relative. Two and a half minutes wallowing naked in a hot tub with a babe would pass in a flash.

But two and half minutes with someone popping caps at you could be an eternity.

His passenger hadn't said anything about having to dodge bullets, but since she was willing to pay big bucks for the privilege of riding with him into a hot LZ, he had to factor in a little gunfire. That meant mounting the chicken plate around his side of the cockpit. The extra weight would add a few seconds to his skit-and-git time, but he had flown into too many hot landing zones to think that he was bulletproof, and he had the battle scars to prove it.

Even though he was taking sensible precautions, he didn't place much credence in a woman's fantasies. If the people there weren't growing dope, and he was certain that they weren't or he'd have known about it, what could be down there that could cause him any real problems?

Picking up a flannel rag and a bottle of plastic polish from his workbench, he walked to the front of the helicopter and started to polish the Plexiglas canopy. When a person was flying fast and low, it was essential that the pilot be able to see clearly. Hooking a skid on a fence post at 160 miles per hour was a good way to tear up a perfectly good little Loach. And that was to say nothing of what it would do to him.

As he polished the spotless Plexiglas, he ran the map route through his mind, visualizing the way he would fly in and out. Flying was as much mental exertion as it was physical, and the faster and closer to the ground one flew, the more of a mental exercise it became. This would be at least a seventy-thirty mental-to-physical ratio this time, and he wanted to be ready for it.

CHAPTER TWENTY-TWO

Grenburgh, Congo

With the Simbas driven back, the Stony Man warriors took stock of their situation. No one had been hurt in the one-sided firefight, and the victory had been won with only a small expenditure of ammunition. But even if every bullet had struck home, every round that they had fired was one that they no longer had. That kind of mathematics had only one conclusion, particularly if they were going to be stuck in Grenburgh for any length of time.

"David?" Calvin James radioed to McCarter, "I want to go down to the plaza and see if I can salvage some AKs and ammunition for us."

"Take T.J. with you."

"T.J.," James radioed, "meet me at the front door."

With Encizo backing them up, James unbarred the massive front doors and walked out with Hawkins to survey the carnage they had created. Someone needed to talk to the Simbas about properly salvaging a battlefield. Every man who had been killed still had his weapon with him, and almost every one of them was the ubiquitous AK-47, the Third World's weapon of choice. Half the bodies wore Chinese-style chest-pack magazine carriers, while the others had their extra magazines stuffed into pockets and pouches.

Going from one body to the next, the commandos stripped the magazine carriers and chose the cleanest AKs from the large selection. The sturdy Kalashnikov assault rifle would fire even if the chamber was packed with mud, which was what made it so popular with the semitrained troops of Third World armies. But with so many weapons to chose from, it made sense to pick the best.

While James's back was turned, one of the Simba "bodies" rose up behind him with a machete in his hand. Hawkins caught the movement from the corner of his eye and spun, his MP-5 spitting on full-auto.

"Behind you!" he yelled.

The short burst of 9 mm slugs caught the lion warrior in the chest and slammed him back down on the ground for good.

"Thanks, partner," James said, sketching a salute.

"De nada."

"Status?" McCarter cut in on the com link.

"One of the bastards was playing possum,"

Hawkins reported, "but I cured him of that nasty habit. We're on the way back with a dozen AKs."

"Get a move on it. I think we might have more visitors coming."

As the two commandos sprinted back for the safety of the old building, they heard the drums start up again, followed by hundreds of men chanting war cries. The rolling sound echoed from the walls of the town until it sounded like distant thunder.

THE COMMANDOS STOOD ready to repel another attack, but the lion warriors seemed content to just drum, dance and chant as they got their fires going again. Some of them waved their AKs above their heads and a few fired bursts into the air, but that was it. Seeing that another attack wasn't in the immediate offing, the commandos stood down. In his rooftop sniper's nest, Gary Manning snuggled up to his sniper scope again. The Simbas might not be in the mood to kill right now, but he sure as hell was. A good sniper was always ready to practice his trade when the opportunity arose. Every one of the bastards he could bring down now was one more that he wouldn't have to deal with later. And now that he wasn't rushed, he could take the time to insure that every shot scored.

At about four hundred meters, the maximum range for accurate aimed fire from his 5.56 mm rifle, he saw a Simba all decked out in feathers waving some kind of decorated stick in one hand and an AK in the other. That guy had to be some kind of officer, which made him a prime target. These guys were going to have to learn that their leaders didn't need to dress up like Mardi Gras to be effective. In fact, on the modern battlefield, standing out in the crowd could be downright fatal.

Manning lined up the scope's crosshairs on the decorated Simba and dialed in the range. Taking a deep breath, he took up the slack on the trigger and let the air out slowly. When he reached the end of his breath, he stroked the trigger. Through the scope, he saw the Simba take the round high in the chest only an inch or so from his aiming point. Not bad for a 5.56 mm weapon at that range.

Satisfied that his eye was in, the Canadian marksman went looking for another target. Popping one of them at random every few minutes would do a lot to keep the bastards off balance and discourage them from getting too close to the fortress. The last thing they needed was for the enemy to make a good close-in recon and discover a way to breach their defenses.

IN THE BASEMENT ROOMS of the administrative building, Frank Bullis was trying to organize his charges. There was little for them to make beds out of except their clothing, so they'd be sleeping rough. But there was a latrine in the basement and, even without running water, it would serve for the short time they would be there. Bullis knew that one way or the other, they wouldn't be staying long.

After distributing an MRE meal, he went looking for Bolan to make his report. "We're right back where we were before," he said. "Short on both food and water."

"We can handle the water easily enough," Bolan replied. "There's an old spring-fed public fountain on the east side of the square that's still running a tickle. Since it's ground water, it should be potable. Get the empty canteens together and one of the men to escort a water detail out there. Food, though, is going to be a problem."

When the group abandoned the patrol boat, they had taken every remaining scrap of the food they had found in the boat's galley, the cornmeal and canned fish. But even with the MREs, Bullis was right. With so many people to feed, it wouldn't last long.

"Go to one meal a day and see how far it will go."

"I already calculated that and came up with two and a half days."

Bolan smiled thinly. "I guess that we'll just have to wrap this up before then, won't we?"

Bullis couldn't help but be encouraged by the commando's professional optimism. No matter what they had faced, Belasko always had a calm assessment of the situation.

"How's the militia coming along?" Bolan asked.

Bullis grinned at the formal term for trying to teach the men in the group how to fire the captured AKs. Now that they had enough extra weapons to go around, everyone was getting a chance to try them out.

"Calvin is doing a hell of a job trying to teach them the basics," he said, "but I'm not sure how effective they're going to be. Except for Joseph, none of them have ever handled a weapon before."

He shook his head. "You'd think that in a land that has constantly been racked with warfare for the past fifty years or more, that every man here would have been born with a gun in his hands. But the majority of the Africans I've met have never fired a weapon in their lives."

"That's part of why there's so much warfare here," Bolan pointed out. "When the locals don't have guns, anyone who does have one is automatically in charge. Just look at Taibu's mob out there. They're not much of an army, but they have guns. No one can defend themselves against them because they don't have anything to do it with."

"We have Joseph, of course, and maybe a couple of others who are coming along. But," he concluded with a shrug, "I don't know how good they're going to be when the bullets start flying."

"No one ever knows that until they have it happen to them," Bolan said. "Combat is the ultimate test. Some pass, some fail and you can never tell how it's going to fall beforehand."

"I'll have a couple of us up there next time," Bullis said, "and I guess we'll see then."

"That we will."

WHEN NIGHT FELL, the Stony Man team gathered on the roof for a battle-planning session. They had survived the first day, but they all knew that it was only going to get worse. They would hold out as long as they could, but their ultimate fate wasn't up to them. The decision would be made in the Oval Office.

"It's too bad that we can't do something to disrupt their sleep," Hawkins said. "You know, I used to be a real drum fan before this shit started."

"We can try the old night-harassment drill," Encizo said. "Sneak down there, kill as many of them as we can and pull back. We can take the AKs we've collected and try to hit their command group. If we can pop Taibu himself, the rest of them will fade away pretty fast."

"We're not really armed well enough to do something like that," McCarter pointed out. "We don't have any fire-support weapons to cover your withdrawal."

"For fire support," Manning suggested, "I could make up a couple of Monsters to toss on the way out to slow them down a bit. The way they're clustered together down there, they could do a lot of damage."

A Monster was a fragmentation bomb made from

blocks of C-4 plastic explosive with nails or small rocks embedded in the plastique, anything to cause shrapnel wounds when the bombs detonated. They were usually a terrorist's weapon, but this was no time to be picky. Anything that would lessen the odds they faced was welcome.

"There's another thing that'll come out of raiding them tonight," Encizo said. "I think we can count on them being drunk, and they're going to go crazy when we hit them. They'll start firing at everything in sight and will probably kill more of their own than we'll be able to."

"Good point," McCarter said. "You want to lead the raid?"

"Sure," Encizo was all grins at that news. "Gary, you make the bombs and—" he turned back to McCarter "—I'd like to take T.J. and Cal with me, as well. The more noise we can make out there, the more panicked they're going to be."

"Go ahead," the Briton said. "Striker and I can hold down the fort while you're gone."

FOR THIS MISSION, the commandos carefully covered all of their exposed skin with matte-black combat cosmetics. They stripped down to their assault harnesses, ammo pouches and weapons so they could move fast and light. The move in would be slow and careful, but they'd have to withdraw as fast as they could and didn't need the extra weight.

"Can I get in on this?" Frank Bullis asked when he saw the commandos preparing.

"Not this time," Bolan said. "This is going to require more training than you have. But I can use you up on the roof to stand guard with David and me."

"Glad to help," the doctor said. "And I'll bring Joseph, too."

THE FOUR COMMANDOS SLIPPED out of Grenburgh and circled to enter the back side of the Simba camp. With their night-vision goggles, they were able to make their way through the darkness without mishap. When they had moved to within seventy-five yards of the enemy, they went to ground and called back their position to McCarter.

They lay prone on the ground quietly and watched the Simbas work themselves into a frenzy.

"Wait for him to get them stirred up a little more," Encizo said, "and when they start firing up into the air, we'll join in. And remember, two magazines on full-auto and we bug out."

The four commandos were spread out in a line a few yards apart so they could cover more targets. Since they were using AKs, the muzzle-flashes would be plainly seen, but spread out the way they were, the Simbas would think that they were being attacked by a larger force.

As Encizo had predicted, a couple of Simbas started firing their AKs into the air on full-auto.

When more joined them in this ceremonial waste of ammunition, the Phoenix Force commandos opened up, as well.

This wasn't combat; this was pure self-protective slaughter as the four AK-47s ripped long bursts into the backs of the lion warriors. Men screamed and fell, but with the drumming, chanting and firing into the air, most of the additional noise was masked.

Halfway through his second magazine, Encizo flicked his AK's selector switch to semiauto and started to deliver aimed single shots. Every time the Cuban pulled the trigger, a Simba fell fatally wounded. Two dozen men were on the ground in as many seconds.

It took a few moments for the Simbas to realize that they were under attack. With the Phoenix Force commandos firing the same kind of weapons they were shooting, the sounds were identical. And the screams and shouts of the wounded were lost in the jubilant cries of the celebration.

It was Taibu who actually first realized what was happening to his followers. He was facing the commandos and spotted the muzzle-flashes of their AKs. Without a thought for how it would look to his worshiping followers, the self-proclaimed Lion King dived for cover. Once he was safe, he shouted for his men to turn and fight.

When heads started to turn their way, the commandos knew that their time had run out. Taking one of the makeshift Monster antipersonnel grenades from his harness, Manning pulled the fuze lighter and hurled the bomb into the crowd. The detonation brought screams of pain as the shrapnel took its toll.

Arming the other plastic explosive bomb, he hurled it, as well.

"Pull back," Encizo called over the com link.

BOLAN AND MCCARTER watched the night attack from the roof of their fortress building. They heard the sudden increase in the volume of AK fire and knew that the ambush had been sprung. A few seconds later, they heard the shouts of alarm and the detonations of Manning's makeshift bombs, followed by cries of pain.

"We're withdrawing," Encizo called over the com link.

" Watch your back trail," Bolan advised.

"Got it covered."

AFTER RUNNING toward the river for several hundred yards, Encizo halted the rest of the team. Spreading out in the dark, they got ready to discourage any Simbas who might have gotten it into their heads to avenge their bushwhacked comrades. Normally, the Simbas didn't like to venture into the darkness, but this might be an exception. Their blood was up, and Taibu would be screaming at them to kill.

Through their night-vision goggles, they saw a

dozen or more Simbas charging into the darkness. Some of the warriors carried torches, but the others ran blindly into the night. This was one time when low tech was at a distinct disadvantage.

The torches were causing temporary blind spots in the commandos' NV goggles, so they concentrated on putting down the men who held them. With the lights extinguished, they could see clearly again and quickly finished off the rest of their pursuers.

"HOW'D YOU DO?" Bolan asked when the raiders got back.

"We probably put bullets into three dozen of them or so," Encizo estimated. "But there's still a bunch of them out there, Striker."

"I'll update the Farm and see if Hal has come up with anything for us yet."

"Tell him to kick someone in the ass and get us out of here," Encizo said. "After tonight, they're really going to be pissed at us in the morning."

CHAPTER TWENTY-THREE

Stony Man Farm, Virginia

The blacksuits at the main gate weren't alarmed when Dimitri Spatkin showed up in a pickup truck instead of his usual loaded company vehicle. But as the work on the Annex had progressed, vehicle control had proved to be difficult with the ever changing transportation needs of the Belmont crew.

"Hey, guys," the Russian agent called out through the open window, "my rig broke down in town, and I need to talk to the boss about getting it fixed."

He shook his head. "Man, it's thrown my schedule all to hell, and he's really going to be pissed."

The lead guard knew Spatkin on sight as Mel Bradley and laughed as he waved him on through. "Good luck, man."

The blacksuit didn't even think to look at what was in the back of the truck. He did, however, follow SOP and call in the change of authorized vehicles to the blacksuit communications center in the farmhouse.

Spatkin slowly drove between the vehicle shed and the farmhouse. No one paid much attention to him as he braked to a halt twenty feet from the farmhouse and got out. He didn't want to try to fake a breakdown here because he knew that the first blacksuit who came by would stop and try to help him get his truck started again. Instead, he got out and acted as if he had business there. According to the timetable Sylvia Thompson-Bracket had given him, she would be making her appearance any time now, so his wait wouldn't be long.

WHEN GREENE WALKED out of the armory, he saw the pickup truck parked by the farmhouse and frowned, as he didn't recognize it. But, if it had been passed in, it had to be a Belmont vehicle. With so many of their people inside the perimeter, it was hard to keep track of all of their rigs. He started over to take a look at it anyway when the Farm's alert siren started wailing.

The siren was rarely heard at Stony Man Farm. It was never sounded for practice so when it went off, every blacksuit on or off duty grabbed his weapon and headed for his alert station at a dead run.

Greene broke into a run and was halfway to the farmhouse when he saw a small helicopter clear the ridgeline to the south and head straight in at him on what looked like a gunship run.

"All blacksuits," he shouted into his com link, "incoming hostile aircraft, take it under fire."

The pickup truck was forgotten as he completed his dash across the open ground for the farmhouse. There was no telling what kind of weapons that aircraft was carrying, and it was already too close to be stopped.

RICK HANSEN HAULED UP ever so slightly on the collective control stick of the speeding helicopter, and the nimble little Loach rose a few feet off the ground to clear the ridge. In the right-hand seat, Sylvia Thompson-Bracket thought that her stomach, contents and all, was going to come out of her mouth as the chopper hopped up into the air.

A split second later, they were back on the deck, the chopper's skids a few feet off the ground. If she could somehow package this experience in a carnival ride, she'd make millions.

She couldn't hear the Farm's sirens wailing over the roar of the turbine, the rush of the wind and the noise of the spinning rotor blades, but she could see the farmhands running for cover. A thrill shot through her, and she felt the power of swooping down on an unsuspecting enemy. She'd show those assholes down there that they couldn't get away with messing with her. She was going to get her story.

Hansen also saw the men diving for cover and instantly realized that he was flying into a shit storm. Whoever those men were, they were well trained and were taking cover against what they thought was a gunship attack instead of panicking. Even though he hadn't fired at them, he knew that in seconds they'd be firing at him.

He unconsciously pulled his trigger finger back against the grip on the cyclic stick, reaching for a weapons firing button that wasn't there. A few bursts of a minigun would clear a path for him, but he wasn't armed and it was too late to try to turn back now. All that would do would be expose his belly to their fire.

He was glad that he had taken the time to rig the armor around the cockpit and hunched lower in his seat. He was being paid very well for this trip, but he was beginning to think that no amount of money was going to be enough to pay for what was coming. The bitch had lied to him, big time. But he was totally committed to the landing, so all he could do was keep on course and hope that he didn't pick up a round before he could put down.

Getting out of there, though, had just become an act of flying suicide.

Thompson-Bracket had unbuckled her seat harness in preparation to jump out once the chopper set down, and she was almost jostled out of her seat when Hansen suddenly jinked the ship to the left. The men on the ground were firing at them! She frantically grabbed the ends of her harness lap belt and clicked the buckle shut again.

Hansen was steadily cursing as he kicked his ship from side to side as he headed for a flare out over the first piece of flat ground he saw. Out of the corner of his eye he saw a man aiming a tube-launched weapon at him and instinctively snuggled deeper into his armor.

Jesus Christ! That was an antiaircraft missile! What in the fuck was he flying into?

WHEN THE ALERT SIRENS went off, the farmhouse crew went into alert procedure and prepared for the worst. Like everything else at the Farm, the house wasn't what it seemed to be either. The blast doors slammed shut and the internal ventilation system cut as did the emergency generators. As long as the chopper wasn't carrying a thousand-pound bomb, the crew could withstand the attack and they went to their alert stations to wait for the all-clear.

DIMITRI SPATKIN WATCHED the speeding helicopter approach. He didn't know who was behind the controls, but the pilot sure knew how to fly. It was too bad that he was going to get his ticket punched hard in just a few seconds. If he wasn't killed outright, he'd be lucky to survive the crash. Miss Hot Shot Investigative Reporter was also going to end up dog meat, as well, but that was the least of his worries right now. The woman had brought it on all by herself, and he had to admit that her bloody corpse might be a perfect diversion.

He saw the launch flare of the Stinger as it left the launcher and streaked to intercept the speeding helicopter. The chopper was too close for the missile's warhead to arm, but it punched through the tail boom right by the transmission case, ripping loose the tail rotor driveshaft.

With the stabilizing torque of the tail rotor suddenly gone, the chopper rolled out of control. Too low to try to autorotate, the pilot fought to land his aircraft right side up, but lost the battle.

The helicopter snapped over onto its side, the tips of the whirling rotors scraping against the ground and shattering. The rotor blades tore loose from the rotor mast and spun through the air like giant sickles. Spatkin wasn't the only man who ducked for cover.

In an instant, the sleek little machine was transformed into a collection of flying junk, scattering pieces over a wide area like shrapnel.

Hughes Aircraft had done well when they designed their Hughes 500D, though. The flimsy-looking bubble cockpit framing was stronger than it appeared and actually formed a very sturdy roll cage. After shedding the tail boom and rotor blades, the helicopter rolled over and over like a runaway basketball, shattering the highly polished Plexiglas, but not collapsing the canopy framing.

When the airframe skidded to a stop, it was only a few feet from the farmhouse where Spatkin had parked his pickup truck.

THE DUST HADN'T even settled before the blacksuits swarmed over the smashed machine, their H&K subguns at the ready. Several of the guards converged on the wreckage with fire extinguishers and started foaming the hot turbine and transmission. Others grabbed hoses and started to wash away the fuel spilling from the ruptured tank. Several blacksuits started to pull the dazed people from the cockpit.

The cameraman had dropped his equipment, and he had suffered a broken arm. When the blacksuits pulled him out, they escorted him to the dispensary straight away.

Sylvia Thompson-Bracket had also been thrown around and battered, but hadn't been seriously hurt. Hands reached in, got her out of her harness, dragged her to her feet and propelled her toward the farmhouse.

Rick Hansen sat in his pilot's seat, staring out the shattered canopy in front of him. Once more, he had survived the crash of a Loach, but from the looks of the guys outside, he would probably never own another one. He recognized a Fed when he saw one and knew that he was in deep trouble. If these guys weren't Feds, though, he was really in trouble because every one of them had a gun in his hand and looked as if he knew how to use it.

Being very careful not to make any sudden moves, he unbuckled his harness, slid back his side armor and slowly pulled himself out of the wreckage, all the time keeping his hands in plain sight. Once he was on his feet, he held his hands out for the cuffs.

He had royally screwed up once or twice before in his life, but never had he done something as outright stupid as this. Staring at the muzzles of the submachine guns aimed at him, he fervently prayed that he would be allowed to live to regret it. The money he had been paid for this stupidity wasn't going to be enough to get him out of this mess. A good lawyer would eat that up in nothing flat.

IN THE RUSH to cover the people in the downed chopper, Spatkin managed to join the blacksuits, most of whom were in their work clothes, too. Only the barracks alert teams were wearing their black combat gear. But they were clustered tightly around his pickup, making it all but impossible for him to get close enough to set the fuses for the bomb as he had planned.

He still might be able to pull this off, but he

would have to wait until things cleared out a little. There was no way that he could light the fuses with so many people standing around.

The fuses he had constructed for his truck bomb were crude black-powder trains and rifle primer igniters, but they would work. He had made extras and had taken them into the countryside to test. Three of the four he tested had functioned properly, and all it would take was one to detonate the bomb. But being made of black powder, they emitted white smoke when they burned.

AFTER CHECKING with the radar operators to insure that no more aircraft were violating their airspace, Buck Greene canceled the alert and went out to take command of the situation.

When Spatkin spotted Greene, he stepped back out of the way so as not to be so obvious. He still wasn't ready to face the man who had hired him.

Now that the danger had passed, the farmhouse unlocked and went on stand down, so the Stony Man crew was coming out to take a look at their unexpected visitor. Yakov Katzenelenbogen and Aaron Kurtzman were the first out the back door, followed by Akira Tokaido. Spatkin had seen Katz and Kurtzman once or twice before, but didn't know what they did for Stony Man. They were just the enemy.

Barbara Price came out to see the chopper that

had dropped in on them, too. Though he didn't expect her to remember him well, Spatkin automatically pulled back farther. The farmhouse crew inspected the wreckage and talked to the blacksuits for a few minutes before going back inside to do whatever it was that they did.

Seeing Barbara Price leaning against the bed of his truck gave Spatkin a start, but he suppressed the urge to warn her away from it. He had to remember that while he wanted her to somehow survive his vengeance, she, too, was one of the Mother Country's enemies.

SPATKIN CONTINUED to hold back from the front of the crowd as the blacksuits hooked the wreckage of the chopper to a tractor to drag it away for further inspection. Other guards were gathering the scattered bits and pieces of the wreckage and hauling them off, as well.

As soon as his pickup truck was free from the clutter, he started for it, the cigarette lighter in his pocket forgotten for now. It had been a good idea to use the chopper as a diversion, but there had been no way that he could have known that the thing would nearly crash on top of his rig.

He had lost his window of opportunity here and would have to come up with another plan fast. With the weather warming up, he couldn't risk letting the crude explosive mixture in his truck get too hot and become unstable. The fertilizer-and-diesel mix shouldn't sit more than twenty-four hours, and his was going on two days now. He had to explode it as soon as possible.

"Who the hell belongs to that truck?" he heard Buck Greene bellow.

Spatkin froze when he heard the security chief's voice, but forced himself to keep walking.

"I don't know, Chief," the blacksuit nearest the vehicle replied.

"Get it the hell out of here. Now!"

"Yes, sir."

"That's my truck," Spatkin said as he stepped up. He couldn't let the blacksuit drive it away and discover what he was carrying in the back.

"Who are you?" Greene turned on him.

"Mel Bradley." Spatkin held out his Belmont ID badge.

"Why's this thing parked here?"

"I was driving through to go talk to Frank Rose about my company truck when I heard the siren. I didn't know what it was so I stopped and got out. I didn't mean to get in the way of your operation."

"Just move it."

"No sweat."

Spatkin climbed into the cab, fired up the engine and carefully drove on to the Belmont work site.

NONE OF THE BELMONT workers were getting much work done. The siren, the spectacular crash and the scramble to get the people out of the wreckage had brought the work to a halt. When Spatkin drove up, the men realized that he had witnessed the incident and swamped him with questions.

He was describing what he had seen when Frank Rose walked up. "Where's your truck, Bradley?" the supervisor asked when he spotted the pickup.

"That's what I was coming to talk to you about, Mr. Rose," Spatkin replied quickly. "The damned thing broke down in town, and I need an authorization to buy some parts locally to fix it."

In the confusion of the moment, it had slipped Rose's mind that Bradley was a person of interest regarding the Farm's security. He just wanted to get his people back to doing their jobs so they didn't fall behind schedule. "Just get the damned thing fixed, okay?"

"Yes, sir."

Getting back in his pickup, Spatkin headed out through the cleared orchard to the back gate rather than drive past the farmhouse again. He would only have one more chance to attack it, and he didn't want to risk being stopped.

The two blacksuits at the back gate were openly carrying their H&K subguns, but they were watching the approaches and waved him right through.

As Spatkin headed toward Wilsonburg, his mind

was racing. He had to find another way to get the explosives inside, and the warm air coming in the driver's-side window reminded him that he had little time to do it.

CHAPTER TWENTY-FOUR

With one burly blacksuit holding each of her arms, Sylvia Thompson-Bracket didn't offer resistance as she was hustled into the farmhouse. Two more of the guards had her pilot, and a third followed them all with a submachine gun in his hands. She didn't know exactly what she had gotten herself into, but this wasn't the first time she'd dealt with gun-toting thugs. If she just kept calm, she might still be able to talk her way out of this situation.

She was led into a small windowless room and told to sit. The two guards took their places on each side of the door, and one of them spoke softly into some kind of communication device. In a few minutes, an older man wearing a suit walked in. He had that look of big money or government, but she wasn't impressed and wouldn't let him take the lead here.

"I assume that you're the man responsible for this outrage?" she asked.

Brognola smiled. "You might say that."

"Who are you?"

He opened his wallet and flashed his ID. "I'm Hal Brognola, and I'm with the Justice Department."

"Am I under arrest?" she asked with just the right tone of righteous indignation for a member of the press who was being put through this kind of ordeal.

"You can call it that if you like," Brognola answered.

"Under what charges?"

"How many would you like?" he asked. "For now, a criminal violation of restricted airspace will do well enough. I might add to that as we go along, though."

"When do I get to talk to my lawyer?"

"Only when, and if, I say you do.' Brognola dropped the banter. "For now, you will be held incommunicado."

"But I have my rights!" she protested.

"This isn't a court of law, Miss Woods. Right now, the only right you have is to answer my questions."

The reporter's heart sank. "What did you call me?"

Brognola maintained an innocent look on his face. "Or are you going by Donna Moore today? It's so hard to know with people like you."

"I don't know what you're talking about." This

guy had done his homework, but she still tried to bluff her way out of this. "My name is Sylvia Thompson-Bracket."

Brognola had known that this wasn't going to be easy, but the woman was one tough cookie.

"Okay, Miss Thompson-Bracket," he said. "But, in case it slipped your mind, your legal name is Tracy Woods and you were born on October 3, 1970, in Los Angeles, California. You didn't start using that phony Thompson-Bracket tag until you were in school in Atlanta. Then, about two years ago, you started calling yourself Donna Moore on certain documents such as the lease on your apartment in Atlanta and the registration on a gray Lexus."

Brognola smiled. "Now, while it isn't against the law in this country to call yourself anything that you want, it does cause problems when the IRS is concerned. And, of course, the DEA gets very interested in anyone who lives under more than one name. Particularly when your father, Vince Woods, was a well-paid cartel mouthpiece for several years."

He leaned over her. "Am I getting through to you yet, Miss Woods?"

"You have my attention," she said stiffly. "Now what?"

"Now you can tell me what you think you were doing hiring that idiot to fly you in here today."

"I wanted a story."

"What story?"

"I really don't know," she admitted. "I only know that you're doing something here that needs to be reported to the public."

"What makes you think that?"

"I'm not one of your local rednecks, Brognola," she snapped. "I know that you're hiding some kind of clandestine operation here. If you weren't—" she shrugged "—none of this would be happening."

"What makes you say that?"

"Jesus, mister!" she said, dropping the Southern accent. "Give me a fucking break! If this is a farm, I'm the Virgin Mary.

"And," she said, meeting his eyes defiantly, "if you know as much about me as you say that you do, you know how improbable that is."

"Okay," he said, "let's say you get a story on whatever it is you think we're doing here, then what?"

"Then I make a big splash in TV journalism because the viewing public likes nothing more than a story about the abuse of power and the secret dirty dealings of its government. The story gets picked up by one of the major network chains and I get offered a job where I don't have to dress like a fucking yokel or talk like I'm mentally retarded."

She shook her head. "Jesus, I hate Virginia."

"And you don't really care what we're doing here?"

"I don't care if you're building atomic bombs or conducting experiments on aliens. I just wanted a big story."

"Enough to risk your life?"

"Mister, if you knew how often I've risked my life, you wouldn't ask a stupid question like that."

"It's a stupid question only if you live to walk out of here," Brognola said. "And whether that happens still remains to be seen."

"But you can't just kill me," she said.

"Not only can I," Brognola said bluntly, "but, should I find it necessary, I will. So I suggest that you start making this as easy on yourself as you can."

"How?"

"By keeping the attitude in check and answering anything we ask you the first time we ask it without adding editorial commentary. You might want to consider this a job interview, and the job you're trying to get is living for a few more years. So far, your first impression hasn't been all that favorable, so if you want the job, you're going to have to convince me.

"And," he said, locking eyes with her, "the first time I hear some smart-assed crack from you about the freedom of the press and the rest of that liberal media crap, you're not going to live to regret it. Do you understand?''

She turned her eyes away. "Yes, sir."

"Good," he said. "That shows more intelligence than you have demonstrated thus far in this incident. There might be hope for you after all."

Brognola glanced at his watch. "Now, I have another appointment, so I am going to turn this over to Miss Price. And I recommend that you don't get smart mouthed with her, either. As I'm sure you're aware, she doesn't care for you very much as it is, and if she advises me that you aren't salvageable, I'll act on her recommendation immediately."

"May I go to the rest room first?" she asked.

"Certainly." Brognola signaled the two black-suits. "These gentlemen will accompany you, and you'll be under electronic surveillance while you relieve yourself. Should you try to do anything stupid, you'll be restrained for the remainder of the time you're with us, no matter how long, or short, that may be."

She swallowed hard. "I understand."

"Good."

WHEN SYLVIA THOMPSON-BRACKET came out of the washroom, the two blacksuits escorted her back to the small room. Barbara Price was waiting for her there, seated behind a table with a second chair a few feet in front of it. "Sit."

The reporter sat.

Price studied her clinically for a long moment, but Thompson-Bracket couldn't read her face at all.

"First," Price said, "I want to go over your background. What is your legal name and birth date?"

The reporter answered that and the rest of Price's questions truthfully and in her native California dialect. This was one time that Southern charm and her famous people skills weren't going to cut it. After each answer, Price consulted her papers or made a note.

"Now," Price said, "explain to me exactly how it was that you decided that there was a story here to be investigated, as you put it."

"I received a phone call from a Mabel Windam," the reporter started out, "about a man in Wilsonburg who couldn't get a job and—"

"Would that be Sonny Barnes?"

"I really don't know his name," she replied. "Mrs. Windam kept calling him 'her sister's eldest.'"

"That's Barnes. Continue."

"As you know, my program focuses in on problems people feel they have in their local communities. I simply saw her call as something that might provide a lead to a story, so I made that call to you."

When Price didn't respond, she continued.

"Then, when I tried to do a little basic backgrounding on this place, I ran into something interesting."

"And that was?"

"This farm is owned by a cutout corporation."

Price made another note. "Continue."

WHEN BARBARA PRICE got tired of interrogating their prisoner, Carl Lyons took over. When he walked in, he took a completely different tack with the reporter. He wasn't called the Ironman for nothing. He leaned back against the table and motioned to the two blacksuit guards. "You boys can wait outside."

When they were alone, Lyons said bluntly, "You don't need to know who I am. All you need to know is that if I decide that you're lying to me, I will cancel your ticket immediately. Do you have any questions?"

"No, sir." Sylvia instantly read this man as being someone she had better not cross. It wasn't his words as much as his demeanor that told her that she was in danger every minute she was around him. She had seen the type before and knew to be very careful with him.

"Good." Lyons nodded. "Now, I want to know about your contacts with the man you know as Mel Bradley. And I caution you again about leaving anything out, no matter how trivial you might think it is."

When the woman heard those words, she finally realized what had happened. She had allowed herself to be sucked into something she knew nothing about. That bastard Bradley had set her up. He had used her desire for a big story to get her to cross the line.

"What do you want to know?"

"When and where did you meet him and why?"

When Lyons was done with her, he left and the blacksuits came back in and stood guard in the room.

NOW THAT EVERYTHING was more or less under control again, Buck Greene was going over the tapes of the chopper crash and its aftermath. He had witnessed most of it himself, but the video cameras would have picked up what he had missed and he knew that he had missed a lot. No one man could witness something like that without missing most of the peripheral action.

Running back to the last minutes before the alert siren sounded, he watched the pickup truck being driven up and parked next to the farmhouse and saw the driver step out. A few seconds later, he reacted to the siren and looked over to see the chopper coming right for him and took cover.

Considering the circumstances, that was a sensible thing to do. But something about that man was still nagging at the back of his mind.

Forwarding the tape, he studied Bradley as he watched from the edge of the crowd as the reporter, her cameraman and the pilot were taken out of the wreckage. The man made sure to stay out of the way of the blacksuits, but his eyes kept going over to his pickup. There was something in that truck he wanted to get to, but what? What could a truck like that carry?

When his eyes caught a view from one of the high cameras, Greene saw that the truck's bed was covered with a blue plastic tarp. Those tarps were as common as dirt around construction sites, but this one was neatly tied down as if to keep whatever was in the back dry, or to keep it from blowing away.

He ran the tapes back and watched Bradley drive up and park again. He hadn't just found that place to park when he heard the siren as he had said. He had parked before the siren sounded, and that meant that he had known that the chopper was coming. Considering the report that he had been the one to prompt Mabel Windam to call Thompson-Bracket, that wasn't surprising.

He was about to key his com link and order the blacksuits to take Mel Bradley into custody when it clicked in his mind. He remembered going over his videotapes before, watching a new probationary blacksuit named Jim Gordon as he went about his treachery.

The walk was the same as Gordon's, as was the general way he carried himself. The face was different, but facial surgery was easy. Even though his photo and description had been sent to nearly every law-enforcement agency in the country, Gordon had never been caught. Greene had no idea why he would have wanted to come back, but he knew that he had and it wasn't to renew old acquaintances.

Running with his hunch, he pulled one of the tapes from the Jim Gordon incident and played a few minutes of the marked sections. He didn't have to watch more than a couple of scenes to be convinced that Bradley and Gordon were the same man.

"This is Greene to all blacksuits. I want the Belmont worker Mel Bradley apprehended and brought into me immediately. I also want his pickup confiscated. He might be armed, so watch him. Don't take any chances, but I have to have him alive. All blacksuits, respond."

The first response to come in was from the pair of guards on the rear gate. "Chief, I think your man just left here a few minutes ago. We passed him out, and it looked like he was headed for town."

"Damn!" Greene said as he punched the intercom button.

"Hal," he said when Brognola came on the line. "I just figured what in the hell's been going on around here."

"It's about time," Brognola said. "We have a mission going tits up in Africa, and I don't have the time to mess with this."

"Do you remember that blacksuit ringer who I took on, Jim Gordon? Well, he's back as Mel Bradley."

"Are you sure?"

"One hundred percent. I've got both of them on tape and they match up."

"Take care of him," Brognola ordered. "Use Carl's people if you have to, but take him down immediately."

"With pleasure."

A quick call to Carl Lyons had Able Team in his office in a few minutes. It took less time than that to brief them and get them on the road.

WHEN ABLE TEAM ARRIVED in Wilsonburg, they had a second truck full of armed blacksuits in their civilian clothing following them. Their first stop was the police station, and Lyons walked right into Chief Baumann's office.

"What's up, Carl?" Baumann asked.

"We have a situation here, Ed," he said. "I need to inform you that the federal Anti-Terrorist Act has been invoked in the Wilsonburg area."

"Oh, shit," Baumann said. The only good thing that had come out of the bombing of the federal building in Oklahoma City had been the enactment of the Anti-Terrorist Act. With it, law enforcement could finally get serious with terrorists both foreign and domestic. The only problem was that under its provisions, the Feds took over until the problem had been taken care of.

"Who are you after?"

"The guy calling himself Mel Bradley. We think he's a leftover KGB agent."

"You're not serious."

Lyons locked eyes with him. "I'm as serious as death, Ed. I've got a dozen federal agents with me, and we're going after him. You might want to inform your people to keep out of the way because we think he's armed."

"I don't need a shoot-out in town, Carl," Baumann said. "I don't have any way to get the people off the streets."

"I'm sorry, Ed. But that's going to be completely up to Bradley. I promise, though, that we'll do our best to keep the collateral damage to a minimum."

"Jesus!"

CHAPTER TWENTY-FIVE

Grenburgh, Congo

When Charles Taibu appeared in front of his assembled Simbas the next morning, he was in his full Lion King kit: naked except for a loincloth, a feathered headdress, bands of feathers on his upper arms and legs and a long bladed spear in his hand. It was the traditional uniform of an African king, and he was wearing it to remind his followers of his power over them.

The attack the previous night had cost him almost a hundred men dead, wounded or deserted, and he was hearing talk about the curse that had been laid on the earlier Simbas who had attacked Grenburgh. To steady the fears of his new Simbas, he had to show them that he was more powerful than the spirits of long dead white priests. One of the Ebola vials was on a cord around his neck, resting against his naked chest like the badge of office of the mayor of London.

When the lion warriors closest to him recognized the vial, they started chanting their war cries and firing their AKs in the air. They were well aware of the power of the yellow liquid it contained. It was the Bleeding Death that killed everyone that crossed its path. It was pure death, and nothing could turn it away, not the medicine of the white men nor the most powerful charms of the African medicine men could prevail against it. But their leader had captured this sure death, and now he controlled it. No African leader had ever been able to do anything like that.

Taibu stood tall as thunderous shouts washed over him. Now that he had his Simbas firmly in hand again, he intended to send them against the Yankees in full strength this time. He wanted this episode to be concluded this day. He still wanted them to capture as many of the Yankees alive as they could, but he couldn't risk further setbacks to his plans. The Yankees had proved to be worthy adversaries, but he had had enough of them.

"Go!" he shouted, and stabbed the spear toward Grenburgh. "But remember, I want them alive! They must be alive so they can taste the justice of the lion!"

With a group roar that echoed from the trees, hundreds of Simbas turned and raced for the city. Taibu shook his spear in the air and shouted encouragement after them. When this day was over, he would have the CNN TV news crew brought to him so he could start showing the world the proof of his power.

"WE HAVE INCOMING," Hawkins radioed from the roof. "There's a whole bunch of the bastards, and they look like they're going to get serious with us this time."

The Simba assault of the previous afternoon had been only a few dozen lion warriors and had been more of a probing attack than a serious assault. That didn't mean, however, that the commandos had treated them any differently than they'd done with the earlier attacks. All it had meant was that they'd taken them down with single-shot fire instead of full auto.

The Stony Man warriors didn't have to be in Taibu's head to know that he was trying to get them to use up their limited stocks of ammunition. Further proof of that tactic had been found when James and Hawkins had gone out to salvage the bodies again early the previous evening. Most of the Simba casualties had had only two magazines with them, so they hadn't been able to resupply themselves with very much.

This time they shouldn't have a problem salvaging the battlefield. They might, however, have a problem living long enough to do it.

"We're on the way up," McCarter radioed over the com link.

Frank Bullis was wearing the team's spare com link, and he, too, responded to Hawkins's warning. "This is Bullis," he radioed. "I'll get my people up there, too."

"Come on up, Doctor," Hawkins answered. "The more the merrier. There's going to be more than enough to go around this time."

"Jesús y Maria!" Rafael Encizo whispered when he got a look at the mass of chanting humanity racing toward the square. All of the streets leading into town fed into the central plaza in front of their fortress, and every one of those streets had its own column of lion warriors howling as they ran.

When Bullis joined the commandos on the roof, he took one look at what was coming their way and felt his guts contract. For the first time, the reality of facing the entire Simba army was hammered home to him. Since the daring rescue when the commandos had pulled them from certain death, he had seen these professionals perform one military miracle after another as a matter of course. But surviving this was going to take more than a routine miracle.

Swallowing his fears, he sought out Bolan. "I have five of my militiamen with me," he said, nodding toward the solemn-faced ex-hostages clustered behind him. "Where do you want us to go?"

"Put your people in between my men and leave one to watch the other side of the building for us. They might try to sneak someone around the back while we're busy out front."

Again, the matter-of-fact way that the man was dealing with this new crisis steadied Bullis. He didn't know where such strength came from, but he was glad to borrow as much of it as he could get.

"I'll put them in position."

Rather than wait for the crowd, Gary Manning started to fire as soon as he could acquire targets on the far side of the square. Again, he was concentrating on taking out the officers and leaders first. This time, though, it didn't seem to matter who fell. The Simbas had their blood up, and each man was in his own little world, caring for nothing but the blood of the enemy.

The rest of the Stony Man commandos also opened up at a longer range, and the next minute and a half was a study in the extremes of human behavior. Had the Simbas been the U.S. troops who had assaulted Omaha Beach on D Day, their actions would have been called courageous. As it was, it was considered suicidal and crazed. The difference lay more in the motivation rather than the behavior itself. But no matter the viewpoint of the observer, it was an extreme example of human willpower overcoming human fears.

With almost a dozen assault rifles and submachine guns blazing fire, the carnage in the square was unending. With their height advantage and the massed target in plain sight, the Stony Man warriors and their ex-hostage allies simply couldn't miss. It was a rare bullet that didn't impact in human flesh. Not all of the resulting wounds were fatal, but they did draw blood.

Even with the slaughter the team was inflicting on the attackers, the charge wasn't even slowed. The sheer numbers gave the Simbas a momentum that carried them all the way to the thick stone walls of the fortress. Whether those old stone walls would withstand them was yet to be seen.

A clot of Simbas stormed the main entrance, throwing their bodies against the thick doors. The locking bar on the inside was solid iron and was held in place by steel reinforced concrete, so there was no chance of their breaking it down. Frustrated, a few of them broke off to try to pull the iron bars over the windows from the stone. Again, the stoutness of the colonial architecture defeated them. Howling with rage, a few of them tried to scale the stone walls, but the Belgian architects had foreseen that threat, as well, and there were few hand- or footholds.

Running in a crouch, Hawkins sprinted across the roof and took cover behind the balustrade over the entrance. Pulling a grenade from his assault harness, he pulled the pin, released the spoon, counted down two seconds and lobbed the bomb over the side. It detonated at head level below and took out at least a dozen Simbas in front of the doors. The survivors roared even louder and fired their AKs blindly at the stone balustrade overhead.

Pulling another grenade, Hawkins tossed it over the side, silencing another dozen of the enemy. A long burst from his subgun cleared the rest from the entrance.

There was plenty of Simba return fire from the plaza. It was somewhat sporadic, though, and Bolan noticed that most of it wasn't aimed accurately. The Simbas were firing their weapons well above the building as if they didn't want to kill them. The thought flashed in the soldier's mind that Taibu might have ordered his minions to capture them alive at all costs. If that was the case, it gave them a greater chance of surviving this assault, but it didn't bode well for the final act of this extended drama.

Being killed outright would be a pleasure compared to what being captured alive would entail.

When the other Stony Man warriors also noticed that the Simbas weren't trying to kill them, they went into a calculated butcher mode. No longer did they try to overcome the mass of enemy by sheer firepower. Switching their weapons back to single shot, they started putting one bullet into every man they could get in their sights. If they could kill them, that was fine, but the purpose of the exercise was to tag each and every Simba that they could. The purpose was to inflict pain on as many of them as possible.

Most of the Simbas stood there and took it, but some of them again vainly tried to storm the windows and doors.

"Grenades!" James shouted when he saw a pair of Simbas take stick grenades from their pouches, pull the friction-cord fuse igniters and rear back to throw them up onto the roof.

A quick burst from Hawkins's subgun cut them down, and the smoking grenades fell from their hands. The crush of warriors was so thick that the two detonations took out a dozen of them and wounded even more.

Encizo and James teamed up to shoot the attackers off the door again and when they were done, a group decision seemed to have been made in the plaza. Slowly, like a pool of thick liquid caught in a receding tide, the mass of Simbas started to flow away from the building.

It was as if the Simbas were operating with a group mind. Those in the rear were the first to fade back into the streets leading away from the plaza. When the warriors in front of them realized that they were being deserted, they, too, turned to go in a ripple effect. Once the ripple started, it quickly spread until only a few dozen lion warriors remained in front of the building.

The Stony Man team quickly shot them down, then ceased their fire. Everyone else was running away, and they needed to save their ammunition.

As SOON AS the plaza was completely clear of live enemies, James, Hawkins and Encizo went outside to salvage more ammunition for their captured AKs. By making the supply run in the daylight, the others could stand guard over them from the roof.

Some of the bodies had been in the plaza for over a day, and the smell was starting to become intense. Rather than venture too far from the safety of the building, the three rifled the bodies of the Simbas closest to them. This time, though, the pickings were good. Almost every casualty had a chest-pack magazine carrier at least half-full of loaded magazines. As they gathered the loot, James started to relay the magazine packs back to the steps where Bullis and his militiamen took them inside.

"I found a cluster of guys carrying Chinese stick grenades," Hawkins called out. "They must have been their mobile artillery section."

"Grab them, too," Encizo said. "They'll come in real handy. Gary can make more Monsters with them."

After collecting at least one hundred AK magazines, the commandos went back inside the walls to await Taibu's next move.

THIS TIME the drumming didn't start up as soon as the Simbas got back to their camp, and after hours of endless noise both day and night, the quiet was startling.

The day was still young, though, so after a quick meal—half an MRE—the fighters were back on the roof to see how this would play out.

"I'm not too sure that we're going to be able to get through another one of those," McCarter said, his eyes looking past the bodies to the now empty approaches.

Bolan's eyes flicked down to the plaza. A couple hundred Simba warriors were scattered over the four-block area. A few of them were still alive, but most of them, if not killed outright, had been trampled to death by their comrades once the panic started. Of the wounded, this wasn't one of those times when the commandos would try to render them aid.

It was a slaughterhouse down there pure and simple, and it smelled like one. But as long as Taibu threw his people into the Stony Man guns, the body count would only mount. The problem, of course, wasn't in killing them; it was having enough ammunition to continue doing so. Another massive attack like the last would have them down to their final magazines for their personal weapons. Then they would have to use the captured AKs and the limited supply of ammunition for them.

"You might be right," Bolan said. "We knew before we holed up here, though, that we couldn't hold out forever. We might want to start planning for the final defense."

"What do we do about the civilians?" McCarter asked.

Bolan met the Briton's eyes squarely. He knew what was being asked. Did they leave the people they had rescued alive for the not so tender mercies of the Simbas, or did they kill them to prevent their capture? It was one of those decisions that went with the job, but one that no one ever wanted to have to make.

"I think we should explain the situation to them and let them make their own choices. We have enough AKs now that no one will have to worry about not having a way to get out of this if they want to."

"That's what I was thinking," McCarter said. "We can pull back to the basement if we have to and defend the stairs as long as we can. That will give them enough time."

Bolan nodded his agreement.

Stony Man Farm, Virginia

THE STONY MAN FARM crew didn't need to have an after-action report from Bolan to know what had taken place in Grenburgh. With the helicopter crash taking center stage, they had missed watching the battle in real time, but the taped images Kurtzman had captured from the satellites told them the story in living color. Even from deep space, the blood soaking the plaza could clearly be seen.

They didn't need the team to send an ammunition inventory to know that the next attack would likely be the last. The body count alone spoke to that fact.

"Now that we have Thompson-Bracket where she belongs and Carl working on that driver," Barbara Price said to Hal Brognola, "maybe we get back to what we're supposed to be spending our time on."

"She's right, Hal." Katzenelenbogen glanced up at the screen displaying the carnage in the Grenburgh plaza. "The Man's going to have to decide once and for all what he's going to do. If he's going to leave them hung out there to dry, we need to let them know so they can try to do something on their own. They don't have much time left."

The Stony Man tactical adviser locked eyes with Brognola. "I still think this situation can be put to bed with a single cruise missile armed with the proper warhead. The target is well grouped, and, knowing how a guy like Taibu works, he'll undoubtedly have the Ebola samples with him. One strike, of the right size, will make that part of Africa a lot safer, as well as save our people.''

Brognola knew what Katz was saying. The big stakes in this game were still not the team and the ex-hostages. As it had been since the WHO research station had been overrun, it was still the Ebola.

''I have to make a report to him anyway,'' Brognola said. ''I need to let him know what went on here and get his guidance on how he wants me to handle our prisoners. Then I'm going to explain that he has to decide the future of Stony Man, and he has to do it right now. Not only have we been attacked here—we are about to lose our main strike force if he doesn't get his head out.''

Brognola glanced back up at the screen. He could see the tiny figures of the commandos on the roof of the building, and they looked even smaller because there were so few of them.

''And,'' he continued, ''if he doesn't act to save Striker and his people immediately, I'm going to ask him to disband this operation immediately. I'm not going to be a part of something that asks men to die without giving help when they need it and it's available.''

''Are you going to fly up there again?'' Price asked.

''No. If I go up there to see him again, I'll have to go through a couple of layers of his flunkies to get to him, and that'll take too much time. This time I'll do it over the red secure phone, because I know he always takes those calls."

"Good luck."

CHAPTER TWENTY-SIX

When Hal Brognola returned from using the secure phone, his face was coldly neutral. "We have permission to use a surgical-low level nuclear strike if we can positively identify the location of the Ebola virus samples. The USS *Seawolf* has been ordered to break from its scheduled cruise in the South Atlantic to divert to a launch position and be ready to fire on command in under an hour."

Yakov Katzenelenbogen let out a low whistle. He had recommended this scenario as a quick solution to the untenable problem facing the team, but his suggestion had been more of a prayer than a plan. He had never expected that it would be approved. While nukes were very useful in situations like this, they were still the big boogey man of domestic politics, to say nothing of international relations.

"Did the Man check that with his friends and enemies in Congress?"

Brognola shook his head in the negative. "He's briefing the National Security Council, but he's going to go solo on this one. He'll invoke the War Powers Act right before the launch, and then argue with Congress about it later. His staff is gathering all the uncensored Ebola footage they can find for a congressional show-and-tell about what he kept from happening to us.''

He shuddered. ''It shouldn't take much of that footage to convince even the most knee-jerk liberal that he did the right thing. I've seen those films and they're grim. Bleeding to death through the pores of your skin and every bodily orifice while your internal organs turn to sludge isn't a pretty picture.''

The political battles that would result from this weren't Katz's problem. He focused in on what was important to him—how this was going to salvage the mission. ''What size war shot did he authorize?'' he asked.

''A 1.5 KT.''

''That's a baby nuke,'' the Israeli commented, ''but it should do the job,''

Even though use of nuclear weapons was still the ultimate taboo, the new dial-a-yield tactical weapons in the American arsenal made them a practical solution for many battlefield situations. With the smaller weapons, one no longer had to eradicate several square miles of real estate to eliminate a small target. A precision nuclear strike was no longer an oxymoron, and a 1.5 kiloton warhead was a good tool for delicate work. It wasn't quite the surgical strike the media so loved to talk about, but it wasn't Armageddon, either.

As the name indicated, a 1.5 kilo ton nuclear warhead carried the same destructive power as one and one-half thousand tons of TNT or about 750 two-thousand-pound aerial bombs full of C-4 plastic explosive detonated all at once. With the nuke, however, you didn't need a fleet of bombers to deliver the blow. A single Tomahawk cruise missile would do the job.

"I'll talk to Striker about how they're going to need to designate the target," Katz said. "That might be a little tricky this time."

"Why?" Brognola looked surprised. "They have a laser designator, don't they?"

"No, it didn't look like there was going to be a need for it on this mission, and they used the weight allocation for extra medical supplies and ammunition. They're going to have to use the lock-on function on the GPS to mark the spot."

"That means that somebody has to be there with it, doesn't it?"

Katz simply nodded.

"Goddamn!" Brognola said softly.

He had used up a lifetime's worth of political credit in hopes of saving lives only to learn now that the life of one of his friends would have to be given up to make it work.

"I didn't know," he said.

"I know you didn't," Katz said gently. "I'll talk to them and see if they can come up with an alternative."

WHEN DIMITRI SPATKIN returned to his Belmont Construction flatbed truck parked along the road outside of Wilsonburg, he tried to think what he needed to do next. From the beginning, this whole expedition had been a spur-of-the-moment thing rather than a well-thought-out tactical operation with a fixed final act. He had been able to wing it so far, but that lack of planning had finally caught up with him. That was the problem of trying to do something of this magnitude solo. His Little Amerika training had supposedly prepared him for individual missions like this, but Little Amerika was a long time in his past.

Even so, he was reluctant to abandon his self-assumed mission. He knew, though, that his chance of surviving it had gone down considerably since the crash of the chopper. Rather than being the diversion he had hoped it would be, it had been a disaster for him. The entire blacksuit security force was on full alert now, and he had no idea how long it would be before they returned to normal status. He knew, though, that he couldn't wait. If he was to try again, it had to be soon.

For one thing, the deteriorating explosive mix in

the back of his truck didn't have much shelf life left. At some point in time it would become so sensitive that merely starting the truck engine would be enough shock to set it off. Whatever he decided to do, he needed to do it quickly.

CARL LYONS HAD the blacksuits spread out in two-man teams to scour the town for Bradley and his truck. While they were searching, he, Gadgets Schwarz and Rosario Blancanales went to the motel room the man had been using. Getting the key from the front desk, they let themselves in.

There was little in the room—shaving gear, a few changes of clothing and a couple of magazines and paperbacks, the sorts of things one would expect of a construction worker. The only thing they found of interest was a half-full can of FFF black powder and a small box of large rifle primers missing at least a dozen of the small metal caps.

"He's been making some kind of explosive device," Schwarz said, frowning. "But, I'm damned if I know what. Unless, of course, he had more powder than that one can."

"Whatever it is," Lyons said, "it's probable cause. Let's toss this place one inch at a time."

"While you guys are doing this," Blancanales stated, "I'm going to have a talk with that barmaid. She might have some idea where he is."

"Do that," Lyons agreed, "but don't let her put

anything over on you. Put the blocks to her and make her understand that her ass is on the line here, too. We've got Bradley, or whatever his real name is, on at least federal explosive charges, and we'll hang them on her, too, if she doesn't cooperate.''

"I'll get her to talk," Blancanales vowed.

LYONS AND SCHWARZ were almost done with the detailed search of Bradley's room when Blancanales called on the com link. "I've got a location," he said. "The Windam woman said that she saw his company truck parked at a turnoff along the side of the state highway north of town. She'd been out there to visit her sister and spotted it.''

"We're on the way."

"I'm coming, too," Buck Greene cut in. He'd been monitoring the radio traffic and wanted in on the final act. "I know the turnoff she's talking about.''

"Alert your people," Lyons said, "and see if we can block that place off.''

BUCK GREENE QUICKLY joined Able Team and guided them to the turnoff. Rather than drive up, they got out of their car and approached on foot. Lyons spotted the Belmont flatbed truck exactly where the Windam woman had said it would be, a turnoff in a dip in the road. He couldn't figure out, though, what Bradley thought he was doing. The ramps for the trailer were down and it looked as if he was going to drive the pickup onto the flatbed. It really didn't matter what he was doing, though. With Blancanales blocking the southern approach with their vehicle and a pickup full of blacksuits around the bend to the north, they had him trapped.

"Bradley!" Lyons shouted. "We have you surrounded."

At the first shout, Spatkin rammed his truck into reverse and stomped on the gas. Tires kicking up dust, the truck shot backward long enough to clear the ramps, and he slam shifted into first. Sliding sideways under the full power of his V-8 engine, Spatkin headed back for Wilsonburg.

If he could break through the roadblock, he would head directly for the Farm, crash through the rear gate and try to make it to the farmhouse. Even if he died in the blast, he would be fulfilling the vow he had made so many years ago to carry the war to the enemies of Mother Russia.

Hunkered over the wheel to keep as low as possible, he didn't bother trying to fire at the blacksuits. His marshal's training had taught him to drive right through ambushes, not stop and fight.

"We need him alive," Lyons shouted as he triggered a .357 Magnum round from his Colt Python at the speeding truck's rear tire.

Spatkin jerked the wheel, causing the slug to miss the tire, punch through the truckbed and hit the primer cap of one of his igniters. The shock of the high-speed round combined with the detonation of the primer was enough to set off the six hundred pounds of unstable explosives.

For a microsecond, the truck could still be seen as the flame-shot black fireball formed. In that instant, both Spatkin and the vehicle ceased to exist except as small chunks of metal and flesh flying through the air.

Able Team barely had time to drop for cover before the shock wave of the explosion slammed into them, driving them into the dirt. For the next few seconds, the air was choked with dust and black smoke, and debris raining over a wide area.

When the smoke cleared enough to see, all that remained of the truck was part of the twisted frame rails and the rear axle driven two feet into the ground. Of the driver, nothing could be seen. Like the government he had so faithfully served, the Russian agent who had sought to take vengeance against his country's enemies no longer existed except as small, tattered remnants.

Lyons picked himself off the ground, his ears ringing, and dusted off his jacket. The pillar of smoke and dust was dispersing, but the smaller bits were still falling.

"Now we know what he was doing with that black powder," Schwarz said, yawning wide to try to clear his ears. "He was making a fucking car bomb."

"And that's why he parked that rig by the farmhouse," Lyons pointed out. "I think he was going to wait till the chopper showed up to divert everyone's attention before he lit the fuse. If that thing hadn't landed damned near on top of the truck, Stony Man would have been wiped out."

Greene shook his head. "I still don't know who in the hell he was."

"I can't say that I really give a shit," Lyons growled. "He's dead, and that's all I care about."

Greene didn't think it was quite that simple. Someone had attacked the Farm, and he couldn't rest until he figured out why. As long as that question remained unanswered, Stony Man was vulnerable.

Grenburgh, Congo

AFTER KATZ TALKED to Bolan, the Executioner took David McCarter aside. "Katz just called and he said that the President has authorized a nuclear-cruise-missile strike if we can get them a clear set of coordinates to fire at."

No one ever wanted to hear the words *nuclear weapon* used in conjunction with the piece of real estate they were currently occupying. While nuclear bombs had been tamed a little since they had first been detonated in anger over Hiroshima and Nagasaki, they were still the ultimate expression of military displeasure. Those who were too close to one when it went off never got a chance to complain about it.

McCarter knew the stakes and didn't hesitate. "What do you think our chances are of surviving it?"

The radiation was the least of the problems. In a nuclear explosion, the blast, heat and shock effects were no different than those of any conventional explosive from black powder to plastique. They were simply several magnitudes greater. If you could pile up enough C-4 and detonate it all in a nanosecond, you would have the same result as a nuclear-weapon detonation—utter destruction over a wide area.

"Well," Bolan said, "we're at least a klick from Taibu's camp and we can take shelter in the basement, so we might stand a pretty good chance of surviving it. If the building comes down on top of us, though, we might have a hard time digging our way out."

"I'll have Gary put some explosives aside in case we need to blast our way clear," McCarter said.

"Good idea."

"Do you want to tell the civilians?"

Bolan thought for a moment. "I don't think we should tell them much. They're barely holding on as it is. If we start talking about a nuclear strike, they'll flash back to Hiroshima, and we don't need any hysteria right now."

"I'd like to tell Bullis, though," McCarter said. "He's proved to be a steady man. He can tell the people that we're bringing on a heavy air strike, and they won't know the difference."

"After we brief the team."

THE PHOENIX FORCE COMMANDOS took the news of the cruise-missile strike calmly. This wouldn't be the first time that they had been in the neighborhood when a nuke went off, either accidentally or on purpose. It would, however, be the first time that they would be so close to ground zero. But when the alternative was waiting for the Simbas to either starve them out or overwhelm them, it wasn't much of a choice.

"The only problem," Bolan explained, "is that we don't have a laser designator with us this time. If we did, we could light up the target from here, take cover and let it home in on the beam. But we didn't expect to have to face anything like this and didn't come prepared for it."

"What's the alternative?" Hawkins asked. He knew there was an alternative, or the Executioner wouldn't have mentioned it. He wasn't a man to waste his mental energy on unavailable options. He was afraid, though, what the answer was going to be.

"The alternative is to use the GPS lock-on signal as a homing device," Bolan said. "The problem is that whoever takes it out there might not be able to get back."

James took a deep breath. "I believe that I'm the obvious candidate for that job, Striker.

"No offense," he said when he saw the looks on the faces of his teammates, "but none of you white guys are going to last thirty seconds in a crowd of homeboys like that. I don't speak any of the local dialects, but I'm sure as hell the right color, and I can borrow a few items from the bodies outside so I'll pass at least casual inspection. None of you guys could even get close. You'd end up on the dinner menu."

"You don't need to do that, Calvin," McCarter said.

"Someone has to go out there," the ex-SEAL said bluntly, "and I have the best chance of pulling it off.

"And I'm not going to go out there to commit suicide," he quickly added. "I figure I can work my way in close enough to lock in the coordinates, switch the GPS to transmit, leave it someplace and get the hell out of there. My mamma didn't raise no suicidal fools."

It was a good story, and most people would have

believed it. But Stony Man warriors knew that there was too great a chance of one of the Simbas discovering the GPS transmitter and shutting it off or destroying it. To guarantee that the missile could home in on its signal, the device would have to be transmitting right up to the last second. For this to work, he would have to stay with it at what would become a nuclear ground zero.

While they all knew that he was planning to go to his death, none of them questioned him or tried to change his mind. He had freely made the decision, and they would all honor his decision to die so that the rest of them and the ex-hostages could hopefully live.

Every man died, but few got the chance to choose his death.

"There's one other thing," Bolan said. "Hal says that the President wants to make sure that this strike will take out the Ebola, as well as the Simbas. Supposedly, we can't call for the fire mission unless we can verify that Taibu actually has the stuff with him."

"That's the biggest load of crap I've ever heard," McCarter snapped. "What're we supposed to do, send two men out there to die? One to find the Ebola and another one to call the missile down on himself?"

"I can do both jobs," James stated calmly, "and get my ass out of there before the package arrives.

Call the Farm and let them know that we can provide the confirmation and target illumination.''

"Are you sure, Calvin?" McCarter asked, his concern plain for his teammate.

"Just call them," the ex-SEAL reassured him. "I'll start getting my gear together."

CHAPTER TWENTY-SEVEN

Stony Man Farm, Virginia

When Hal Brognola got the call from Carl Lyons about the explosive end of Mel Bradley, he sought out Barbara Price. "I'm going to the interrogation room to wrap up the loose ends," he told her. "The President wants us to put a lid on this episode ASAP."

"Good luck dealing with her."

Brognola didn't smile. Even with the Bradley situation concluded, he was in no mood to be messed with by anyone. Not when one of his men was soon going to die in Africa. "I think I can handle it."

SYLVIA THOMPSON-BRACKET didn't know how long she had been held, but knew that it had been several hours. During that time, the guards had been changed and she had been offered a meal. She'd not been particularly hungry, but ate it out of boredom. When she'd asked how much longer she could expect to be held, the guards hadn't answered her. The only time they had spoken to her had been to offer her the meal and to okay another trip to the washroom.

When Brognola finally walked in, his face was grim and the woman braced herself for whatever bad news was coming. She'd tried to stay positive, but had finally allowed the fact that she was in more than serious trouble sink in.

"Miss Woods," Brognola said formally, "it is my duty to inform you that you are now being held under the provisions of the Anti-Terrorist Act. In case you were too busy exposing abuses of governmental power to pay attention to that law's enactment, let me point out a few of its salient points. First off—"

"But," she sputtered, "I'm not a terrorist, you know that."

"You have aided and abetted an act of terrorism, and that makes you an accomplice to it. You can save your pleas of innocence for the judge."

"But what happened?" She wanted to scream, but was keeping a grip on herself. "My trying to fly in here was stupid, but it wasn't a terrorist act."

Brognola ignored her and continued. "As I was saying, you are now in federal custody and are being investigated for a federal felony. You will be transported to a federal secure facility as soon as we can arrange it. Once there, you won't be allowed to make bail as long as this matter is being investigated, and there is no limitation on how long the investigation can take. At the end of the investigation, a determination will be made as to the disposition of your case. If, at that time, an indictment is made against you, you'll be provided counsel as required by law. Until then, it isn't required.''

She couldn't believe what she was hearing. ''You're saying that I'm going to be locked up and no one can tell me for how long?''

''I'm afraid that's about the size of it, Miss Woods,'' Brognola said.

''But I don't understand.'' She was close to tears and had suddenly become very frightened.

''Knowingly or not, you have been a part of an attempted terrorist attack against Stony Man Farm. The President has invoked the provisions of the Anti-Terrorist Act, so it is out of my hands.''

''What will happen to me?''

''To be perfectly honest with you, Miss Woods, I don't know. The President has asked that the Attorney General lead this investigation, so it will be up to his office now, not mine.''

''Oh, Jesus,'' she said softly.

''Miss Woods?''

''Yes?''

''Should you ever find yourself a free woman again, may I suggest that you find another career? You haven't shown good judgment in this one. You have to understand that even in the United States of America, the freest nation on Earth, there are those times when the good of the many outweighs the good of the few. Particularly those few who seek to exploit necessary national secrets to further their own selfish goals.

"You'll never learn what we do here, Miss Woods, but let me assure you that we work for the greater good of millions and not only the good of Americans, but for people of the whole world. We do important work here, and it must continue. The nation, and the world, cannot allow you, or anyone else, to keep us from doing our job."

"I had no idea." She was close to sobbing, something she hadn't done since she had made her escape from the cartel in L.A. "I truly am sorry for whatever I've done."

"I'm sure you are, but I am afraid that doesn't alter what's going to happen. As I said, this is no longer in my hands."

With that final pronouncement, Sylvia Thompson-Bracket broke down and started to sob. She hated herself for doing it, but she'd had all that she could take.

Hal Brognola wasn't a pushover, but he did have a thing about crying young women. "For what it's worth," he said, "if it turns out that you weren't actively involved with the attempt that was made against us, I'll do what I can to see that you are freed. Should that happen, however, you'll be required to sign a lifetime agreement never to disclose anything about this incident. To forget that would result in your being immediately imprisoned again.''

The woman's sobs had subsided, but silent tears still fell.

"Good luck," he said sincerely.

"HOW DID SHE TAKE IT?" Price asked when Brognola entered her office.

"I think I finally broke her," he said. "She's tough, but I think she now realizes that she's lucky to be alive. I really don't think that she knew what Bradley, or whatever his name is, was planning to do. She just let her naked ambition take control of her common sense."

"Do you think she'll keep quiet about this?"

Brognola nodded. "I think so. I'll have her put on the list for lifelong surveillance and periodic visits. She'll never be allowed to forget her agreement to keep her mouth shut about all of this."

"We'll see." Price wasn't easily convinced.

"Have we heard back from Striker yet?" he asked, changing the subject.

She nodded. "The message just came in. Calvin's going to illuminate the target for them tonight."

"I'll be in the Computer Room."

Congo

IN GRENBURGH, the afternoon passed quickly for Calvin James. He cheerfully kept up the fiction that he would be able to get away from ground zero in time before the missile showed up. Though the commandos knew it was only a facade, they understood and honored his unrealistic optimism. No matter how desperate the mission, people always liked to think that they might have a way out.

James caught a nap that afternoon and, upon waking, enjoyed an MRE for an early dinner. "Damn I like that Cajun-rice-and-sausage entrée," he said, grinning.

Hawkins shuddered. "Man, that stuff isn't anything like real Cajun food. When we get back, I'll show you some real Cajun."

James met his eyes and smiled. "I'll hold you to that."

Hawkins looked away.

AS SOON AS DARKNESS FELL, the drums started again. The day had been quiet without any probing attacks, but now Taibu needed to get his people back with the program. But with all the Simbas busy chanting and dancing around their fires, the way to them should be clear.

After James made his final farewells, the Stony Man commandos went up to the roof to cover him as long as he was in sight. Frank Bullis met him at the front door as he was heading out to salvage a bit of finery from the Simba bodies littering the plaza. The doctor was wearing his AK and a full chest-pack magazine carrier. "I'll cover you out there," he said.

"You don't have to do that, Doctor."

"It's Frank," Bullis said. "And you don't know if any of those bastards are hiding in ambush out there."

Bullis had kept his head before, so James didn't mind the company. "Okay, but be ready to bug out if it gets sticky out there."

"Don't worry, I will."

"You're clear in front," Gary Manning called over the com link from his sniper's nest on the roof. The Phoenix Force warriors were keeping a sharp eye out in case some of Taibu's people tried a silent sneak attack.

"Bullis is escorting me," James sent, "and we're on the way."

The square in front of the building was clear of living enemies, but not of debris and most of that debris consisted of Simba bodies. Taibu didn't seem to be concerned with recovering his dead.

The first of the bodies was wearing a feathered headband, but James hesitated to take it. He was sure that the feathers had to signify something, probably rank, and he didn't want to stand out.

The second Simba casualty was wearing a vest cut down from some kind of khaki uniform shirt. James stripped it from the corpse and found that it almost fit his broad chest. Worn over his dirty camouflage pants, it looked authentic. The rope sandals the Simba was wearing were too big for *him,* but they looked to be close to James's size. He added them to his disguise.

The last thing he needed was an AK and a magazine carrier. Taking one of the team's H&Ks would again invite unwelcome attention. Although the commandos had salvaged several of the assault rifles from the Simba casualties, they would be needed if the missile attack was canceled at the last moment. And, as they all knew, that was a distinct possibility. What the Man promised wasn't always what got delivered.

"There," James said as he turned to Bullis after he had donned the last piece of his disguise. "How do I look?"

"Just like most of these bastards," Bullis said without smiling.

James held out his hand. "It was nice getting to know you, Doctor. Good luck when this is all over."

Bullis took his hand and said. "I can't say that I've enjoyed any of this, Calvin, but I'll never forget what you've done for me and the rest of us.

And—" he smiled "—I'll cover you to the other side of the plaza."

"Keep your butt down," James growled, but he was glad for the company.

Keeping low and moving cautiously, it took several minutes for the pair to reach the buildings on the other side of the open ground. With the cobblestones littered with corpses, it was difficult to walk without treading on a body. They stopped at the head of a street that ran directly to the Simba camp. The sound of the drums and the chants of the warriors were louder.

"It sounds like he's whipping them up into a frenzy again," Bullis said. "You'd think that shit would get old after a while."

"But he has to do it," James explained. "After that butt kicking we gave them today, if he wants to send them against us tomorrow, he's got to get them pumped up again. No one wants to die, not even Simbas, and he's got to make them forget what happened back there today. It's not easy to make men go into a situation like that.

"But," James added, "at least with all of that going on, they're not going to be paying too much attention to one more black guy wandering around in their midst. This should be a piece of cake.

"Well," James said, taking one last look at the administration building, "I guess I'll let them know

I'm launching.'' Keying his com link, he spoke quietly to McCarter.

Bullis stepped back a pace to give James some privacy and him some room. Though neurology wasn't his specialty, he was a medical doctor and he knew his way around the human body. He knew exactly where to strike a blow to incapacitate a man, but not injure him severely. It was never as simple as it looked in the movies, and it had to be done with care, but it could be done.

Clasping his two hands together, he waited until James had finished saying his goodbyes before striking him behind the left ear. The commando went down with a grunt and lay still.

Now that James had just become his patient, Bullis automatically knelt beside him, checked his pulse and found it strong. After making sure that James was laid out comfortably, Bullis took the GPS unit and tucked it in his belt. He checked the magazine in his AK again before slinging it over his shoulder.

He didn't expect that he would need it, but the past several days had taught him to be prepared for the unexpected.

Now that he was equipped for his mission, Dr. Frank Bullis headed toward the sounds of the drums to face the greatest unexpected event any man would ever have to face, his own death. He was surprised at how calm he felt.

JAMES WOKE with a sore head and, when he saw that the GPS transmitter was missing and Bullis was nowhere in sight, he realized what had happened. The doctor had gone to make the sacrifice in his place. He was almost ashamed that he felt a wave of relief sweep over him, but it was also tinged with great sadness. Bullis was a good man and he deserved to live. A man who had given so much to try to help others was now giving everything to save lives.

"Striker," James called over the com link, "is Bullis with you?"

"No." Bolan sounded surprised. "Why?"

"He bushwhacked me and took the GPS unit. I think he's gone to light up the Simbas for the missile."

"Get back here as fast as you can then, we need to take cover."

"On the way."

Grabbing his AK, James hurried for the protection of the building. Hawkins and Encizo raced out the front entrance to cover him as he came back in. McCarter and Bolan were waiting for him right inside the doors.

"What the hell happened out there?" McCarter asked as the doors were barred again.

"Man, I don't know." James rubbed the back of his neck. "I had just finished talking to Striker and the next thing I knew, I was waking up with a sore head. For a doctor, he coldcocked me good.''

There was little to be said. Bullis had decided that he should guide the missile, and they would honor his decision. Their job now was to see that the people Bullis was giving his life for were protected from the wrath he was calling down out of the sky.

"Let's get down to the basement.''

OUTSIDE TOWN, the drums and chants echoed in the dark and drew Frank Bullis toward the Simba encampment. He was running on pure adrenaline, and it was taking him to a place he hadn't known even existed. A man in his situation might be expected to be paralyzed with fear, and he was surprised that he felt little of that. It was almost as if he were outside his body looking down at what he was doing from a distance.

He was a fully accredited American doctor and a noted medical researcher, but Johns Hopkins and the CDC labs seemed like a faint dream of another life to him. Even his work for the WHO at Donner's Station just a few days earlier was alien to him now. The past few days had stripped that from him and had reduced him to almost a primeval man. He was closer to the Simbas now than he was to any American civilian he had ever met.

His movements were quick and sure, more like

those of the hunter than of the hunted. All of his physical senses were greatly enhanced; his vision was that of a night cat. The pounding of the drums resonated in his ears like a giant heartbeat, and he felt the cool night air caress his skin like butterfly wings. Over the odor of the fires and the reek of too many unwashed humans, he could smell the river, the jungle and the rich, red earth.

He couldn't remember ever having been this aware of life before, and now he understood why some men reveled in jumping out of airplanes, racing cars and running with the bulls. He also understood Belasko and his men much better and felt a kinship with Calvin James. He didn't, however, regret that he had denied James his solitary walk to the beat of the drums.

The commando had made that walk many times before while it was the first, and would be the last, for him and every man needed to feel it at least once in his life.

CHAPTER TWENTY-EIGHT

Frank Bullis continued to be unafraid when he reached the fringes of the Simbas. Though he didn't speak any of the Congo dialects fluently, he had picked up a few words of greeting in several of the local languages during his stay at the research station.

When a lion warrior turned and looked his way, Bullis quickly greeted him in Tutsi. "I see you, my brother."

"I see you," the Simba called back.

Having passed muster, Bullis headed deeper into the crowd to lose himself.

Several large fires had been set in an arc, and the Simbas clustered around them. On the other side, he saw Taibu, but this time the Simba leader was wearing full tribal regalia, not his military uniform. The firelight glinted off the sweat streaking his face as he harangued his listeners.

A Simba walked by holding two sharpened sticks with chunks of roasted meat on the ends. When the man saw that Bullis had nothing to eat, he held out one of his sticks and offered its morsel.

"Eat, brother."

Rather than gag at the sweetish, burned smell of the meat, Bullis took it, thanked the Simba and the man walked on. Once he had disappeared into the crowd, he dropped the meat and moved on.

He had heard Belasko tell James that the GPS transmitter should be no further than a hundred yards from the target to insure that the Ebola was completely vaporized in the fireball. As far as nuclear devices went, the missile's warhead was about as small as it could be and still function. He knew, though, that he shouldn't get too close to Taibu. The Simba leader knew him too well, and he couldn't risk being recognized. But he vowed that he would get closer than a hundred yards to him; twenty would be more like it.

When he'd first thought of this idea, he'd had some vague plan of taking the GPS reading from the middle of the Simba encampment, then hiding the unit while he made his getaway. He now realized that wasn't going to work. With hundreds of men crowding around Taibu, there was no place to put the device where it wouldn't be found or damaged. To insure that it was functioning when it needed to be, he had to keep it with him.

That meant that he would die in the nuclear blast along with Taibu and his Simbas, but it couldn't be helped. And in the back of his mind, he'd known from the start that he wouldn't come out of this alive. The only question had been how he would die, and dying in a nuclear instant was far preferable to being hacked to bits by crude weapons or being roasted alive over an open fire.

He had worked his way to within thirty yards of the Simba leader when he found his way blocked by a line of dancing, chanting warriors. Looking past them, he spotted what he had wanted to see and stepped back out of the throng. Shielding his mouth with his hand, he held the microphone of the com link up to his lips.

"He's got the sample box right next to his throne," he whispered. "I recognize the biohazard markings on it."

"Roger." Bullis recognized Belasko's voice. "I copy that you have confirmed the samples. Prepare to take the GPS reading on my command."

"I'm ready."

"Do it now."

Switching on the GPS transmitter, he shielded it with his body while he called up the NavStar satellites in deep space. Once he was in contact with three of them, the readout gave his exact location to within three yards. Taking a deep breath, he pushed the transmit button that would send his location out in a radio signal the cruise missile could home in on.

"Signal transmitted," Bolan told him. "Stand by."

Off the Western Coast of Africa

EIGHTEEN MILES off the coast of West Africa, the attack submarine USS *Seawolf* cruised at war-alert depth, her antennaes riding on the surface. Her captain had received orders from the National Command Authority to prepare to launch a War Shot at a target on the African continent, and now he had the coordinates for the target.

A copy of the encoded War Shot message was taken to both the sub's captain and XO. The two officers decrypted it independently and, when they compared the results, saw that they were the same. They were to launch one Tomahawk III cruise missile loaded with a 1.5-kiloton nuclear warhead at the coordinates they had just received.

After bringing his sub up to launch depth, the captain scanned the horizon through the periscope. Seeing that the sea lanes were free of shipping, he gave the command to fire. At the weapons console, the weapons officer readied his firing key. The captain inserted his own firing key and turned it, completing the firing circuit.

The Tomahawk III cruise missile leaped from the silo on a blast of compressed air. When it surfaced, its wings snapped open and the jet engine ignited. Once the missile had oriented itself, it headed east toward Africa at a mere five hundred feet above sea level and cruising at a little less than six hundred miles per hour.

After the successful launch, the *Seawolf* slipped back under the waves and took up its station again to wait out the missile's flight.

The nuclear clock was ticking.

THE TOMAHAWK HAD a leisurely flight as its terrain-following radar guided it along the Congo River. Anyone looking up as it flew past would more than likely spot it, but probably wouldn't know what it was. Even if they did, its diminutive size, a little over twenty feet long and almost nine feet wide, made it very difficult to hit even with radar-directed antiaircraft guns.

The missile was vulnerable to other missiles, though, particularly the shoulder-fired antiaircraft weapons like the Stinger and Strella. But it had to be seen in time to get a lock on the fire. At the extremely low altitude it flew, its exposure time was measured in seconds.

The Tomahawk's guidance system was taking it to a target that had been preset in its computer memory. An onboard GPS system was making sure that it was staying on track, but when it came within twelve miles of its intended target, it would switch over to seeking a final ground-based signal. When it received that, it would take its final heading and go into its dive.

Grenburgh, Congo

FRANK BULLIS WAS very much aware of what was coming his way, and it still didn't quite seem real to him. But nothing that had happened since the Simbas had shown up at the Donner's Station facility had seemed real to him. His captivity, the daring escape through the jungle, the aborted river trip and even the defense of the building behind him was more like a movie than a memory.

Bullis wasn't worried about suffering before he died. He knew that when it came, he would feel no pain and that it would be a cleaner death than any of those he had witnessed over the past several days.

He was a little concerned, but not worried, though, about what would happen to him after that. Like all humans, he was having difficulty imagining his not being in existence somewhere, somehow. During his residency days, though, he had attended enough dying patients to know that most of them had faced their deaths with a calm dignity, devoid of fear. If they could do it, he would, too.

He dug his bare toes into the red earth that he was soon to become a part of. In a way, it was comforting to know that he was about to become one with the land of his ancestors. He had never felt nostalgic for the mythical homeland that so many African Americans yearned so passionately for. Everyone in America, even the Indians, had come from somewhere else and blacks were no different. But there was a kind of a continuity to his being in the birthplace of man's earliest ancestors.

Since he knew what to listen for, Bullis recognized the faint sound of the Tomahawk's turbine engine as it approached. It sounded like the hum of a rather large bumblebee. It was the last thing he heard.

The glaring nuclear fireball appeared over the bank of the river like a misplaced sun instantly displacing the night. Those looking in its direction lost their sight a microsecond before they ceased to exist. Those looking away had the same amount of time to ponder what the bright flash behind them had been.

Even over the pounding of the drums, Taibu, too, had heard a faint hum where none should have been and turned his head toward it. The flash of the detonation melted his eyeballs and burned into his brain. He didn't even have time to scream before he ceased to exist.

LIKE ALL THINGS MAN-MADE, the small sun that formed in the night sky over the Congo Basin didn't last long. But in its short life, it burned hotter than any Hell ever imagined. In a heat that could only be found on the surface of the sun, every living thing that the man-made sun touched was converted back to its component atoms. And that included the virus that man had no defense against.

Just as man couldn't withstand the invisible killer, Ebola couldn't withstand the nuclear fire that man had caused to spring into existence. The metal of the biohazard box containing the Ebola samples protected them from the nuclear radiation pulse, but not the heat flash. Being almost directly below ground zero, the box and its contents were instantly vaporized.

As with all explosions, both nuclear and nonnuclear, the flash was followed by the shock wave.

While the massive building bearing the proud name of a dead Belgian king blocked the radiation and heat pulse, the shock wave rocked it. A rolling thunderous roar filled the air as a several hundred-mile-per-hour wind smashed against the masonry. The Belgian masons had never imagined a nuclear blast, but their work withstood the fury as if they had specifically built for it. The battlements on top of the roof were scoured off, some of the stones cracked under the stress and the few remaining panes of glass in the windows disappeared in a spray of microscopic shards, but the building stood.

Stony Man Farm, Virginia

THE COMPUTER ROOM at Stony Man Farm was crowded to capacity with people watching the big screen that displayed Kurtzman's spy-satellite images. He had set the screen to automatically blank out at a certain light level rather than risk burning it out from overload. The screen was showing a multisensor, composite image of the bonfires in the Simba encampment when it flashed white and blanked out.

When the screen came back on, it was night again in the Congo, except for the glowing circle half a mile wide that was centered on what had been the Simba camp. As they watched, the glowing cloud of superheated dust started to move as the surrounding air swept back.

"I'm having difficulty getting a clear digital picture," Kurtzman said tersely, "and the IR's going crazy with all the heated dust in the air. I'm switching over to radar mapping to see what it can pick up."

The radar pulses punched through the glowing dust cloud and showed the city of Grenburgh.

"The building's still standing," Kurtzman announced. "It looks like there's been some damage to the roof, but it doesn't look serious. They should be okay."

Katzenelenbogen stood ready by the satcom radio receiver, knowing that it would be some time before they would hear anything from the survivors. A nuclear blast rendered atoms into their atomic particles, which ionized the surrounding atmosphere, making both transmission and reception of radio signals impossible until the energy was dissipated.

The team's tight-beam satcom radio was shielded against the EMP of the nuclear blast, so it would still work. But even it would have to wait until the torn atoms spent their brief energy.

Congo

THE PEOPLE in the basement had huddled for cover as the nuclear storm raged around them. The rolling roar of savagely displaced air echoing through the stone walls had shaken them like an earthquake, and the sudden silence left them marveling that they were still alive.

Leaving the others to check over their charges, Bolan looked for Gary Manning. "Bring the satcom radio," he told him. "We're going to the roof to see if we can get through to the Farm."

On the roof, the glow hanging in the sky over the Simba encampment gave a twilight effect to what should have been the middle of the night. Fires raging in the jungle added to the light, and they could see that most of the town had survived the blast more or less intact. A few of the smaller buildings showed structural damage, and one had collapsed.

Manning quickly erected the tight-beam antenna on the radio and handed the mike to Bolan. "Give it a try."

"Stony Man Base, Stony Man Base," Bolan said, "this is Striker. How copy, over?"

"Striker," Katz's voice said through the static, "this is the Farm. We have you with a lot of static, but we copy, over."

"Everyone made it okay," Bolan reported. "Even Calvin. I'll explain later. We need food, water and transport ASAP, over."

"Roger. Hal says job well done and the choppers will be in at first light."

The soldier's eyes went out to the glow where a damned good man had died so that others wouldn't. It was the oldest story in the world, but it would continue to be played out again and again as long as there were men who lusted for power. This chapter of it, though, was closed. The specter of Ebola had been turned back, and maybe there would never be another outbreak of Simbas. Time would tell.

"We'll be here."

Follow Remo and Chiun on more of their extraordinary adventures....